A Front Page Affair

Radha Vatsal is the author of *A Front Page Affair* and *Murder Between the Lines*, the first two novels in the Kitty Weeks mystery series set in World War I-era New York. Her fascination with the 1910s began when she studied women filmmakers and action-film heroines of silent cinema at Duke University, where she earned her PhD from the English Department. She was born in India and lives in New York City. She is also co-editor of the Women Film Pioneers Project. Radha is a member of Mystery Writer's of America-NY, Sisters-in-Crime NY, and International Thriller Writers.

Also by Radha Vatsal

A Kitty Weeks Mystery

A Front Page Affair
Murder Between the Lines

A FRONT PAGE AFFAIR

RADHA VATSAL

CANELO CRIME

First published in the United States in 2016 by Sourcebooks Landmark

This edition published in the United Kingdom in 2020 by

Canelo Digital Publishing Limited
31 Helen Road
Oxford OX2 0DF
United Kingdom

Print ISBN 978 1 78863 536 3
Ebook ISBN 978 1 78863 425 0

Look for more great books at www.canelo.co

Printed and bound in Great Britain by Clays Ltd, Elcograf S.p.A.

"History is nothing if not far-fetched."

– Albert O. Hirschman

Chapter One

"*This* is whom they've sent to cover my party?" Mrs Elizabeth Basshor was in her forties, plump, and well-preserved. As befitting a queen bee, she was dressed in crisp yellow silk, and the plunging neckline of her gown revealed an ample, bejeweled bosom.

"Hotchkiss?" She turned to her secretary, a boyishly handsome fellow who coughed into his palm by way of reply. Behind them, workers put final touches on the dais for the band, and waiters scurried about, pushing chairs into place and arranging floral centerpieces on tables dotted across the lush lawns of the Sleepy Hollow Country Club.

Mrs Basshor trained her gaze on Capability Weeks. "Are you sure you are up to this?"

Nineteen-year-old Kitty squared her shoulders. Today's Independence Day gala – held on Monday, July 5, since the Fourth fell on a Sunday – would be her first solo outing as a reporter. In a simple tea dress, her glossy chestnut hair pinned away from her heart-shaped face, her brown eyes sparkling, Kitty felt ready. "Miss Busby wanted to attend, but she sent me because she's indisposed. I've been working for her for the past six months."

"I know your Miss Busby." Mrs Basshor sniffed at the mention of Kitty's editor at the Ladies' Page of the *New York Sentinel*. "She gives me a nice write-up." Her gaze drifted to the workmen on the lawns. "Too close, too close," she called, frowning and pointing to a string of lanterns, patterned in red, white, and blue. Her attention returned to Kitty. "Did Miss Busby tell you we're having a display of Japanese daylight fireworks this afternoon? You must observe them carefully and be sure to give them their due. They're quite spectacular, not at all flashy like the nighttime ones.

"Hotchkiss." She swung around to him. "See to it that Miss Meeks receives a copy of the guest list and the program. If you need further help, Miss Meeks, my secretary will be happy to assist you."

"It's 'Weeks,' actually," Kitty corrected, but Elizabeth Basshor had already stepped off the terrace and was busy making sure that the lanterns were being hung to her satisfaction.

"You mustn't take it personally." Hotchkiss tried to smooth things over as soon as his employer was out of earshot. "Names aren't her strong point – I'll leave you to imagine what she called me when I first started working for her." He shuddered at the ghastly memory and handed Kitty a page from his clipboard.

She glanced at the notes: *Guests to arrive at three. Japanese fireworks from four to five. Illumination of the clubhouse terrace and Italian gardens at six. Dinner and dancing to follow.*

"Have you been with Mrs Basshor for long, Mr Hotchkiss?"

"About five years, Miss Weeks." He took a deep breath. "I must point out that we've had some cancellations because of Saturday's incident on Long Island."

Kitty nodded. He was referring to the shooting of Mr J. P. Morgan, the nation's foremost financier, who had been attacked by an intruder who barged his way into the Morgan mansion. The story had made front-page headlines and pushed aside news of the war in Europe.

"Fortunately, Mr Morgan seems to be recovering well." Hotchkiss pulled a handkerchief from his pocket. "Otherwise – who knows – we might have had to call off the party." He wiped the perspiration from his forehead. "Do you know how much work it took to get to today, Miss Weeks? Months of agonizing. Menus changed and changed again. The guest list vetted, entertainment fixed – and we have the impossible task of ensuring that each year everything is the same, and, at the same time, *utterly* different."

"It sounds extremely demanding, Mr Hotchkiss." Kitty looked around her. "But this is a beautiful location." The patio gave way to green lawns, which sloped toward formal gardens and the Hudson River, and backed up against the majestic brick-and-stone clubhouse, which had once been home to a Vanderbilt granddaughter.

"It is much more pleasant than trying to do something in Manhattan."

"Hotchkiss!" Mrs Basshor trilled just as a long-haired Oriental beckoned to her secretary from the far side of the terrace.

"If you will excuse me" – he sounded flustered – "I should go take care of business."

Kitty left him to negotiate the competing demands for his attention and wandered off to explore the grounds before the party began. She made her way past trimmed topiaries, through a vine-covered pergola, and down neatly graveled paths that led to a fountain burbling at the center of a peaceful Italian garden.

In the distance, ships steamed up and down the broad expanse of the Hudson. Kitty watched the water surge in their wake for a few quiet moments. Just a year and a half ago, in the spring of 1914, she had been nothing more than a recent boarding-school graduate arriving by sea to set foot on home soil for the first time. She had been born abroad and, as a child, had followed her businessman father on his travels through the Indies and the Orient; then, for almost a decade, she boarded at the Misses Dancey's school in Switzerland until he sent for her to join him in New York.

She had applied for the position at the Ladies' Page after she had settled in and grown accustomed to her new town. Without any practical experience, she had been certain she wouldn't be selected. But somehow, Miss Busby had hired Kitty as her apprentice – and then set her to opening mail, reading proofs, judging cookery contests, and, every now and then, writing a piece about domestic matters.

The Morgan shooting, which reawakened Kitty's urge to write a real news story, seemed like just the latest instance of how the world could turn on a dime. Last summer, an assassin's bullet in far-off Sarajevo had launched the entire continent into war. This May, a torpedo from a German U-boat had struck the majestic ocean liner *Lusitania*, which sank in a mere eighteen minutes, killing nearly twelve hundred passengers – 128 of them Americans – and it felt as though the United States might be sucked into Europe's madness.

Kitty turned away from the river to a shady path that wound its way toward the club's golf course.

"The example of America must be a special example," the president had said in his rousing speech in the aftermath of the *Lusitania* tragedy. "The example of America must be the example not merely of peace because it will not fight, but of peace because peace is the healing and elevating influence of the world and strife is not."

The clack of hedge cutters jolted Kitty from her reverie. A gardener trimming bushes with a ferocious pair of blades scowled as she walked by.

She came across a groundskeeper shoveling manure into a wheelbarrow outside a two-and-a-half-story yellow-brick building. With its tiled roof and arched windows reaching all the way to the roofline, it looked formal, but the layout didn't seem right for a residence. "What is this place?"

"It's the stables, miss."

"Is that so?" Kitty smiled to herself. Some horses had all the luck.

A couple strolled along arm in arm. He was big and burly in his formal attire; she was about half his size and wore a lavender gown with muttonchop sleeves that overwhelmed her petite form.

"I don't know what we're doing here," the woman said to her companion before her words were drowned out by the sound of touring cars crunching down the gravel drive.

Kitty hurried back to the party, where the band had begun to play, and chose an inconspicuous position beside a pillar on the terrace from which to observe the goings-on.

The lawns soon filled with gentlemen in dark suits and ladies in wispy organza gowns. Pearls glowed around necks; diamonds sparkled on languid wrists. Silver trays bobbed up and down as waiters made their way through the crowd, proffering bubbly drinks and savory appetizers. Children darted between the grown-ups' legs.

Bang! "You're dead, Willie!" A gunshot went off. Kitty searched for the source of the sound.

One of the boys had fired his toy pistol.

"I'm not Willie," his playmate cried indignantly.

"Are too."

"Why don't you play Cowboys and Indians?" Kitty suggested.

The boys stared at her in confusion. "Why would we want to play that?"

"Look at us," the first one demanded, "and tell me who looks like Kaiser Bill and who" – he stuck his hand in his pocket and assumed a debonair pose – "resembles King George."

Kitty laughed. No one seemed to care for the German kaiser these days. She wondered whether he was as bad as the press made out.

The boys ran off, continuing their battle, and she found herself drawn to another conversation. Two men, one with a chest full of medals, discussed the details of the Morgan shooting. How Mr Morgan's attacker panicked and fired when he saw the 250-pound banker charge toward him – and then found himself pinned below the massive financier, who toppled forward when the bullets hit his groin and thigh. How the Morgans' butler had conked the fellow on the head with a lump of coal after Mrs Morgan pried away his guns. The would-be assailant was in police custody.

"Wouldn't you know, he's German," the man with the medals said. "Thank goodness he's safely behind bars," the other replied.

"Doing a little eavesdropping, were we?" Hotchkiss startled Kitty by materializing noiselessly beside her.

"I'm just doing my job." She felt her cheeks flush.

"Aren't we all?" Tiny moon-shaped gold cuff links flashed from under his cuffs as he clasped his hands together. "Would you like me to help you put names to faces?"

"That would be wonderful." Although Kitty and her father went to parties from time to time, they didn't hobnob with New York's high society, and it would be important for her to identify the most important guests in her article as well as to say who was wearing what.

"The woman with the turban" – he nodded toward a striking figure in iridescent Turkish-style pantaloons – "is Mrs Poppy Clements. She's the wife of Mr Clement Clements, the theater producer, and is a playwright herself. The handsome buck to her left is Justice Stevens, a cad of the first order.

"He's with his grandmama," Mrs Basshor's secretary continued with a smirk, as a good-looking fellow with an old lady on his arm made eyes at all the pretty girls going by. "She's richer than Croesus, and he has to keep on her good side." He turned to another cluster of guests. "Those over there are the Goelets in conversation with the Burrall-Hoffmans.

"Mrs Wilson Alexander is behind them in red and blue. Mr Wilson Alexander has the white beard. There's John Parson with the glasses. Miss Winnie Slade is wearing a wonderful bracelet – do you see those emeralds?"

Kitty nodded. She wished she could take notes, but Miss Busby had forbidden her from writing anything. "Notepads and pencils staunch the flow of conversation, so it all stays in here." She had tapped her temple.

"And... Oh no." Hotchkiss pretended to take cover. "Here comes Hunter Cole with his wife, Aimee."

Kitty spotted the couple she had seen wandering about the grounds stop to speak to the turbaned Mrs Clements.

"What's wrong with them, Mr Hotchkiss?" she said, surprised that he would be so indiscreet in front of a reporter.

"Have you seen her dress?" The secretary sneered. "He's a bully, and she's a nobody – but, of course, you didn't hear me say that."

Kitty watched the couple for a few moments; when she looked up once more, the secretary had vanished.

What a strange man, she thought to herself before she stepped out onto the lawns.

Kitty felt the urge to mingle. These were people whom a girl in her position might be expected to know, that is, if her father took more trouble to socialize. Realizing that she didn't have to wait to be introduced because she was there on business, Kitty approached the first lady she saw heading her way – Mrs Goelet. The older woman seemed amused by the young reporter and was soon joined by the inquisitive Mrs Burrall-Hoffman. Kitty had no illusions that the women were interested in her for her own sake. From their remarks she could tell that what they really wanted to know was how someone who dressed well and spoke well could be there to work, and that they wouldn't mind a mention in the Page's Social Scene column.

"Isn't she delightful?" Mrs Basshor joined the group and took Kitty's arm as well as the credit for her being there. "I told dear Frieda Eichendorff that her husband's paper must send someone other than that beanpole, Helena Busby, who usually comes."

Kitty didn't care to hear Miss Busby described so disparagingly, but this was hardly the moment to leap to her boss's defense.

Mrs Basshor beamed at her friends. "The fireworks will start in fifteen minutes or so." Her smile hardened as she turned to Kitty. "I look forward to your description, my dear. Don't let me down."

The women drifted away to find their husbands, and Kitty returned to the terrace, pleased with the results of her first foray into social reporting. She hadn't gone into journalism to become a society columnist, but she had to admit that the profession had its pluses: one could speak to whomever one wanted, for starters.

Given her lack of formal training, Kitty realized that she couldn't afford to be choosy. Moreover, the skills she required today – to observe, ask questions, come forward when necessary, and disappear into the scenery when not – were all skills required for any good reporter, even a newswoman.

A sudden flurry of movement caught her eye. A feminine voice, shrill enough to be heard above the din of the party, called, "I'm sorry!"

A figure in a lavender gown with muttonchop sleeves pushed her way through the guests.

"She bumped into me on purpose," Mrs Cole hissed to her heavyset husband as they made their way toward the terrace.

Chapter Two

"Don't make a scene, Aimee. They're all watching us," Mr Cole said.

"What do I care about them?" she retorted, her pale complexion blotched with anger. "I hate it here. Let's go back to Manhattan."

Mr Cole held his wife by the wrist. "We're not going anywhere. Clean up your clothes, and let's pretend that none of this happened." He dropped her arm.

Kitty stepped forward. Mrs Cole's dress had been soiled by a greasy spill that ran down the front of her bodice. "I beg your pardon. I couldn't help overhearing—"

"And who are you to be listening in to our conversation?" Mr Cole demanded.

"I'm Capability Weeks, from the Ladies' Page of the *New York Sentinel*."

Husband and wife stared at her, aghast.

"I could help," Kitty offered. "I'm good with stains."

"You make them, or you clean them?" Mr Cole said.

"Well, both, I suppose." Kitty couldn't tell if he meant to be funny. In any case, his tone wasn't very nice.

"That's very kind of you, Miss Weeks." Mrs Cole smiled brightly. "I could use a hand." She couldn't have been much older than Kitty, twenty-one or twenty-two at most.

"I have no time for this nonsense," her husband muttered. "Do what you want, and come find me when you're done." He strode back toward the crowd on the lawns.

"Don't mind Hunter." Aimee Cole turned to Kitty. "His bark is worse than his bite. And he thinks he can get away with anything because the Coles go almost all the way back to the *Mayflower*... Shall we?"

Kitty followed her into the clubhouse.

"Have you heard of them?" Mrs Cole opened the door to the powder room.

"The Coles? I'm afraid I haven't."

"Don't worry." Aimee Cole giggled. "Before I married Hunter, neither had I. My family goes back a whole two generations. All the way to Brooklyn!" She stared at her reflection in a gilt-framed mirror above a porcelain sink and said wistfully, "You wouldn't believe that I was rather pretty once."

Kitty felt sorry for the young woman. "Let's clean up this mess."

"You don't look like a reporter." Aimee Cole turned around.

Kitty smiled and asked the attendant for talcum powder and a towel.

"You seem pretty competent for someone your age."

"I'll take that as a compliment." In addition to a basic education, Kitty's boarding-school teachers, the Misses Dancey, had taught their charges how to speak, read, and write in French, German, and Italian; memorize poetry; sketch from life; play an instrument; and run a household. They hadn't taught the girls politics, algebra, or any of the sciences.

Mrs Cole wiped the greasy residue from her dress, and Kitty dusted powder on the stain.

"That Lizzie Chilton bumped my arm and made me spill my canapé." Mrs Cole frowned, then added, "Don't put that into your report."

"I won't be writing about any of this." Kitty waited for the powder to soak up the grease and then brushed off the remains. "Better?"

Mrs Cole stood back and looked in the mirror. "Much better, thanks."

"I'm so clumsy, I rarely eat at parties," Kitty confessed to her.

"If I didn't eat at these things, I wouldn't have anything to do." Mrs Cole laughed. She seemed in a more cheerful mood.

Kitty checked the time on her watch. It was almost four o'clock. "I think we should get back."

There was no sign of Mr Cole when they came out on the terrace.

"Where could he be?" Mrs Cole looked around. She said she would wait for her husband at the children's tables and thanked Kitty again for her help. "It means a lot to me."

"It was no trouble at all." Kitty returned to her position by the pillar.

From a stage on the lawns, Mrs Basshor rang a bell. The crowd went quiet.

"Your attention please." The hostess addressed her guests. "Please join me in welcoming our visitors who've traveled here all the way from Yokohama to delight us with the daylight fireworks that are the specialty of Japan!"

Mrs Basshor brought her hands together, and everyone joined her in an enthusiastic round of applause. Two kimonoed men in wooden sandals emerged from behind the trees and took a quick bow in military unison. They were joined by a third with a bandana wrapped around his head, who slowly and deliberately beat a round brass gong.

The sound faded into silence.

All Mrs Basshor's guests waited under the blazing summer sun. A toddler in a sailor suit cried out and was hushed by his nursemaid. The air was still, and the waiters seemed frozen, trays suspended in midair. Groundskeepers looked on from behind the bushes, and even the stable lads had come up to watch the proceedings from a safe distance. When nothing happened, some of the ladies exchanged glances, smiling to hide their embarrassment.

Then a bomb blast went off, startling everyone, and jets of pink and blue smoke shot into the heavens. A collective gasp ran through the crowd as tiny packages of paper and wire unfurled below the clouds, and orange goldfish, golden carp, and green serpents floated downward. Another explosion rang out, and this time dwarfish goblins and gorgeous butterflies came to life. Bursts of smoke in different hues filled the atmosphere. The show went on and on, like a rainbow continuously changing its colors, shape and form. One explosion followed another, and the patterns bloomed and dissipated as if by magic. Finally, the pièce de résistance: an ephemeral vision of red, white and blue stripes pierced by a quick succession of exploding stars.

A shower of tiny tissue-paper figures rained on the guests. The children shrieked and scrambled to catch silhouettes of turkeys, George Washington, trumpets and flags. Many of the adults couldn't resist either and held out their hands for a souvenir.

Kitty had never seen anything quite like it. The display ended almost an hour after it had begun, and she decided that she ought to head back home. The drive to Manhattan might take some time, and Miss Busby had told her she could leave once the fireworks were done.

She went to look for Mrs Basshor but spotted Hotchkiss instead. The secretary stood at the edge of the lawns, his hands behind his back, surveying the delighted crowd with pride.

Kitty walked over and held out her hand. "Congratulations, Mr Hotchkiss."

"Thank you, Miss Weeks. Are you leaving us already?"

"I think I have the best part for my story."

"Yes." He nodded. "Those daylight fireworks are quite a sight."

"Someone seems to need to speak to you," she said, looking over his shoulder at the groundskeeper running toward him.

"Mr Hotchkiss!" the groundskeeper panted, out of breath, holding his cap in his hands.

Hotchkiss turned. "What's the matter, man? Don't you know better than to interrupt in the middle of a conversation?"

"I'm sorry, sir" – the fellow shot a glance at Kitty – "but it's one of the guests."

"Yes?"

"The lads found him in the stables."

"Go on." Hotchkiss sounded impatient.

The groundskeeper seemed to be struggling to find the right words. Then he came out and said it: "He's dead, sir. He's been shot."

Chapter Three

Kitty didn't ask for permission to follow. She picked up her skirts and hurried after the men, thankful not to be wearing a gown or Louis heels that would sink into the soft grass.

Her thoughts were jumbled. *Someone murdered? In the stables? Who could it be? How did it happen?*

A crowd of lads had gathered by the entrance to the attractive brick building that Kitty had admired just a few hours before. Sunlight bathed the copper-domed monitors atop the tiled roof, and Kitty caught her breath. It didn't seem possible that there could be a dead body inside.

The men parted to make way for the secretary and his escort.

"I wouldn't go in there, if I were you, miss," a stable hand said, but Kitty didn't listen. One moment, she was out in the bright sunshine, surrounded by voices; the next, she was enveloped in darkness and silence broken only by the clatter of hooves and the occasional whinnying of a horse.

It took Kitty's eyes a second to adjust. Then she caught sight of a figure, stretched out like a beached whale along the wooden aisle between two rows of stalls. Her reluctant gaze traveled from the soles of polished shoes, up a pair of sharply creased black trousers, over the mound of a belly, to a slack jaw and glassy stare. A single bullet hole pierced the forehead.

Kitty felt her legs give way. She had never been to a funeral, let alone seen a corpse. She held on to the door of a stall and forced herself to look again.

The body was that of Hunter Cole, someone to whom she had spoken not more than an hour before.

She turned to Hotchkiss. The secretary's face was ashen.

So forceful in life, Mr Cole was nothing now. "I should go." Kitty tottered from the barn. She sat on a nearby bench, lowered her head in her arms, and waited for the dizziness to pass.

Around her, the stable hands chattered. The man must have been killed while they were out watching the fireworks. They had been gone for forty minutes. Not one of them had stayed back. No one saw any stranger come or go. They had discovered the body only when they returned to check on the horses.

Kitty looked up to see one of the club's employees arrive on the scene and announce that the police had been called and that everyone must remain on the premises and nothing should be touched.

Hotchkiss said something to him about breaking the news to Mrs Basshor.

Kitty made her way back to the party in a daze. She couldn't, and didn't want to, leave now.

The news had evidently filtered through the guests. They huddled together, whispering in uneasy clusters, as children were packed off with their nursemaids and chauffeurs. The band had fallen silent.

18

"How could this happen?" someone said.

"Where's the killer now?"

"I hope they don't think one of us is involved."

"Must we stay to talk to the police?" A lady's sharp voice signaled her disdain for lawmen.

"If horses could speak, then everything would be resolved," another remarked.

Kitty looked for Aimee Cole and found her sitting at one of the children's tables beside the pantalooned playwright, Mrs Clements.

"Now, now, my dear," Poppy Clements said, patting the widow's shoulders gently. "Now, now." She snapped her fingers at a waiter, who jumped to attention, and ordered him to bring a cup of tea with rum.

Aimee Cole stared blankly into space. She appeared to be in shock.

"What in damnation was Hunter doing at the stables?" a man beside Kitty said.

Another replied, "Just like him to be lurking off."

A uniformed policeman approached Mrs Cole a short while later. "I'm sorry to disturb you at a time like this, madam, but I'm afraid that I will have to ask you some questions." He flipped open his notepad.

Aimee Cole responded dully to his questions. "I don't know why my husband went to the stables."

"Did he have any enemies, Mrs Cole? Anyone who might want to do him harm?"

"No one that I know of."

Kitty was amazed by the speed of it – a flesh-and-blood person had just been killed, and now it was straight down to the facts.

"When did you see him last?" the policeman inquired.

"Shortly before the fireworks began." She noticed Kitty and pointed. "This young lady was with me at the time."

"Wait for me, miss," the policeman said to Kitty just as one of his colleagues handed him a small bundle wrapped in a handkerchief. He placed the bundle on the table and then opened it.

Aimee Cole's hand flew to her mouth. "It's Hunter's," she said, staring at a small gray revolver. "Where did you find it?"

"On the floor of the stables, madam. Was Mr Cole in the habit of carrying guns to garden parties?"

"No, he wasn't. And I begged him not to bring it here, but he wouldn't listen. He told me he had to be prepared." Her voice cracked. "He said – because of the Morgan shooting – that there were too many crazies running about."

The waiter brought over a cup of tea.

"Drink this," Mrs Clements ordered.

Aimee Cole took a sip. "Did Hunter fire it?" Her eyes never left the pistol. "Was he able to defend himself?"

The policeman lowered his gaze. "We're not certain, but we believe that this is the weapon that killed him, madam."

Horror flooded the widow's face.

"Enough!" Mrs Clements put an end to the conversation. "The poor girl has had plenty of suffering for one day." She held her hand out to Mrs Cole. "Clement and I will drive you home. Officer, you can speak to her tomorrow."

The policeman raised an eyebrow but didn't argue. "A moment of your time, miss." He beckoned to Kitty after Mrs Clements led Mrs Cole away. "Have a seat." He nodded toward the chairs that the women had vacated and took down Kitty's name and occupation. "So, are you and Mrs Cole friends?"

"We just met." Kitty explained how she'd bumped into the Coles on the terrace and helped Aimee Cole with the stain on her gown.

"And that was when exactly?"

"About a quarter to four."

"You're certain?"

"I didn't want to miss the fireworks so I checked my watch."

"And that's the last you saw of Mr Cole?"

"Yes."

"There was no sign of him after you returned from the ladies' room?"

"No."

"Anything else you can tell us?"

"I don't believe so."

"Well, if anything comes to mind, please give us a call." He handed her a card.

Kitty rose from her seat as Hotchkiss hurried by, clipboard under his arm.

"Can I be of any use?" she asked.

"The police want names of all the guests. It's too ridiculous." He brushed a lock of hair from his forehead. "They were here watching the fireworks. What can they possibly have to say about what happened?"

It occurred to Kitty that she should put a call in to the *Sentinel*. There ought to be a telephone in the clubhouse. When she arrived at the reception area, a long line had formed outside a single booth. Kitty waited her turn, filled her name in the ledger, and under "Guest of" wrote "Mrs Basshor."

She made her call as quick as possible – long distance rates could be astronomical – and since it was nearly seven o'clock and Miss Busby wasn't in, she told the operator at the paper to let the City Desk know what had happened.

She returned to the lawns, where the evening had taken on the character of a wake. Waiters brought out trays laden with food, and everyone ate and drank while the police made their rounds. By the end of it, Kitty noticed plates of pastries and meat being ferried out to the chauffeurs and staff. It was past nine o'clock when the guests were finally allowed to depart.

On the drive home, Kitty asked her chauffeur, Rao, whether he had seen or heard anything strange.

"No, Miss Kitty," he replied. "We were all watching the fireworks. We only found out what happened afterward."

As the car raced through the darkness, it occurred to Kitty that, save for his wife, no one seemed to have mourned Hunter Cole. Sure, she had heard a few whispered murmurs of sympathy here and there, but those had been what any stranger might have said upon hearing about the murder. For the most part, there seemed to have been a sense among the guests that Mr Cole's fate was of his own making. It was almost as though someone who had wandered off to the deserted stables in the midst of the party was thumbing his nose at his hostess, and deserved whatever happened to him.

Since her own impression of the man hadn't exactly been favorable, Kitty could hardly find fault with the others who had known him longer and evidently never cared much for Mr Cole while he'd been alive.

Still, she thought, pulling her jacket tightly around her. They should have pretended to be sorry, if not out of common decency, then at least for the sake of his wife.

Chapter Four

Sparrows chirped beneath the windows of the New Century Apartment House on the corner of West End Avenue and Seventy-Ninth Street, where Julian Weeks sat at the head of the breakfast table reading his newspaper. He lowered it when Kitty came in, dressed for work in a pale green skirt and white shirtwaist with a floppy bow at the neck. "Did you manage to sleep?"

"A little." Kitty took her seat beside him, shook out her napkin, and swallowed an Aspirin with her water. Try as she might, she hadn't been able to wipe away the image of Hunter Cole on the floor of the stables. His puffy face with the wound below the hairline. The scuffed soles of his shoes with the neatly tied shoelaces. "Is it in the papers yet?"

"Just a one-paragraph write-up." Mr Weeks's usually stern face registered concern as he looked at his daughter. "I still can't believe that you witnessed a shooting."

Kitty tried to make light of it as she helped herself to toast from the caddy and their cook, Mrs Codd's, home-made jam. "It's not so bad, Papa. I didn't actually see the deed take place, you know."

She had told him about what had happened when she returned from the party last night, but she didn't want to discuss it any further, partly because she needed time to come to terms with it herself and partly out of fear that he would insist that she stop working. A proud, self-made man, Mr Weeks had been surprised when Kitty announced that she wanted to apprentice at the Ladies' Page but hadn't complained once he realized that her work wouldn't interfere with their domestic routine. Mrs Weeks had died from complications due to childbirth, so now that she was an adult, it fell to Kitty to run the household. She had arranged her schedule so that she came home every day by lunchtime to take care of her responsibilities. Fortunately, both Mrs Codd and Grace, the maid, didn't need much direction, and they made sure that Mr Weeks's meals were served on time and that his linens were always ironed.

Kitty took a bite of toast and switched the conversation to her father's favorite subject. "What's the latest news on the *Lusitania*?"

"It's a stalemate, but it shouldn't be." Julian Weeks scratched his chin. His rugged features were weather-beaten from years spent outdoors in Malaya. Since May, he had been following the tense back-and-forth correspondence between Washington and Berlin regarding the sinking of the passenger liner.

He tucked his napkin into his collar as Grace brought in his steak and eggs. "The Germans should be responding to the president's second note any day now."

"What do you think they will say?"

"I can't tell for sure, but I understand why they're angry. Frankly, I'm amazed that the president continues to insist on our right to travel unmolested as passengers on merchant vessels, of any nationality, even in a war zone."

The *Lusitania*, an English ship, had been struck just a few miles away from the coast of Ireland.

"I find it all so confusing," Kitty said. "Is the president trying to say that we deserve to be unharmed because we're neutral?"

"That's correct." Julian Weeks looked Kitty in the eye. "But there's a war going on, Capability. And the simple fact of the matter is that even neutrals aren't innocent."

—

Rao drove Kitty to work in the Weeks' touring car, a Packard, and dropped her off at the corner of Forty-Ninth Street and Broadway. She pushed her way through heavy brass revolving doors into the *Sentinel*'s towering office building. A three-faced clock in the center of the entry hall told the time in New York, London and Tokyo, and a compass rose with the paper's motto, *Guarding the Truth*, had been inlaid in mosaic tile on the marble floor below.

The *Sentinel* had moved its offices uptown from Newspaper Row shortly after the *Times* had set up its headquarters at Broadway and Forty-Second Street, now known as Times Square, after its famous tenant. Before arriving in New York, Kitty had heard that the city was awash with crime, with dirt, foreigners, skyscrapers, and money, and all of which was true. But to her, more than anything else, New York was awash with news. Its citizens consumed staggering amounts of the stuff, and she had been amazed by the newsboys who stood at every street corner and shouted out headlines all morning, evening and afternoon. New Yorkers devoured the *Sentinel* and the *Times*, the *Herald*, the *Tribune*, William Randolph Hearst's *Journal*, Pulitzer's *World*, the *Wall Street Journal*, the *Sun*, and the

Post, not to mention dailies in Yiddish, Chinese, Croatian, French, German, Hungarian, Italian and Russian.

Kitty came into work every day thrilled to be a part of such a vital enterprise. The paper's archivist, Mr Musser, had told Kitty that the *Sentinel* printed nearly 337,000 miles of paper each year. As the custodian of every article ever published by the *Sentinel*, grizzled Mr Musser knew something about everything. He worked from a room in the basement, otherwise known as the morgue, and supervised a team of boys who cut, pasted, and filed away each story, carefully arranged by subject matter.

Kitty thought she might visit him today as she waited in front of a bank of elevators, the only female among advertising men and mail clerks. When she stepped out on the third floor, she turned left, away from the smell of fried eggs and bacon wafting from the cafeteria and toward the cacophony of metallic clacks and clings resounding from the cavernous typists' hall. She skirted past the rows of women in starched shirtwaists tirelessly pecking away at their machines – which gave the hall its name, the "hen coop" – and hung her purse from a seat at a desk in the front of the room.

"We heard all about it, Miss Weeks!" From the table behind Kitty, Jeannie Williams's pale round face shone with excitement. She wore her flaxen hair twisted around her head in braids like an Alpine milkmaid and was built sturdily like one too. "You were at the party, and you called in the story. Do you think the City Desk will allow you to assist with the reporting?"

"I doubt it." Kitty couldn't permit herself to hope. Like other respectable papers, the *Sentinel* didn't allow women into the newsroom. Even her guidebook, *Careers for Girls*, stated in no uncertain terms that the problem with women reporters was that they couldn't be sent out at all hours and couldn't stand the strain of working under deadlines like men. "Don't look so disappointed, Jeannie. It will all change some day."

"You think so, Miss Weeks?"

"It has to, doesn't it?" Kitty said in order to buck her up. Usually it was the other way around – buoyant Jeannie, a shop girl who had studied nights and weekends in order to land her job as a typist at the paper, encouraged Kitty while she labored with her assignments.

Kitty picked up her pad and pencil and made her way to Miss Busby's office, which was in an alcove connected to the hen coop via a narrow corridor.

Gray-haired Helena Busby stopped sifting through her papers when Kitty knocked at the entryway. "Come in and sit down, Miss Weeks," she squawked. "I have a bone to pick with you."

"Have I done something wrong, Miss Busby?" Kitty pulled up a chair.

Miss Busby wagged a scrawny finger at her. "I sent you out to cover a party, and you called in a murder?" The bracelets on the editor's wrist jingled, her dangling earrings swinging as she shook her head. From his portrait behind the editor's desk, even President Wilson seemed to disapprove. "The Ladies' Page has no connection to crime of any sort. It all belongs to News. And now, Mr Hewitt wants to speak to both of us." She rummaged in a drawer for her medicine bottle.

"What for?" Kitty asked, taken off guard. Mr Hewitt was Miss Busby's supervisor.

"I have no idea, Miss Weeks." Miss Busby gulped down a spoonful of Rowland's Remedy. "All I will say is that I will do the talking and you will remain silent. Is that clear?"

"Yes, Miss Busby."

"I hope I won't have to regret sending you to the party yesterday." Miss Busby rose from her seat, and Kitty followed the lanky figure down the hall toward Mr Hewitt's office.

They knocked on the door and found a florid man with a full head of pomaded hair, picking his teeth with an ivory toothpick while Mr Hewitt rocked back in his chair.

"Good morning, ladies." Mr Hewitt sat up straight, and the stranger leisurely slipped the toothpick into his breast pocket.

"Miss Busby," Mr Hewitt said. "Meet Mr Flanagan from the newsroom."

Miss Busby nodded, while Kitty remained silent as directed.

"Should we sit?" Miss Busby said.

"Please do. I have a favor to ask of you," Mr Hewitt began. He was the only rooster among hens on this side of the floor. A balding, unintimidating man, he wore spectacles and supervised the weekend section of the paper, which included the Ladies' Page, photography, cartoons, and theater, motion picture and book reviews.

Kitty sensed Miss Busby's back stiffen – Mr Flanagan's presence didn't bode well for the Ladies' Page editor. She wished she could sit on her hands; instead, she twined her fingers loosely in her lap and tried to appear unaffected by the conversation.

"The City Desk has its men camped outside Mr Morgan's hospital room," Mr Hewitt said. "The rest are at the Morgan estate or down at police headquarters – it seems that a bomb went off there today, and the Anarchists are up to their old tricks."

"What does this have to do with me, Mr Hewitt?" Miss Busby sounded as sweet as the syrup she drank by the bottle.

"We need to borrow your girl for a couple of days. Or rather, Mr Flanagan does. He's out of reporters."

Kitty thought she had misheard him.

"Miss Weeks attended the party," Mr Hewitt said. "She saw what went on. She can assist him."

"Impossible." The tendons on Miss Busby's stringy neck tightened. "I have one girl working for me. One. And City has how many men? Over a dozen? And still, they want to steal *my* one apprentice?"

"No one is stealing anyone, madam." Mild-mannered Mr Hewitt wouldn't allow the situation to escalate. He polished his glasses and put them back on. "It's just for a few days. And since I don't get the chance very often, I'd like to be able to oblige my colleague in News."

Mr Flanagan spoke up. "All I need is some assistance with background material. We wouldn't have asked if it weren't for the fact that your girl was present when the shooting took place."

Kitty observed the proceedings with the nervous tension of a spectator at a tennis match. The only difference was that it was her fate being smacked back and forth across the net.

"With all due respect, sir," Miss Busby addressed Mr Hewitt, "when I agreed to take on help, we both agreed that my apprentice would work solely for me."

"And she does." Mr Hewitt kept his voice low. "This won't be for long."

"We're busy, Mr Hewitt."

"With what, may I ask? Articles about hats, hemlines, holidays?" Flanagan smirked.

"Laugh away, young man," Miss Busby retorted. "My stories bring in more advertising revenue than yours do."

"So you won't reconsider?" Mr Hewitt pushed his glasses up the bridge of his nose.

"Have you thought that *I* might be stretched to my limits, Mr Hewitt? Isn't that why you wanted me to hire an apprentice in the first place? So that I'd have help if things went" – Miss Busby hunted for the word – "south."

Kitty had no idea what her boss was referring to.

"All I need is a day or two at most," Mr Flanagan said. "If you can't give me that" – he shrugged – "well, I'm sure I'll manage."

Kitty felt her chance slipping away. Miss Busby had outplayed the gents.

"Let's do this." Mr Hewitt adjusted the notepad on his desk. "Since your girl only works until lunchtime at present, she can stay later and work for both of you until this case is closed." He turned to Kitty. "Does that suit you?"

Kitty hadn't realized he knew she worked there, let alone that she worked only in the mornings. "Me?" Three sets of eyes stared at her.

"Well?" Mr Flanagan said.

Kitty turned to Miss Busby for guidance.

"I can't prevent you from taking on longer hours, Miss Weeks. Clearly what *I* want doesn't matter," her boss snapped.

"Then I'll do it," Kitty replied without missing a beat.

"Good, that's settled then." Mr Hewitt pulled a pile of papers toward him.

"Just to check, Mr Hewitt. You'd like me to report to Miss Busby in the morning and Mr Flanagan in the afternoon?"

"Manage it however you like, Miss Weeks. You're free to go now."

"I'll speak to you in five minutes," Mr Flanagan called to Kitty as Miss Busby closed the door behind them.

The editor's face twisted in disappointment once they were alone in the hallway. "I didn't think you would be so treacherous, Miss Weeks. City must be really desperate to have poached from me. And if you think this is going to end well, you are sadly mistaken."

Sorry it had come to this, Kitty watched Miss Busby head off to her alcove. But, rebuke or no, she could no longer contain her delight at finally being allowed to assist on a news story.

Chapter Five

Kitty met Mr Flanagan in the cafeteria, one of the few spots at the paper where employees from different divisions could mingle. Generally, staff from unrelated departments didn't cross paths: the Circulation and Administration departments were on the lowest floors, followed by the Weekend Supplement on third and other, less time-sensitive – and therefore less prestigious – divisions on the fourth and fifth. The City Desk occupied the sixth floor, along with International News, while Business, Advertising and Management were right at the top of the hierarchy.

"Do the police have any leads, Mr Flanagan?" Kitty leaned across the metal table. She had spent hours the night before running through the events at the party, trying to come up with potential leads to the murder.

"They have some ideas, yes."

"Everyone was so excited to see the fireworks, and I've been wondering what prompted Mr Cole to leave the lawn," Kitty went on. She hadn't been able to wipe away the grim memory of Hunter Cole's body between the rows of stalls. "Do you think he went to the stables to meet someone in secret?"

"That's not for you to worry about." Flanagan rubbed the fleshy pads of his fingers together. "What I need from you is *texture*. Details about the evening: who came, what was said, emotional reactions and such. How did the guests respond when they heard the news? How did the police handle matters? The feminine viewpoint on things."

"Ah, yes, I see. The woman's angle." Kitty swallowed her disappointment. "Well—"

"Don't tell me – write it down. Write it down," he repeated. "And then, I need you to speak to a few of the key players – let's say the widow, the hostess and another guest at the party – and get some reactions. If you've already spoken to the first two, well, now's your chance to pay them a personal visit. Call on them, sit down, show some interest, and get them to talk. You'd be amazed at the things people say."

"Yes, Mr Flanagan."

"Have you conducted an interview before?"

"Ah…" Kitty wasn't about to draw attention to the fact that the first time she actually spoke to anyone on official *Sentinel* business had been yesterday, at the party.

"Tell me, how does one go about it?" Flanagan didn't notice her hesitation.

"An interview," Kitty began, "is a journalistic form first attempted on this side of the Atlantic."

"I'm not asking *what*, Miss Weeks. I am asking *how*. Please, answer the question precisely."

"Yes, Mr Flanagan." Kitty quoted from Shuman's *Practical Journalism*. "The reporter meets his man, has a talk with him on the subjects desired, and instead of taking a faithful record of every word, watches to catch the spirit of what is said and the manner in which it is uttered. He jots down the speaker's exact words only on vital or technical points."

"Exactly," Flanagan murmured.

"With his materials mostly in his head, he goes to his desk and writes the interview. Half of the words credited to the speaker may not in fact have been uttered by him, yet if the work is well done, it will be more just and infinitely more readable than any dialogue reproduced verbatim."

"That's correct." Flanagan ran a hand through his leonine mane.

"The most difficult part of the task is getting the subject to talk," Kitty continued. "You must remember what he has said while keeping up your side of the conversation and keeping in mind the questions that remain."

"All right, Miss Weeks, you know your stuff. Now all that remains is for us to see if you can do as you say."

"Yes, Mr Flanagan." Kitty's heart raced. "You'd like me to speak to Mrs Cole and Mrs Basshor and one guest" – her thoughts immediately flew to the turbaned Mrs Clements – "and have my report for you by—"

"This afternoon."

Her eyes opened wide.

Flanagan groaned. "This is real news, Miss Weeks. Not your Ladies' Page stuff. We have hard deadlines." He relented. "All right. Since you're new to it, you can give me the third report tomorrow. Hand in your notes on the other two by three o'clock today." He pushed back the bench. "You're familiar with the term 'Sob Sisters'?"

"Yes, Mr Flanagan."

"They're the four lady reporters who covered the trial of Harry Thaw for murdering Stanford White back in '07."

"Yes, Mr Flanagan." Kitty knew their names: Miss Greeley-Smith, Miss Dix, Miss Patterson, and Miss Black. "Isn't Mr Thaw to have another trial soon?"

"I believe so, but that isn't my point. What I want to bring to your attention is the type of writing that those females produced. They did your kind a great disservice by splashing their personal opinions on every line. They churned out page after page of purple prose that made me sick to my stomach. Not that you will be writing anything other than notes, but you cannot forget" – he slowed down – "the *Sentinel* does not tolerate that kind of… garbage. While you're working for me, you keep it simple, keep it dignified, and you keep to the facts. Can you manage that?"

Kitty had no intention of doing anything else. "Absolutely, Mr Flanagan."

Kitty decided it might be easier to speak to the hostess first, since she felt uneasy about conducting an interview with Mrs Cole at a time when what she really ought to be doing was paying a condolence visit. It seemed that the freedom from social niceties that came with being a reporter might also have its drawbacks. How did one bring oneself to question a widow the day after her husband had been murdered?

She took a cab to Mrs Basshor's apartment house on Park Avenue.

"Lovely, ain't it?" the cab driver observed as they motored down the broad boulevard, which was flanked on either side by gracious apartment buildings and bisected down the middle by a tree-lined pedestrian path.

Kitty agreed. This avenue and nearby Fifth were the most desirable residential stretches in Manhattan.

"You wouldn't know that twenty years ago, trains belched smoke and soot right here," the driver said. "They chugged along tracks dug into the ground where the trees are planted now. And these apartment houses?" He gestured out the window. "They only came up once the rails were buried underground and the street was paved over. There used to be tenements here before."

"So we're driving over hidden railway tracks?" Kitty liked the idea.

"Oh yes, miss." He pointed to the imposing terminus behind them. "The trains going in and out of Grand Central Station are clattering along beneath us."

He pulled up at Mrs Basshor's a few minutes later. Kitty hunted in her purse for the fare and added a tip. The very sidewalks seemed to radiate heat as she stepped out into the muggy summer air, and the cool interior of Mrs Basshor's building provided welcome relief. A uniformed caretaker buffed the marble floors, while a liveried doorman ushered her to an elevator, which whisked her up to the hostess's fifth-floor triplex.

Kitty rang the doorbell. A maid answered the door and asked her to wait in the vestibule – an octagonal room papered in silver-leaf wallpaper painted with herons, lily pads, and bridges in an Oriental theme.

A tall vase of irises stood on a table in the center. The last home Kitty had visited in this part of town belonged to her friend Amanda Vanderwell's family. Their slender brownstone stood in the Seventies between Park and Madison Avenues. Mrs Vanderwell liked to call apartments "tenements" and declared that they were only for Johnny-come-latelies. Looking around her, Kitty suspected her claim might be fueled by envy. The Vanderwells were among the last of the old guard to jump ship from points further south in Manhattan, which was why, when it came time to buy, they couldn't afford much. Kitty guessed that Mrs Basshor's opulent apartment might have cost more than the Vanderwells' freestanding house.

Footsteps clicked down the hall, and a few moments later, Hotchkiss appeared with a poppy in his lapel. His youthful, handsome face looked haggard.

"Miss Weeks." If the secretary was surprised to see her, he didn't show it. He asked Kitty to follow him to an anteroom where he drew back heavy velvet curtains to let in the light.

"You will understand, of course," he said, adjusting his sleeves, "that Mrs Basshor is quite overcome and as such is unavailable to members of the press. We are all shocked and dismayed by what took place yesterday and offer our sincerest condolences to the Cole family." His words sounded mechanical, and only a slight tremor of his long-fingered hands betrayed his agitation. "If there's anything you need, I will be happy to assist. My employer has asked me to make myself available for questions. Is there anything in particular that you'd like to inquire about, Miss Weeks?"

Kitty didn't know how to begin, how to get past the secretary and to Mrs Basshor.

"I'm shocked too," she said, trying to buy some time. "That something so terrible should have happened… and it must be much worse for you. You knew Mr Cole and you had been preparing for the party for ages."

"I gave it everything I have, Miss Weeks," the secretary said. "Mrs Basshor is a true patriot, and this event is the most important in her calendar. As you say, we prepare well in advance. Those fellows who did the fireworks – they didn't just trot up from Chinatown. No, *I* found the best in the business; we paid for their passage from Japan."

Hotchkiss removed a doily covering a jug. "Will you have some water?"

"No, thank you."

He poured himself a drink.

"The fireworks were wonderful," Kitty said to keep the conversation going. "Really spectacular. I hadn't seen anything quite like them."

"Mrs Basshor wanted something that would be novelty for her guests and given that crowd, I can tell you, it wasn't an easy order. I had hoped to take a short vacation afterward. Nothing elaborate, just a trip to the coast to recover from the strain. But I can't, not after what's happened. To be honest, Miss Weeks" – his lower lip trembled – "it's hit both Mrs Basshor and myself very hard indeed."

"How could it not, Mr Hotchkiss? And that's why you must let me speak to her." Now that Kitty had stumbled onto her ploy, the words came out in a rush. "All the other papers are going to print something about what happened last night. And they have no scruples. They'll say anything to sell an extra copy. But together, you and I can help her. With your assistance, she can share her perspective with our readers. I'm sure she will want her side of the story faithfully represented to the public."

"And why should I trust you over the others, Miss Weeks?" Hotchkiss replied. "They've been calling, you know, since eight this morning."

"You forget that Mrs Eichendorff, our publisher's wife, is a friend of Mrs Basshor's."

The secretary blinked. "That's right. Yes."

"And that's exactly why you must trust me, Mr Hotchkiss. Our paper would never allow anything to be printed that might do Mrs Basshor an injustice." Kitty hoped she wasn't telling a lie.

–

"Hunter Cole was the black sheep of a good family," Elizabeth Basshor said, sounding neither out of sorts nor devastated. She lay on a pale silk-covered chaise in her morning room with a shawl wrapped around her shoulders and a light throw draped across her legs. "He was a bit of a bore and a show-off, but I invited him for his parents' sake."

She held out her teacup, to which Hotchkiss added an extra squeeze of lemon. "Do take that poppy off," she commanded as he bent over her. "You know the smell makes me quite faint."

Her secretary turned to a wastebasket in the corner.

"No, not here! Outside." She returned her attention to Kitty. "So, yes, it's Hunter's marriage to that girl that was his undoing. Not that Dr and Mrs Cole ever complained about it. They're far too well-bred for that. But the wedding, in Connecticut, was much smaller than it ought to have been – no one but the closest family and friends were invited. I remember it as though it was yesterday. Had the circumstances been different, they'd have done things on a much grander scale."

"You were at the wedding?"

"Naturally. And then I had to telephone last night to break the news. Quite terrible to have to tell parents that their own son has been killed. But between you and me" – Mrs Basshor leaned in conspiratorially – "I always thought Hunter would come to a bad end. Not like this, of course. It's just that his marriage was the last straw. He never settled, if you know what I mean. Never occupied himself with any one pursuit. Always skulked around on the fringes of things.

"I couldn't say that to Dr Cole, of course. I just told him that it must have been a tragic mistake. Hunter must have gone off to take a look at the horses, and some deranged madman mistook him for someone else."

"That's what you believe?"

"I don't know what to believe."

"Did Mr Cole have a special fondness for horses?"

"He loved them. It's the one thing one really knew about him. An avid horseman and always at the races. But there was talk, you know." She paused.

"What kind of talk, Mrs Basshor?" Kitty asked, pleased with the flow of the conversation. She hadn't anticipated that conducting an interview would be so straightforward.

"Hunter lived beyond his means," Elizabeth Basshor said. "Spent far too much money gambling. It's true, but it's sad that he should be killed for it. A gentleman makes mistakes, my dear, but if there's one thing he has, it's his word. If Hunter said he'd pay his debts, then he would. There was no need to come after him with pistols loaded."

41

"I'm sorry, Mrs Basshor, are you suggesting—"

"It had to have been his bookmakers or someone else from the racetracks," the hostess declared with certainty. "Why else would he have been killed there? You agree with me, Hotchkiss?"

"I beg your pardon, madam?" The secretary came back, *sans* the offending bloom.

"Don't you agree that Hunter was killed because of his gambling?"

"It's possible, Mrs Basshor." Hotchkiss stared at his feet.

"Either that or some Germans mistook him for someone else and did him in." She finished her tea and handed her man the empty cup. "One thing I know without a doubt is that none of *my* guests had anything to do with it. Please make sure you put that in your article, young lady. I want all my friends to be quite certain that they are completely above suspicion."

"I'll let Mr Flanagan know," Kitty replied. "He will write the final story."

"That's a nice dress you have on." Elizabeth Basshor took a moment to rearrange her shawl. "I liked your frock yesterday too. What did you say your name is again?"

"Capability Weeks," Hotchkiss replied before Kitty could answer.

"Capability?" Mrs Basshor's eyes widened. "As in Capability Brown?"

"You're familiar with his work?" Kitty hadn't expected the hostess to recognize her name's origins. Mr Brown was England's most famous designer of landscapes, but an eighteenth-century gardener nonetheless.

"He's a man!"

"Yes, but the name isn't very common, so most people don't realize—"

"I've seen examples of Mr Brown's brilliance in parks all over Britain," Mrs Basshor cut in coldly, "particularly at the grounds of Blenheim Palace. The Duchess of Marlborough, whom I've known from when she was just little Consuelo Vanderbilt, is a great friend of mine. It's not done to give a girl a man's name. And your surname is 'Weeks'?" The hostess waved a dismissive hand. "Never heard of it."

Kitty's head spun with the speed at which Mrs Basshor jumped between topics.

"Allow me to tell you something for your own sake, my dear," she went on. "Don't get ahead of yourself. You will never marry if you continue in this vein."

The pronouncement caught Kitty off guard. "I beg your pardon, Mrs Basshor?"

"I have no quarrel with women who do what they need to in order to take care of themselves. But girls like you who don't need to work but do so anyway? That's intolerable. It's showing off. What does your mother have to say about it?"

"My mother has passed away, madam." Kitty had lost control of the conversation and didn't know what she had done to prompt the change.

"Well, that explains it. And your father hasn't remarried?"

Kitty's ears burned. "No, he has not. But perhaps we might return to the matter at hand?"

"In a moment, my dear. Given your situation, I feel it is my duty to warn you that your problem will be – if it isn't already – that you will never fit in. You're obviously much too well-off to have working friends, and you work too much for the rich ones. You can't be in two worlds at once. If you try, you end up in neither. I *know*. I learned that the hard way. Today's young men don't have the courage of their convictions. They may flirt with a girl who seems different, but they'll never marry her. Aren't I right, Hotchkiss?"

Kitty had heard enough. "Well, thank you, Mrs Basshor. I'll try to keep your advice in mind." She stood.

"Are we finished then?" The hostess sounded disappointed.

"Yes, we are." Kitty kept her voice carefully neutral.

"I hope you haven't taken any offense, my dear. I may have my faults, but varnishing the truth is not one of them."

As she left the room, Kitty heard Mrs Basshor call, "Mark my words, you will benefit more from scrutinizing your own life than from any amount of inquiry into Hunter Cole's murder."

Chapter Six

By the time Kitty was seated at Tipton's tea shop on Madison Avenue, she had calmed down a bit. She pressed the glass of ice-cold water that the waitress served her against her forehead. She couldn't fathom Mrs Basshor's behavior. *Mark my words* indeed. What was she, a punching bag for the older woman to beat about as she pleased?

"What will you have to eat, miss?" asked the young waitress in her starched cap and white apron. Kitty ordered a roast beef sandwich. At the tables around her, women in small groups laughed and chatted easily to one another.

It occurred to Kitty that there might be another reason Mrs Basshor didn't want her poking around in the circumstances surrounding Hunter Cole's death. The hostess might be protecting someone. But whom? One of her guests? Hotchkiss?

She recalled the secretary's remark about Hunter Cole being a bully.

Perhaps, Kitty thought, Mrs Basshor was worried that Kitty had seen or heard something incriminating during the party, and that's why she had deflected the attention away from Mr Cole.

Kitty took a bite of the salad that came with her sandwich and looked around at the smiling, laughing faces.

Young or old, not one of them sat alone. All the ladies had come out with company. *Perhaps Mrs Basshor was correct.*

She reached into her purse for a pencil and pulled out a postcard advertising *The Romance of Elaine*, the new series featuring her favorite motion-picture actress Pearl White. "Fearless, Peerless Pearl" had been set loose in a hot-air balloon, kidnapped by bandits, and regularly faced all sorts of perils. She would never allow any setbacks to deter her – let alone one middle-aged woman's disparaging comments.

Kitty put away the postcard, taking solace in the fact that Pearl and the intrepid characters she played probably had occasion to eat alone in tea shops and hotels. That was the price they paid for their independence. She finished her sandwich and left a dollar bill on the table.

Mrs Basshor's stinging attack could have been nothing more than the older woman's attempt to protect herself or someone close to her – but she, Capability Weeks, had seen through it.

–

The smell of frying onions wafted through the sixth-floor landing. Kitty hadn't expected the Coles to live in such a modest place. The building was on a noisy side street in the Fifties, just west of Broadway. The stairwell looked like it hadn't been painted in years, and the elevator creaked and shuddered all the way up. Kitty was quite relieved when the operator – who also doubled as the building's doorman – shut the metal grille behind her with a clang, and she stepped out to safety on the landing.

A small, hard-faced woman peered out from behind the Coles' door when Kitty knocked.

"From the *Sentinel*?" she asked after Kitty introduced herself.

"Let her in, Mama," a girlish voice called from within.

Kitty entered the flat with trepidation. It was small and compact: a simple foyer opened into a living room, which was connected by French doors to a dining room.

Aimee Cole sat in an overstuffed brown sofa beside an army of fragile porcelain shepherdesses. Her skin looked sallow, and her dull hair hung uncombed around her shoulders.

"It's so kind of you to come." She introduced Kitty to her mother, Mrs Henderson, who mustered a grim smile. "It's so nice for me to have a friend here."

Kitty thought it odd that Aimee Cole thought of her as a friend when they had only met the day before and under such strange circumstances. Then she wondered whether the widow hadn't realized that Kitty had come as a representative of the paper.

"Have one." Mrs Henderson held out a plate of brightly wrapped bonbons in a cut-glass serving bowl.

Kitty demurred. She found the atmosphere in the apartment oppressive and would have liked to open the windows to let in some fresh air. More Dresden shepherdesses filled the sideboard in the dining room. Aimee must have a real fondness for them.

"Go on, take one," Mrs Henderson insisted.

Kitty unwrapped a chocolate and put it into her mouth. It tasted dusty and dry like some her father had once sent her from Russia. She swallowed quickly and offered both daughter and mother her condolences.

"I'm so sorry for your loss, but I'm afraid I'm here on business."

"I know all about business," Aimee Cole managed with a laugh. "How can I help you?"

"I'll leave you young ladies to yourselves." Mrs Henderson withdrew to the adjacent dining room, where she busied herself dusting the porcelain figurines. Another girl peeked in, only to scurry away when Aimee's mother flashed her a warning glare.

Kitty asked Mrs Cole whether she would mind talking about her husband so that the *Sentinel* could print an accurate, respectful report of the tragic occurrence.

"I'd be happy to." Aimee twisted the fringes of the throw draped over the sofa around her finger. "You know, we haven't had any visitors so far. The police were here earlier this morning, and other than that, it's just been me, Mama and Alice, my sister."

"The Learys brought cake," her mother spoke up from the other room.

"That's right. The Learys are our downstairs neighbors. Hunter's parents called on the telephone but decided to remain in Connecticut."

"It must be dreadful for you." Kitty perched on the far edge of the sofa, leaving the cushion between her and Aimee vacant.

"I've been up all night, asking myself why we went to that party."

"Was it Mr Cole's idea to attend?" Kitty felt like a vulture circling for a tidbit, but she reassured herself that the public ought to know more about the man who had been killed.

"We went every year for the three years we've been married. It's just something we did," Aimee replied. "Although Hunter never enjoyed it."

48

"He wasn't one for society?"

"My husband despised Mrs Basshor and her friends. But he liked to get dressed up and appreciated good food and drink… Hunter had been jittery ever since he heard about the Morgan shooting on Sunday," she added in a quiet voice, "which is why he decided to bring his pistol with him. The police told me this morning that they're certain he was killed with it."

"That's terrible." Kitty paused for a moment. "And you arrived early to the party?" She phrased it as a question, but of course she'd seen them strolling about.

"Hunter hated to be late. But I didn't want to be a nuisance, so we walked around the grounds."

"Do you recall who Mr Cole spoke to during the party and what kind of mood he was in?" Kitty asked.

"Well, let me see. Things weren't any different than usual. Hunter seemed content once we arrived. He said hello to Mrs Basshor and some of the men, and we both spoke to Mrs Clements. She's always been very kind to me. As you've probably gathered by now, Miss Weeks" – Aimee Cole's pale skin flushed red – "even though I married Hunter, the others have never let me forget that I'm not one of them."

Kitty sympathized with the widow. From her years abroad, she knew what it was like to feel like an outsider.

Mrs Henderson stared in from the dining room, but Aimee turned away from her. "This morning, the detective asked why I didn't go looking for my husband when the fireworks began. I said that Hunter often went off on his own and that he liked his privacy. Was I wrong in remaining where I was, Miss Weeks? Would you have gone if you had been in my shoes?"

Kitty glanced at the frumpy blue slippers on Mrs Cole's feet. They matched her dark blue housecoat. "No," she said. It made no sense to add regret to the widow's grief. "How could you have known what would happen?"

"Hunter had very little patience for society and no interest in fireworks. He must have decided to see the horses just to amuse himself." Aimee's voice cracked. "Sometimes, I think he loved them more than he loved people. You'll hear people say that Hunter went too often to the races, but I never faulted him for it, Miss Weeks."

In the background, Kitty could see Mrs Henderson shaking her head.

"He grew up riding," Aimee Cole went on. "What else was he to do?"

"Aimee's too generous." Mrs Henderson couldn't hold back any more and rejoined them in the living room. "I don't like to speak ill of the dead, but I'll tell you this: my son-in-law was no good either as a man or as a husband. He went to the racetracks, frittered away whatever little fortune he might have had, and even though we heard so much about the great Coles of Connecticut, his people never helped my daughter one bit. Whatever they have, Aimee brought to the marriage. People like to say that she connived to get him, but that's a lie. My girl didn't do anything underhanded to win his affections. He met her, he fell in love and he asked her to marry him. She said yes, and that was the problem."

"Mother," Aimee protested, but Mrs Henderson wouldn't be silenced.

"It's true, Aimee. He got the better half of the bargain. What were you ever but a good, decent wife to him, and what did he give you? Nothing!" Mrs Henderson waved an arm across the room. "Even this apartment is rented. Now, if you'd accepted that nice Padrewski fellow like your father and I told you, you'd be lording it over everyone in a mansion, and he'd be smothering you in furs from head to toe."

"Paderewski, Mother." Aimee smiled unguardedly for a moment, her watery blue eyes lighting up, and Kitty thought she might have caught a glimpse of the spark that had attracted Hunter Cole when he met her. "And I never married in order to be smothered."

"He still wants to marry you, my dear."

"Mother." Aimee's tone turned sharper.

"I'm just saying, Aimee. I'm just saying."

A dwarfish maid brought tea on a tray, and Mrs Henderson poured three cups.

"I hope I don't seem like I'm prying," Kitty said delicately, "but did Mr Cole have an occupation?"

"Hunter didn't really work," Aimee replied. "But we got by. We always managed."

Mrs Henderson pursed her lips. "It's nothing like what you'd have had if you'd married the furrier. And you'd be living just down the street from us in Brooklyn."

Kitty took a sip of her tea. It was probably time to leave mother and daughter to each other's company. "I should be on my way."

"Can I show you around the apartment?" Aimee said.

"Of course." Kitty put down her cup and rose.

The tour didn't take long, since all that remained for Kitty to see were the dining room, the bedroom (to which Mrs Cole didn't open the door), and Mr Cole's study.

To Kitty's surprise, she felt most at ease in the dead man's private room. It had been sparsely yet tastefully furnished with a rolltop chestnut desk, swiveling chair, rich Persian carpet, and curtains that reached the floor. An antique clock with a mother-of-pearl face sat on his desk. An eye-catching canvas of a muscular stallion posed against mountains hung on the wall above low walnut bookshelves.

"Is that a Stubbs?" Kitty stepped in to take a closer look.

"Hunter's grandmother left it to him in her will. I don't know much about art, but I do know that it's the one good piece we have from them."

The widow put her hand on Kitty's arm. "I hope I can trust you to be kind, Miss Weeks. The public will say cruel things about me. They may even point fingers in my direction."

"Mrs Cole—" Kitty pulled away.

"Call me Aimee. After all we've been through, I think we might allow ourselves that."

"I just work for the *Sentinel*." Kitty hoped to avoid the invitation to be intimate. "I'm not in charge of what they print."

"I understand."

"I do hope the police will apprehend the culprit—"

"You have a lot to learn, Miss Weeks," Aimee Cole burst out in anger. "Where I'm from, we know what the police do and what they don't, how they pin the crime on whoever happens to be convenient. What I want is *justice* for my husband." She spoke with force. "I'm not interested in watching them haul away some poor sod just so that they can cross the case off their list."

Kitty took her leave of the widow shortly afterward.

Mrs Henderson walked Kitty to the landing and waited with her for the elevator. "We're supposed to go to Connecticut on Friday for the funeral, but none of them will come here to see my daughter."

The rattling machine arrived, and the operator pulled open the fretwork grille. Kitty stepped inside.

"The Hendersons may not have come here on the *Mayflower*," the older woman continued as the gate shut between them with a clang, "but Aimee will be so much better off without Hunter."

With a jerk, the elevator lurched downward, slowly erasing Kitty's view of Mrs Cole's bitter parent.

–

For once, the typists' incessant clacking didn't drive Kitty to distraction. She filled two sheets of paper with neat script and brought them upstairs to the sixth floor, where a glass wall partitioned the newsroom off from the rest of the hallway. Behind it, the real reporters, all men, went about their business. Some spoke on the telephone; others sat at their desks, writing or chewing on their pencils; still others smoked cigarettes or chatted with their colleagues.

Kitty knew she wasn't allowed to enter, so she tapped on the glass, caught the attention of one of the reporters, mouthed the words "Mr Flanagan," and then, acutely aware of sidelong glances in her direction, waited until Flanagan emerged from within.

"Not bad," he murmured, glancing over her notes. "I can do something with this." He looked up. "You'll speak to a third party tomorrow?"

"Yes, Mr Flanagan. First thing." Kitty planned to telephone Mrs Clements to set up an appointment.

"All right then. You're free to report to Miss Busby."

But the Ladies' Page editor still seemed miffed by Kitty's disloyalty, and when Kitty went in, she said that all she needed was the result of this week's home cookery contest.

"Did Mr Flanagan like your work?" Jeannie asked when Kitty returned to her desk.

"I think so." Kitty sifted through the entries and picked a recipe for breaded mutton cutlets with onion sauce. It didn't sound too appetizing, but she was in a rush. She dropped it off on Miss Busby's desk.

"I'll see you tomorrow, Jeannie." Kitty left the hen coop without looking back, so she didn't notice the typist staring after her.

Chapter Seven

Kitty hurried home and changed into her leather boots, a split skirt, and a linen shirt. Then she telephoned Mrs Clements before calling for her Stutz Bearcat, the sporty yellow roadster that her father had given her for her birthday. Like riding a horse, Kitty drove for pleasure. She went downstairs, hopped into her car, and covered the distance to Durland's Academy on the west side of Central Park at top speed, only to find Amanda Vanderwell already mounted on Lucky Number 7, waiting for her.

"Sorry I'm late." Kitty parked the car. A lad brought Damsel forward, and she hoisted herself into the saddle. Kitty and Amanda had met the previous summer and struck up a conversation over the rose garden plantings at the Botanical Gardens. Kitty had been dazzled by Amanda's beauty and effortless confidence; what Amanda admired in her had been less obvious – perhaps it was Kitty's freedom to move about the city, which was so foreign to Amanda's rarified and tightly controlled experience of New York, although the Vanderwells and their set had been on the island for generations.

"I hope you have a good excuse." Amanda flicked Lucky with her crop, and the horse trotted along with Amanda poised elegantly sidesaddle.

"Work," Kitty said, following a few paces behind, acutely aware, as always, how awkward she appeared in comparison astride on Damsel. But Mr Weeks insisted. It was safer to ride in the mannish style, he said, for both horse and equestrienne.

"I don't know why you carry on with that nonsense." Amanda turned and raised an eyebrow behind her veil, but her lips parted in a smile. Coppery hair glinted from below her hat.

"How was your weekend?" Kitty asked as they headed toward the bridle paths that crisscrossed the park.

"Lovely." Amanda shrugged. "As was to be expected. Did you know that this was the first big party the Astors have held since Colonel Astor drowned on the *Titanic*? And then we found out about what happened to Mr Morgan, and I can tell you, it gave everyone quite a scare. But" – a roaring sound from one of the automobile mowers trimming the lawns in the distance distracted her – "I did have a fascinating time at Saturday's dinner."

"Did you meet someone?" Kitty grinned at her friend. Amanda had no shortage of beaus, all of whom she found some reason to reject sooner or later.

"Not in the way you're thinking, naughty girl." Amanda laughed. "I was seated next to the most intriguing little man though, one of those newfangled psychoanalyst fellows. He regaled us with one story after another, the best of which was that the kaiser started the war in order to win his mother's approval."

"Really?"

"Oh yes. Of course, the kaiser, King George, and Tsar Nicholas of Russia are all cousins, related through their grandmama, Queen Victoria—"

"Yes, yes." Amanda sometimes treated Kitty like she didn't know basic facts, as though attending boarding school in Europe had somehow stunted Kitty's intelligence.

"And Princess Victoria, Queen Victoria's daughter who was married off to the German emperor," Amanda went on, "had to have her son, the present kaiser, pulled out of her with forceps. He was born with a crippled arm as a result and had to undergo excruciating treatments to straighten it. They say he always felt like he was never good enough for his parents. When he was five years old, his mother decided he must learn how to ride. He had British royal blood, so it was unthinkable that he couldn't. But his mother was determined that her son learn to ride like a British king. Of course, it's hard when you have one arm that doesn't work. And although he kept falling off and begged her to stop, she wouldn't give up until he learned how to do it to her satisfaction."

"And that's why he declared war on Russia, France, and England?" It was Kitty's turn to be skeptical.

"He wants to prove that he can keep up with the rest," Amanda replied. "That neither he nor the German nation are to be trifled with. Don't look at me like that," she said to Kitty. "I'm just repeating what I heard."

"I thought you found your dinner companion fascinating."

"He was. You should have been there to hear him tell it in person."

"So no new beaus?" Amanda's parents had their hearts set on her making "a good match," which meant a wealthy match, since the Vanderwells, although they were descended from a distinguished line, had very little cash at present.

"It was the same old boring crowd: Jerry, Potty, and Neville, prattling on as usual. But I did make a decision that I want to tell you about. I said it in front of everyone at our table, including Mummy and Daddy, so I can't back down now."

"What is it?" Kitty turned to face her friend.

Amanda's cheeks were flushed, and her eyes sparkled. "I plan to enroll in a nurse's aide course at the YWCA, and when it's over, I'm going to go to Europe to tend to the wounded."

"You?" Kitty slowed down. The Amanda she knew barely deigned to tie her own shoelaces, let alone tend to others.

"Yes! And why not? I'll be twenty-four this year, Capability. I haven't met anyone who suits my tastes and Mummy and Daddy's requirements, and I won't have people calling me a spinster. Besides" – she resumed her breezy manner – "nursing is terribly glamorous. Who knows? I may even meet a wounded nobleman who dies in my arms, leaving me his fortune."

"You mean debt, don't you?"

Amanda grinned. "All the best girls are becoming nurses these days, which is why I want you to give up the paper and come join me."

"Excuse me?"

"That's right. Give up the paper. You've been complaining about that Miss Busby since you started."

"She's not so bad…" Kitty began to regret anything unkind she might have said about the Ladies' Page editor.

"You told me she doesn't give you any real work. Just makes you judge contests and open mail."

"Not any longer."

"Is that so?" Amanda flicked Lucky with her crop, and he broke into a canter.

After a moment's pause, Kitty urged Damsel forward and followed her friend down the empty path, free and fast on her mount with nothing but greenery around her and snippets of clear blue skies overhead.

They came to a turnoff in the trail, interrupted by a low wall. It was against the rules to ride there, but many of the young bucks did, to get in a jump. Amanda sped up her horse some more, and one-step, two-step, she was in the air, soaring across the barrier as Kitty watched, her heart in her mouth.

Her friend looked so precarious, perched there with both legs on one side of the horse – she could slide off or her skirt might get caught in the stirrups. A moment later, she was safely back on the ground.

"So what's changed for you at the paper?" Amanda called, exhilarated.

Kitty gathered her reins, took the jump herself, and rejoined her friend on the path.

"A man was killed at a party I covered."

"Hunter Cole at Bessie Basshor's do?"

"How did you know?"

"Mama is a great friend of Bessie's. The only reason we weren't there was because we had been invited to the Astors'."

"I've been asked to help out with the story. I spent this morning speaking to Mrs Cole and Mrs Basshor."

Amanda snickered.

"What's wrong with that?" Kitty couldn't fathom her friend's response.

"She was a dance-hall girl."

"Mrs Basshor?"

"No, silly. Aimee Cole. I bet she didn't tell you that, did she? 'Rising star of burlesque stage marries Hunter Cole, American blue blood and ne'er-do-well.' It caused quite the scandal."

"I had no idea."

"She was called Fatima, or something of that sort, and performed exotic numbers with a serpent and veils. They say" – Amanda lowered her voice even though there was no one else around – "that she was half-naked when Hunter first set eyes on her."

Kitty couldn't picture timid Aimee dancing on a burlesque stage – or any other stage, for that matter. "You're teasing me."

"She was scantily clad."

"Oh my." The description didn't fit the drab woman Kitty had met. They had come to the end of the loop and paused near the turnoff to the stables.

"If you ask me," Amanda said, "she's the one who did it. Fatima Cole strangled Hunter with one of her scarves."

"He was shot," Kitty corrected.

"Shot, strangled, what's the difference? He's dead. She's not and is probably waiting to collect what remains of the Cole bounty. Anyway, don't forget: four o'clock next week at the YWCA on Fifteenth Street." Amanda blew Kitty a kiss before she trotted off.

Kitty watched her friend disappear around the curve. Then she gave a pull on her reins and began another round. She knew that Mrs Vanderwell disapproved of their friendship. Amanda didn't say as much, but from the hints she dropped, Kitty guessed that Mrs Vanderwell thought she was a nouveau-riche upstart from the wrong side of town, which was why Amanda never came to Kitty's place, and only rarely invited Kitty over. Mostly they met at Durland's or out shopping.

Kitty wondered whether Amanda wanted her company at the YWCA only to aggravate her family. Then she dismissed the thought as uncharitable. Stuck in her world of endless social commitments and obligations, Amanda needed a friend from outside her circle just as much as Kitty needed someone to talk to. She considered attending the introductory session to humor her, even though she had no intention of leaving the paper. Especially not at the moment.

Damsel clopped down the turf in the dappled shade, and Kitty urged her to go faster. The horse's speed matched Kitty's galloping thoughts: Aimee Cole might have been a burlesque dancer who married above her station, but that didn't make her a murderess. Still, the widow's past would explain why others dismissed her. It would also explain why Mrs Cole had seemed so worked up when she told Kitty that the police would pin the murder on someone convenient – after all, who would be more convenient than a dance-hall girl?

Chapter Eight

"Your name, please, sir?" Prentiss, the photographer, said to Mr Weeks.

"Julian Conrad Weeks," Kitty's father replied.

Kitty paced up and down the stifling front office on Broadway, staring at the sample portraits displayed on the walls. She had a nine thirty appointment to speak to Poppy Clements, the theater producer's wife who had been at Mrs Basshor's party, and here she was, waiting for the punctilious Prentiss to fill out official passport application forms.

"Occupation?"

"Businessman."

"Your age, please, sir?"

"Forty-seven."

"And date of birth?" Prentiss's nib scratched against the cheap government-issue paper. He wrote carefully, blotting each entry so that the ink wouldn't smudge.

Kitty couldn't see what all the fuss was about. When she'd arrived in New York the previous year, all she'd carried by way of identification were two letters, one from school and one from her father's attorneys, and the nervous young customs official who boarded the ship had seemed embarrassed to check even those.

But this morning, Mr Weeks explained that the State Department had issued new regulations. Since the war broke out, it had become mandatory for all Americans traveling abroad to carry a passport, and by the end of the previous year, the rules had become even more rigid, requiring a sworn application before a clerk of a court and the inclusion of two unmounted photographs.

"And will you be traveling with your wife, Mr Weeks?" Prentiss said.

"My wife is deceased. I will be traveling with my daughter."

Julian Weeks provided Kitty's particulars: Capability Violet Weeks, nineteen years of age, born February 10, 1896, in Selangor, Malaya.

The scratching nib paused. "Selangor?" the photographer said. Then he added, "No matter, sir. Miss Weeks's citizenship follows yours. Your place of birth, Mr Weeks?"

"Dover, Delaware."

"And you have a birth certificate to prove that?"

Kitty suspected that Prentiss enjoyed the liberty of asking the many questions that the form required of his customers, although he presented it as a courtesy that he offered gratis to those requiring a photograph.

"I don't have a birth certificate," Mr Weeks said. "Do you, Mr Prentiss?"

Prentiss coughed. "So many men of our generation don't possess one. Was your father native born or naturalized, Mr Weeks?" Pen poised, he waited for a reply.

Julian Weeks said, "That's a bit much."

Kitty read from a news clipping, pinned beside a list of the photographer's services and prices:

> Statement from Secretary of State Bryan, November 13, 1914: The President, upon the advice of the Secretary of State, has this day signed an order under which the rules governing the granting and issuing of passports in the United States are made much stricter than they have been in the past. The immediate cause of the amendment to the passport regulations was the fact that the Department of State had been recently informed of several cases in which aliens holding themselves as native American citizens have obtained, or attempted to obtain, American passports for purposes of espionage or otherwise in foreign countries.

"I don't believe this," she said and read out loud: "'Under the former rules it was not difficult to obtain passports fraudulently.' Anyone claiming citizenship through birth in the United States only had to make a sworn application before a notary. 'It was not required that either the applicant or witness be known to the notary.'"

She turned to her father. "Now you will need a witness, who must also be an American citizen, to make a sworn statement in support of your application. And that individual must be known to the clerk of the federal or state court."

"The new regulations have been instituted to keep us all safe," Prentiss observed.

"My father was native born, Mr Prentiss." Mr Weeks checked the time on his pocket watch. "Miss Weeks will fill out the rest of the form. Why don't we go ahead and take that photograph?"

"As you wish, sir." The photographer blotted the document and slid it into an envelope. He pulled back a black curtain. "This way, please, sir and madam."

He instructed the Weekses to remove their hats, posed them in front of an off-white backdrop, and requested that they face the camera head-on.

Kitty joked, "Just like criminals."

"No smiling, please," Prentiss said.

Kitty tried to keep a straight face.

"Just keep your expression neutral, Miss Weeks." He ducked behind his camera and held up a flashbulb. The negative was exposed in a burst of light. For good measure, he repeated the process.

"Well, that's that." Mr Weeks put his hat back on as they left the studio. "Thank you for being patient. It's something I've been meaning to take care of for a while."

They climbed into the waiting Packard, and Kitty gave Rao Mrs Clements's address. The playwright lived on Central Park West, so she might not be too late after all.

"Where did your father originally come from?" Kitty didn't know much about her family's ancestry. Her mother didn't have any relatives, and Mr Weeks preferred not to talk about his parents, who had died when he was young.

"I'm not sure." Julian Weeks picked up his paper. The headline had to do with Muenter, the man who had shot J. P. Morgan, committing suicide in his jail cell. "What do you make of this business?"

"It's horrid." Kitty had read the story this morning: Muenter had climbed the bars of his cell and jumped to the floor, cracking open his skull. "They say he had a history of mental problems and tried to kill himself earlier this week by digging into his wrist with a jagged blade he made from the metal eraser holder of a pencil." She winced at the gruesome image.

"And the police left him unsupervised long enough that he could try again?"

"The constable in charge walked away for a few minutes—"

"Why did the constable walk away, Capability? *That's* the real question." He shook his head and opened the paper, but not before adding, "I'm afraid the unfortunate Muenter was dead meat the moment he barged into Mr Morgan's mansion with his guns drawn."

Kitty thought hard. Among the documents that had been found on Erich Muenter's person was a press clipping announcing the Morgan bank's recent flotation of a hundred-million-dollar war bond on behalf of the British government. When reporters had questioned him about it, Muenter said that he didn't support one side over another. All he wanted was to put an end to America's export of war materials to Europe and to "persuade" Mr Morgan to use his "great influence" to put a stop to the United States's role in Europe's bloodshed. The result of his good intentions? Mr Morgan lay in the hospital, recovering from his injuries, while Mr Muenter had been found in his jail cell with his head smashed on the concrete floor.

–

"Welcome, my dear, welcome." Mrs Clements greeted Kitty with open arms. She wore a brocaded caftan with Japanese lacquered chopsticks holding her hair in place. A couple of unruly locks fell onto her forehead. "I can't believe it's been almost two days since Hunter passed." She closed her eyes. "I can't bring myself to say 'killed'… Come this way."

She led Kitty down a hallway lined with books on every conceivable topic, from art to politics, science, and literature. Above the bookshelves hung framed posters of Mr Clements's productions: *The Lost Girl*, *Beauty's Demise*, *Antigone by the Lake*, and others.

"I'm so glad that the *Sentinel* has put a girl on the case," Poppy Clements went on. "In my heart, I believe that this is a woman's story."

"What makes you say that, Mrs Clements?" Kitty asked.

"I just sense it. My Clement tells me that I should follow my instincts, and so I do – even if they're contrary to popular opinion. My entire career as a playwright is based on that principle. For instance, my current project has to do with the sinking of the *Lusitania* – but from the U-boat captain's perspective."

Kitty must have looked surprised, because Mrs Clements laughed.

"You see? I already have your attention."

Kitty followed Mrs Clements past a souk-like living room. The floor was covered with Turkish rugs, and colorful throws had been flung across every piece of furniture.

"No one thinks about the men who live in those tin cans," Poppy Clements continued in her lazy drawl. "And I can tell you that it's awful – they're stuck inside for days on end, unable to stand straight, no sunlight, no fresh air, no fresh food. As a matter of fact, they have so little oxygen that they're ordered to sleep when they're not on duty in order to conserve it. And that's not all."

Kitty marveled at the Bohemian decor as they walked through the apartment. It all seemed slightly haphazard and yet of a piece, in keeping with Kitty's sense of Mrs Clements's exotic tastes, and perhaps, her penchant to shock.

"The toilets blow back refuse into the user's face, which makes me thankful for our American plumbing," the playwright continued, "and the sailors are forced to wear a single leather uniform for the duration of the journey, which must stink like hell by the time they get home." She threw open a door. "Welcome to my den." The Oriental theme continued here too, with a low-slung divan in one corner and filigreed lamps hanging from ornate metal hooks.

"Excuse the mess." Mrs Clements cleared away a pile of pillows with a sweep of her hand. "Come sit." She leaned against an embroidered bolster and patted a seat beside her. "Do the police have any leads on who killed poor Hunter?"

"Not as far as I'm aware," Kitty replied. All she knew was what she'd read that morning, and the story had been short. "Mr Cole died of a single bullet to his head. And there were no signs of struggle on the body, so he must have been expecting whomever it was that assaulted him."

"How awful." The playwright frowned. "There weren't any fingerprints? That's normal police procedure, isn't it?"

"I believe so." Kitty was hardly an expert, but she answered, "Apparently, the pistol had been wiped clean."

"And he was killed with his own gun?"

"Yes." The woman certainly had a lot of questions.

"And it's certain that he was killed while the fireworks were in progress?"

"That's what is being said. Mrs Clements?"

"Of course, you need to ask me things, not the other way around. Forgive me, my dear. It's my instinct as a writer. Ask, ask, ask. Never rest until I'm satisfied." She took out a cigarette from a silver case. "Do you mind?"

"Go ahead."

"Would you like one?"

"No, thanks."

"Too young? You'll get the hang of it soon enough." Mrs Clements fitted the cigarette into an engraved silver holder and struck a safety match to light it. She inhaled deeply and blew out a long stream of smoke from between her lips.

"I've been asked to gather background information. Details about Mr Cole and how he was regarded—"

"You mean the woman's angle."

"That's right." Kitty nodded.

"Well, let's see." Mrs Clements picked a fleck of tobacco from her tongue and, with a flick of her elegant fingers, tossed it into the air. "Let's start with Mrs Cole. You could say I always made it a point to speak to her."

"She did tell me you were very kind."

"And I spoke to Mr Cole too."

"Did you talk to him the afternoon he died?"

"Oh yes."

"Do you recall what he said?"

"He'd had one too many to drink, you know. And he was rambling on. He seemed preoccupied with some-thing, but – and I've been thinking about this ever since it happened – for the life of me, I can't remember the specifics of our conversation. The thing is, I never paid much attention to what Hunter said. He was the kind who always went on about something or other, and I pretended to listen, because nobody else would, but mostly I observed. How he held himself, how he moved. It's useful for my writing."

"And how did he seem to you that afternoon?"

"As I said, preoccupied. Excited about something or other. But then again, maybe I'm imagining that because of what happened afterward."

"Do you have any idea what he might have been excited about?"

"You're a persistent one, aren't you?" Mrs Clements seemed amused. She shrugged. "Some people are just like that. They get into a tizzy over nothing. I'm sorry I can't give you anything particular to work with."

"Did Mrs Cole mention anything?"

"No, she kept her mouth shut. And quite rightly, I'd say. Look, Miss Weeks, I meet all kinds of people in my line of work, and I don't hold anyone's past against them. So Aimee did what she did—"

"By that you mean she was a dance-hall girl?" This would be a good time to verify Amanda's information, since Mrs Clements didn't seem the least bit prudish.

"She was indeed a dance-hall girl. One of the naughtier ones, possibly." Mrs Clements seemed unbothered by the insinuation. "But what you must understand, Miss Weeks, is that it doesn't matter. People used her as an excuse to avoid *him*."

"I'm sorry—"

"If Hunter had more to offer, they'd still gossip, but in the end, they'd overlook Aimee's past. If he had real money or influence, do you think they would care what his wife did?"

"I see." Kitty considered the point. "And Mr Cole had neither money nor influence?"

"Exactly."

"And not many friends."

"True again."

"But he was from a good family."

Mrs Clements shrugged. "That only gets one so far these days."

"Have you heard that he liked to bet on horses?"

"That's what they say."

Mrs Clements seemed frank and intelligent. She knew everyone and was held in high esteem. Kitty wanted to learn what the playwright really thought had happened. She knew she wasn't supposed to be investigating the murder, but Mr Flanagan hadn't explicitly forbidden her from asking the witnesses about their suspicions.

"Would you have any idea who might want to see him dead, Mrs Clements?"

"His wife?" Poppy Clements laughed a throaty laugh. "I'm only joking. But wouldn't you, if you were her? The thing that bothers me, Miss Weeks, is that Hunter really wasn't worth killing. Unless I'm missing something, and I don't believe I am, Hunter was a big, hearty, somewhat stupid but not evil man. Maybe he was short of cash and had some debts. But to shoot him at the stables at a party?" She shook her head. "It doesn't make sense."

She stubbed her cigarette into a chased copper bowl and pressed down on it until the final spark had been extinguished. "What's sad is that he was killed after he was feeling so much better—"

Kitty perked up. "Was he ill, Mrs Clements?" Finally, something to "work with," as Poppy Clements said.

"Yes, he was. He must have been. He told me that he had been seeing a doctor when we met at an exhibition back in March or April. He told me that he had been seeing this man regularly and that he never felt better."

"Did he tell you what for?" Kitty leaned forward. If Mr Cole had been cured of a serious illness, that would add a poignant twist to the tale.

"Someone pulled him away in the midst of our conversation. I remember clearly because Mr Clements's physician had recently retired, and I was looking for a replacement. What's strange is that when I asked Hunter about it a few weeks later, he denied that he'd been seeing anyone."

"Do you think he had something to hide?"

"Possibly."

"You didn't happen to catch the doctor's name?"

"Yes, I did. It was Michael… Or Lawrence. No, that's not right. It was one of those names that could either be a Christian name or a surname." She struck a match to light another cigarette. "It was Albert. Dr Albert." The match hovered in the air.

"Dr Albert. You're certain?"

"Positive. But the oddest part is that I asked all my friends, and no one seems to have heard of him."

—

"Come now, that's not possible." Mr Flanagan flipped through Kitty's notes. "This Dr Albert must be in the telephone directory. Look him up and find out what kind of doctor he is. If Cole suffered from a serious illness, then our readers need to know."

"Have the police made any further progress, Mr Flanagan?" Kitty said. The fact that her usefulness to him wasn't over, that he was treating her like one of the boys – straight to the point and no-nonsense – was more than she could have wished for.

"If they have, you will be the first to find out. Now run along. You have work to do." He turned back to the newsroom, and Kitty raced down the stairs, the cool metal banister gliding beneath her fingers.

She found her workplace confidante, Mr Musser, eating a sandwich in his basement lair.

"May I borrow your telephone directory, Mr Musser?" she asked the grizzled archivist.

"*Was?*" The old man brushed a crumb from his beard. "*Keinen 'Guten Tag' heute Morgen?*"

"*Guten Tag, Herr Musser,*" Kitty replied, unable to wipe the smile from her face. "Have you heard of a Dr Albert?"

He put down his sandwich, shuffled out from behind the counter, and pulled a volume from one of the stacks. "Why do you ask?" He thumped a copy of the *Bell Telephone Book for Greater New York, Including All Five Boroughs* in front of her.

"Hunter Cole." Kitty flipped through the pages. "The man who was shot at the Sleepy Hollow Country Club – he may have been seeing a physician by that name."

"Albert." Musser stroked his droopy walrus mustache. "Sorry, it doesn't ring a bell."

Kitty took out her pencil and began to copy a list of subscriber numbers.

Musser looked over her shoulder while she wrote. "Did you know that the Bell system has ten times the number of telephones, proportionate to the population, of course, as in all of Europe? The company's cables, buried underground, carry as many as *eighteen hundred* wires?"

Kitty kept her finger on the page of tiny type to make sure she didn't lose track. The one drawback to coming to Mr Musser for advice was that he was lonely and liked to chat about his current preoccupations. Usually, she didn't mind. In fact, for the most part, she enjoyed his little lectures.

"Their switchboard," he continued as she copied the information she needed, "used to require a roomful of boys to handle just a few calls and now needs only two or three girls to serve much larger numbers faster, and with far less confusion."

"That's progress." Kitty finished and returned the directory.

"And what is this?" He pointed at her notes.

"It's a list of every Dr Albert in the city."

"What do you plan to do with it?"

"I'm going to call each one of them and find out who treated Mr Cole."

"Miss Weeks." Musser's blue eyes twinkled. "You think they'll tell you?"

"I'll find out if you allow me to use your telephone."

"Help yourself. I have work to do." He shuffled off to the back.

Kitty sat in his chair and took a moment to formulate her plan. This was no different from being in drama class, she reminded herself. All she was doing was playing a part.

She picked up the receiver and asked the operator to connect her first call.

"May I speak to Dr Albert?" she said when a male voice came on the end of the line. It turned out that there was no *Dr* Albert at the residence, only a Mr Albert, but Kitty decided to pursue the conversation regardless.

"I beg your pardon," she said into the instrument. "My brother passed away recently and left a note for his doctor, but he didn't leave an address. I thought I would try every Albert in the telephone directory to see whether I could track him down."

Silence.

"My brother's name was Cole. Hunter Cole. You don't happen to have known him?"

"I'm sorry, miss. I just own a dry-goods store."

Kitty thanked him and hung up the receiver.

"Mr Cole's sister." Musser ambled out to the desk. "That's a nice touch."

Kitty grinned. The next Albert was a doctor, but he was out of town on vacation, and his nurse said he had never had any patients by that name. The third was an astronomy professor, who told her that the only Cole he knew was one of his students, and that young man had been fit as a fiddle when he came to class that morning.

Kitty kept going. There were only five names left, and her approach didn't seem to be setting off any alarms. She told herself that she was entitled to make such inquiries, and any doctor would surely want to know what had been written to him by a recently deceased patient.

She struck gold on her fourth attempt.

"Cole, but of course!" the male voice on the other end of the line exclaimed. "Have the note sent over. I'll give you my address."

"I'd like to verify a few details first, sir." Now it was Kitty's turn to be cautious. "Would you mind telling me my brother's Christian name?"

"Don't *you* know?"

"Of course I do. I'd just like to be sure that you do as well so that I don't send his letter to the wrong individual."

"Are you accusing me of lying?"

"No, sir. It's my duty to my brother's memory. I'm sure you understand."

There was no reply.

"Sir? His Christian name, please?"

The voice turned sullen. "I don't recall the Christian names of all my patients."

"Could you describe him for me?"

"Five foot ten, brown hair, brown eyes."

Hunter Cole was taller. "Where did you meet?"

"At my club."

Kitty heard someone speak in the background. The man giggled. A woman came on the line. "I beg your pardon. May I help you?"

Kitty explained.

"I'm sorry," the woman said. "Dr Albert suffers from a weak mind. He isn't allowed to speak on the telephone. Please don't call again."

Disappointed, Kitty hung up the receiver. Before she could move on to the next name on her list, a mail boy popped his head in.

"Miss Weeks, Miss Busby wants you."

Kitty slipped the list into her pocket and hurried upstairs. She would finish later.

-

"Good to see you again, Miss Weeks." The Ladies' Page editor seemed in a chipper mood that afternoon. Her hair was up in curls, she wore dangly tourmaline earrings, and she appeared ready to forgive and forget Kitty's betrayal. "Have you had lunch?"

"Not yet."

"The longer day isn't proving too difficult?"

"Not so far, Miss Busby."

"Wonderful, wonderful. Well, with all this excitement, I hope you haven't forgotten about your meeting with Mrs Stepan tomorrow."

Kitty's blank look must have suggested that she had, because Miss Busby said, "Mrs Stepan, the chairwoman of the ladies division of the Early Risers Riding Club. You are to meet her and report on their plans for the upcoming season, as we had discussed."

"Of course."

"You have the address?"

"Mrs Stepan lives on Madison Avenue."

"And you're prepared?"

Kitty hesitated to remind her boss that she had already undertaken three interviews for Mr Flanagan in the past twenty-four hours. "I am. I'll meet her at eight, right after her ride."

"All right then, Miss Weeks." Miss Busby handed her a sheaf of notes on "What to Wear This Summer." "I'd like you to put this into article form for me by four o'clock. Twelve hundred words, no fluff."

"Yes, Miss Busby." Kitty paged through the disjointed ramblings of a prominent ladies' dressmaker: *wide skirts will stay with us until August…pleating is in high demand…knife pleats…three-quarter sleeves or double sleeves (opaque above, transparent below)*. This would take all her ingenuity to convert into something coherent.

Her mind swimming with visions of chiffon and muslin, skirts and sleeves, Kitty returned to the hen coop. She would take care of Miss Busby's article, then finish her telephone calls from home.

Chapter Nine

Julian Weeks picked Kitty up from work. "You seem busy these days." He stared out of the window as Rao drove them to the west side. Kitty's father had never learned to operate a motor vehicle. He said it was too much trouble; she suspected that he preferred to be chauffeured.

"I've been asked to help out a bit on the Hunter Cole story," Kitty said. "It's nothing much, just a little background since I was at the party and met some of the people involved."

"That's good." He seemed distracted. "You know, I've been thinking that it might be time for us to travel again. Did you know that it's not too difficult to take a trip through Europe? I looked into the matter, and it seems that all we would require is a stamped *sauf conduit* – and then, with American passports, we can go wherever we like, even sightsee on the battlefields."

"I hope you're not serious." Kitty turned to him, but his face was impassive. "That sounds morbid."

He shrugged. "Some of the smaller countries over there still rely on tourist dollars."

"And how do you intend for us to get there? Swim?"

"Don't be silly. We'd sail on an American vessel. The Germans aren't about to blow those up."

"Their U-boat captains do make mistakes."

"That's true. It's possible there might be some danger."

"It's more than possible." Kitty knew he said these things just to get a rise out of her.

Rao slowed the Packard and let them off in front of the New Century's colonnaded entryway before driving around the corner to park in the garage at the rear. Not for the first time, Kitty reflected that Mr Weeks had selected the perfect place for the two of them to live when he finally decided to settle down after a lifetime of doing business abroad.

New York was the business hub of the East Coast, and Manhattan its center. Within the island, the east side was too snooty and downtown too commercial, but the area west of Central Park consisted of the perfect blend of families and self-made men like Mr Weeks: doctors, lawyers, politicians, and artists from all corners of the globe. He could have picked a gracious home on Riverside Drive, but they required too much maintenance for a no-frills individual like himself. The apartments on Central Park West would have been lovely, but the New Century on West End Avenue turned out to be perfect. Just a block to the west from the stores on Broadway and a block to the east from the park and the river, the New Century combined old-world comfort with new-world conveniences. Filtered water poured out of every tap, and the garage at the back offered facilities for charging one's batteries should one happen to drive an electric vehicle. The construction was solid and entirely fireproof. Each floor contained only two apartments, and in addition to the three main bedrooms, Kitty's home featured a comfortable foyer, a sizable dining room, living room, and study, as well as a pantry and kitchen, two servants' rooms, and a servants' bathroom.

Grace opened the front door, and Mr Weeks handed her his hat and cane. He told Kitty that he had an appointment that evening and wouldn't be in for dinner.

Kitty looked in on Mrs Codd and gave the order for a light supper. She didn't mind being on her own too much, and she wanted to finish telephoning in privacy and then write some long overdue letters to her friends in Europe.

Kitty had converted the two bedrooms at the back of the apartment, overlooking the garage, into a suite for herself. She went inside to change. Opening the bureau for a fresh blouse, she caught sight of a photograph in a tiny blue-and-green-enameled frame. A woman in a broad-brimmed hat that cast a shadow over her features smiled at Kitty. It was the only picture she possessed of her mother.

Julian Weeks had said the photograph was taken before he and Violet were married; it was an early one from when she arrived in Malaya as a penniless young governess. He met her a few years later out in a remote area where, friendless and alone, she hired him to help manage the modest rubber estate left to her by the late Mr Hiram Smith, her first husband. They fell in love, married, and had planned to have another photograph taken with the baby, but since Mrs Weeks died shortly afterward, that never happened. Julian Weeks had given the photograph to Kitty when she left for boarding school.

Kitty changed into a clean blouse, put on a pair of knickerbockers, and did her exercises: jumping jacks, marching in place, neck and hip rolls, ankle stretches.

She heard footsteps in the hall. Her father must be on his way out. She called goodbye, washed the perspiration from her face, put her skirt back on and, after making sure that Mrs Codd and Grace were safely in the kitchen, walked across the foyer to his study, slipped inside, and shut the door behind her.

The apartment had been wired for two telephones: one in the foyer, right outside the pantry, and the second one in Mr Weeks's study so that he could speak in private. He kept his room dark, with the heavy curtains drawn. It was the one room in the apartment that Kitty hadn't been allowed to decorate and wasn't supposed to be in on her own. She switched on the desk lamp.

Books interspersed with souvenirs that Mr Weeks had gathered on his travels filled the wall behind his desk. Real estate guides gave way to an ivory Chinese coolie pulling a cart loaded high with fruit, cloisonné bowls stood on top of atlases and almanacs placed sideways, and an antique jade dagger leaned casually against Adam Smith's *An Inquiry into the Nature and Causes of the Wealth of Nations*.

Kitty particularly loathed one piece that her father had placed on a shelf so that when he sat at his table, it appeared to be looking over his shoulder: a jet-black human figure whose milky eyes seemed to follow one everywhere. She felt its gaze bore into her back as she pulled back his chair and reached for the telephone.

It rang and she flinched, then laughed at herself for being foolish. He couldn't possibly know she was here – that's not who was calling. She lifted the instrument and felt inexpressibly glad to hear Amanda's voice.

"You didn't tell me whether you'd come to the YWCA training, Capability. It's just the introductory session, and I can't go by myself. Promise me that you will be there?"

"Remind me when it is again?"

"Next week." Amanda gave her the date and time. "I'll pick you up. And if you like what you hear, might you consider joining?"

"Amanda!"

"I'll quit while I'm ahead."

Kitty smiled. If Amanda ever chose to go into journalism, she would be a force to be reckoned with. She never gave up. On the other hand, she didn't listen – or she did, but only when it suited her.

Kitty removed the list of Alberts from her pocket and resumed making her calls. Dr Albert number five turned out to be a dentist; Albert number six was a chemist; and number seven ran a clinic for the needy on the Bowery.

The final Albert, Dr Beverly Albert, was a woman for whom the name Cole rang a bell. "Is this the Mr Cole who was recently murdered?"

"Yes," Kitty replied, her excitement mounting. "Were you acquainted with him?"

"I'm afraid not. I just heard about the shooting from a friend who attended the party."

Kitty replaced the receiver and stared at the sheet of paper. Something was wrong. Either Mrs Clements hadn't heard the doctor's name correctly, or one of these people had lied to her. Or perhaps, just perhaps, the Dr Albert she was looking for wasn't on this list.

She pushed the chair back into its place, stuck her tongue out at the statue, and made sure her father's desk was exactly as she had found it before she switched off the light and left the study.

She wrote her letters to her friends from boarding school and, alone at dinner, mulled over the events of Monday, July 5. Why did Hunter Cole go down to the stables that evening? That seemed to be the central, unresolved question. Was it just to get away from the other guests, or had something or someone pulled him away while everyone else was busy enjoying the fireworks?

–

Kitty spent the next morning chatting with Mrs Stepan in the back garden of the Stepans' home on Madison Avenue. The chairwoman of the Early Risers Riding Club was a young mother, pretty and active with three boys, ages four, six and eight who dashed into the garden and hugged her around the legs before going off to play under the supervision of their nurse. She glanced at them fondly and resumed her story about the glanders virus that killed her childhood pony. "It came as such a shock. One day little Zsa-Zsa was there, and the next day she was gone. I've never cared for any animal as much since, although I do ride every day."

"That sounds awful, Mrs Stepan."

"It was tragic. A terrible disease, but tell me, what would you like to know about our group?"

"Can you describe the events you have planned, who the members are, and some of the benefits of early morning equestrian exercise?" Kitty said.

"With pleasure." Mrs Stepan rattled off a list of fetes, charity breakfasts, and a gala. She mentioned names – some were prominent women who Kitty had heard about

– and then the benefits of regular riding: improved circulation, better complexion and a chance to begin one's day in communion with the natural world, away from the commotion of the city.

"Of course, we're in the city." Mrs Stepan laughed as they finished, and she led Kitty to the door. "We ride in Central Park, but that's an oasis, don't you think? Do you ride, by the way?"

Kitty nodded.

"Well, then you must join us sometime if you can be there by six. We're a friendly group, I promise."

Kitty walked back to the *Sentinel*. It wasn't that far, and the route wasn't complicated. Most of Manhattan's streets and avenues were organized along a rational, unswerving grid. Numbered streets ran from east to west, bisected at sharp right angles by avenues that ran north to south. There were those who said the plan was motivated by shameless commercial considerations (it resulted in nice rectangular plots for development) and had none of the grandeur of avenues radiating outward from the city center, like Haussmann's Paris.

But Paris was Paris, Kitty thought, picking her way down the sidewalk, dodging litter, peddlers, and a steady stream of businessmen and women. There were some people who didn't care for New York, who found it too crass, too brash, and visually unappealing. Kitty had to admit that she had felt the same way when she first arrived. She'd been alarmed by the throng of humanity in all colors, by the metal trains that rattled along overhead rails, and by the skyscrapers, some twenty, thirty, and even forty stories high, that pierced the heavens.

But she had become accustomed to it all; even the smell of rotting garbage on a hot summer day no longer repelled her. She smiled as she pushed through the heavy revolving doors at the *Sentinel*. This was home. She lived in a city that always looked toward the future.

Kitty was in one of the stalls in the women's restroom when she heard a couple of the typists enter and start chattering away at the basins.

"Who does she think she is?" The sound of running water threatened to drown out the words, but Kitty could still hear them.

"All hoity-toity and never in like the rest of us. Where is that pricey miss this morning?"

Kitty's face flushed.

"Give her a chance." The voice belonged to Jeannie Williams.

"What chance? She's already been here six months."

The taps shut off; there was a shuffle, and then the door closed behind them.

Kitty emerged from her cubicle and washed her hands. Her cheeks burned. It was one thing to suspect that the others didn't care for her, another to have one's guess confirmed.

Jeannie was the only decent one of the lot, the only one who bothered to speak to her or show any interest in what she was doing. Because Kitty worked for a shorter day, she didn't take the eleven o'clock break with the typists, and even if she did, she wouldn't have known what to say because their lives were so different.

She walked through the hen coop without looking left or right and knocked at the entryway to Miss Busby's alcove.

"I just got off the telephone with Mrs Stepan," the Ladies' Page editor trilled, looking up at Kitty. "She was most pleased with you. 'So pleasant, so personable, such a good listener.' Her words, not mine."

"I'm glad I made a good impression."

Miss Busby's coral earrings swung back and forth as she nodded. "Good impression? She thought you were just right! And so it seems that my plans are coming to fruition sooner than I expected."

"Just right for what, Miss Busby?" Kitty pulled up a chair. "What plans are you referring to?"

"Just right to interview Miss Anne Morgan about her new book."

"I beg your pardon – *the* Miss Anne Morgan?" Kitty dropped into the chair.

"That is correct." Miss Busby looked like a girl who had won the first-prize ribbon at a school contest.

"Why me, Miss Busby?" Anne Morgan was the philanthropist daughter of the first J. P. Morgan, the sister of the current, wounded J. P. "Jack" Morgan. She was known around the world for her personal fortune and charitable endeavors. "Why would Miss Morgan want a girl like me to interview her about her book?"

This was all happening too fast – in less than a week, Kitty had gone from spending all morning behind her desk to covering a party, interviewing a bereaved widow, a hostess, a playwright, a horsewoman – and now an heiress? And not just any heiress but quite possibly the wealthiest unmarried woman in the world.

Miss Busby thrust a slim volume in front of Kitty. "Because her book has been written for and about girls." She ran a finger beneath the title: "*The American Girl: Her*

Education, Her Responsibility, Her Recreation, Her Future.
And Miss Morgan would like an American girl to discuss it with her."

"I don't know what to say. I'm overwhelmed. And honored."

"As you should be."

Kitty panicked. "And I'm not very American. I wasn't raised here."

"Really?" Miss Busby paused, but just for a moment. "Well, no one can tell."

"Do you think I'm up to it, Miss Busby?"

"Well, you better be up to it, Miss Weeks, because I'm not about to refuse Miss Morgan, and I hardly qualify as a girl myself."

"Yes, I see."

"Take a deep breath, Miss Weeks."

Kitty did as she was told.

"There's just one rub."

"Yes, Miss Busby?"

"Miss Morgan maintains a busy schedule. The only time she has available to speak to you is Monday morning."

"This Monday?" The words came out in a squeak.

"That is correct."

"But that's four days away."

"I am aware, so you will not come in to work tomorrow. As soon as we're finished, you are to go home and start preparing. Don't think of doing anything else. You must study the book from cover to cover and formulate a list of questions. I'll do the same, and we will discuss it first thing on Monday morning. The interview is scheduled for ten thirty, and I'll expect you here at eight o'clock sharp. That should give us enough time. Or if you prefer, I can come in on Sunday to help you."

Kitty flipped through the book. It was short, just about sixty-five pages. She could read it in an afternoon. "That won't be necessary, Miss Busby. I can manage."

"Music to my ears. And you never know – you might find some advice in it that could be of value to you personally. Lord knows, if I were your age, I'd jump at the opportunity." She twirled a strand of gray hair around her finger. "Sadly, *my* best years are almost over."

"I hope I can be worthy of your confidence, Miss Busby."

The editor's eyes moistened. She blinked. "Go on. You better finish up."

Kitty returned to the hen coop in a daze, the volume clutched to her chest. *Responsibility… Education… Future.* These were momentous topics. And she would have the chance to discuss them with no less a personage than Miss Anne Morgan.

"There's someone here to see you." Jeannie Williams looked up from her work when Kitty came in. She stared at the book in Kitty's hands. "Is that *The American Girl*? Is it for the Ladies' Page?"

Kitty nodded. "I'll be doing the interview." The words didn't seem real.

"Oh my!" Jeannie's hand flew to her mouth. "I admire Miss Morgan so much. She's such a fine lady."

Kitty put down the book. "Did you say that someone wants to see me?"

"Silly me." Jeannie glanced at a chit beside her type-writer. "A Mr Lucian Hotchkiss. He said to tell you it's urgent."

Chapter Ten

It never rains but it pours. Kitty ran down the stairs. She had been stuck behind a desk and bored for months, and now it seemed as though everyone clamored to speak to her. What could Hotchkiss possibly want? She pictured the handsome, fretful secretary before she saw him adjusting his tie beside the three-faced clock in the *Sentinel*'s lobby. He looked nervous. A young man, likely a reporter, sauntered over and murmured something to him.

In response, Hotchkiss reached into his breast pocket and pulled out a lighter. The young man put a cigarette in his mouth and bent over the secretary's cupped hands.

"Mr Hotchkiss." Kitty approached them.

Mrs Basshor's secretary fumbled and dropped his lighter.

"Thanks." The young man strolled off, puffing away.

Hotchkiss picked up his lighter and put it back into his pocket. "Good morning, Miss Weeks." He sounded more than a little flustered.

"What brings you here, Mr Hotchkiss?" Kitty said. "May I help you with something?"

The secretary wiped his forehead with a handkerchief. "Can we speak in private?"

"This way." Kitty led him to a marble bench in a quiet corner of the atrium.

"Mrs Basshor doesn't know I'm here." The secretary remained on his feet. "She'll worry if I'm not back soon. You might think it odd of me to be so concerned, but I owe her everything. I'd be nowhere and nothing without my employer."

"I understand, Mr Hotchkiss."

"Yes, well." He coughed into his hand. "Let me start by saying that I came to you, Miss Weeks, instead of anyone else because I thought I might be able to count on your discretion. You seem to me like a young lady of tact and understanding."

"I appreciate the compliment, Mr Hotchkiss, but I haven't got all day."

"Of course." His smile was apologetic. "I believe you are aware that when Mrs Cole was questioned by the police detectives, she said that she'd been waiting for her husband at the children's tables for the duration of the fireworks?"

"Yes." As far as Kitty was aware, no one had been able to confirm Mrs Cole's claim. On the other hand, no one had disputed it either.

"I have reason to believe that that may not be entirely accurate."

"Go on," Kitty urged.

"When I was at the club yesterday, wrapping up some housekeeping matters, one of the waiters approached me and said that he had something troubling to report. Apparently, one of the ladies had lost her bracelet and asked him to search for it. He hunted around the children's tables for at least five or six minutes while the fireworks were in progress. During that time, the tables were empty. He said there was no one sitting there at all."

"Why didn't he tell the police?" Kitty's mind raced through the implications of this new information.

"He didn't think it mattered at the time."

"I see. Well, perhaps you should report it now."

The secretary smiled nervously. "Mrs Basshor would fire me on the spot if she knew that I was talking to you out of turn, let alone bringing one of her guest's movements to the authorities' attention. The waiter won't say anything for the same reason – the club frowns on it. I could have kept quiet," he added, "but instead, I decided to come to *you*."

"What can I do about it, Mr Hotchkiss?"

"You could speak to Mrs Cole and find out what happened. She won't mind if it comes from another young lady. And in the end, it might be nothing. She may have needed to powder her nose, or something like that. Something she wouldn't have wanted to tell the detectives."

"And suppose she doesn't have a convincing answer?"

"Then perhaps you could inform the authorities?"

"Really, Mr Hotchkiss." He wanted her to do his dirty work. He wanted her to question Mrs Cole and then point fingers if necessary.

"I leave it in your hands," the secretary replied. "But I would appreciate it if you didn't mention to anyone that you heard this information through me."

Kitty sighed. He looked so anxious, and Mrs Basshor probably would be furious if she found out. "I won't tell anyone about our conversation, but what I do with what I learn is my decision."

"That's all I can ask." He seemed relieved to have transferred the burden and shook Kitty's hand. "Thank you, Miss Weeks."

Kitty watched him leave. So devoted to Mrs Basshor, and yet he wasn't without his own scruples and, perhaps, grudges.

She waited for the elevator to the sixth floor. If Hotchkiss was correct and Mrs Cole had indeed been absent for some time during the fireworks, Mr Flanagan ought to be informed. The tidbit might offset her news that the Dr Albert lead hadn't amounted to much.

She tapped on the glass partition and mouthed Flanagan's name, but a tall, scholarly man emerged in response to her summons.

"Miss Weeks?" He looked down at her from his rimless, President-Wilson-style pince-nez. "I'm Rathbone, Mr Flanagan's colleague. He's asked me to give you a message."

"Is he out?"

"He's up in Connecticut with the police. It seems that the Cole case is about wrapped up. He says to tell you that they're hot on the killer's trail and should have him in custody by this evening."

Chapter Eleven

"I beg your pardon?" The revelation transported Kitty to a moment in the misty past, when her native *ayah* had taken her to prayer hall in the mountains. Kitty had been absorbed in the rich orange of the monks' robes, their strange droning chants, the golden statues draped with silky white scarves. She hadn't noticed her father barge in until he'd grabbed her wrist.

"You have to remember who you are," he'd said through gritted teeth. Seven-year-old Kitty had been terrified; she'd never seen him look so grim. It wasn't long after that that he packed her off to Switzerland, and Kitty never saw the *ayah* again. She had promised herself that she would never make the same mistake: she would never believe that she was part of something, or that she belonged somewhere, when she didn't.

The problem was, her hopes got the best of her sometimes, and judging from the stab of pain she felt in response to Mr Rathbone's abrupt announcement, she realized that she had forgotten her childhood vow and had imagined herself to be more central than she really was to Mr Flanagan's investigations.

"One of the stable hands did it." Rathbone twirled a pencil between his fingers.

"A stable hand? Why? Why would a stable hand want to shoot Mr Cole?"

Mr Flanagan's associate shrugged his shoulders. "Calm down, Miss Weeks. I'm not conversant with the details, but I believe it has something to do with the fellow being Cole's acquaintance from the racetrack. He was dismissed from his job there because of some wrongdoing and only found employment at the country club by providing a false name. Mr Cole recognized him... Really, it's best you wait until tomorrow. There will be a full account in the papers, and you can read all about it."

Kitty shook with anger. *How dare he?* How dare he treat her like another member of the news-hungry public?

"It's all I can tell you." His tone was dry as he returned to the newsroom.

But she wasn't a little girl anymore, Kitty thought as she made her way downstairs. And she no longer had to accept others' valuation of her place in the world and what she should or shouldn't do as a result of it.

–

Kitty collected her things and hailed a cab to take her home. She had gone less than half a block before she changed her mind and redirected the driver to Aimee Cole's address.

She had a role in this story too. She had met the dead man. She had met his wife. No one had been charged with the crime yet. She still had opportunities to have her questions answered.

A striking woman with sparkling eyes and red hair arranged in ringlets opened the door to the apartment. "Can I help you?"

Kitty tried to contain her disappointment. Mrs Cole probably wasn't in.

"It's me – Aimee!" the woman squealed once it became clear that Kitty hadn't recognized her. She pulled off the wig and transformed back into her unremarkable self. "I know you must think I'm awful, playing around so soon after what's happened, but I'm all alone, and I've nothing to do except look through my old things."

She flung the door wide open, and Kitty followed her inside. Open boxes and cartons littered the living room. Flouncy garments spilled out of one; another overflowed with shimmery bits. Aimee tossed her wig into a box of hairpieces.

"It started with my not being able to find my black gown," she explained. "The funeral is tomorrow, and I need something decent to wear. Mama's gone to the shops to buy me proper mourning."

She cleared a pile of scarves from the couch. "Souvenirs from my former life. Will you have some tea?"

"I don't want to trouble you."

"It's no trouble at all. Here, take a look at this while I put on the kettle." She handed Kitty a linen-bound album.

Kitty opened it, expecting to find photographs from Aimee and Hunter Cole's marriage. Instead, the album was filled with page after page of clippings, photographs, and postcards of Mary Pickford, the motion-picture actress famed for her long, red curls – no doubt the inspiration for Aimee's wig.

Kitty leafed through the pages: here was thoughtful Mary in an advertisement for *Mender of Nets*; there she was looking saucy in *Female of the Species*. She was on alert in *Tess of the Storm Country*, forlorn in *Cinderella*, and ready for romance in *Hearts Adrift*. Reviews from *Photoplay* and *Motion Picture Weekly* had been interspersed with the pictures. Some had been starred with a thick red pencil, while portions of the others had been circled or underlined for extra emphasis.

"*The Eagles Mate* is a lively feature without a real kick," Kitty read a marked review to herself, "but it has Mary Pickford, the best kick or punch that could be put in."

"Isn't she wonderful?" Mrs Cole returned to the parlor. "She looks like she's not much more than a child, but she's America's highest-paid motion-picture heroine."

"I'm partial to Pearl White myself." Kitty put the album on the coffee table. She loved Pearl's films, but she hadn't created a shrine to her like Aimee Cole had for Miss Pickford.

"Pearl doesn't hold a candle to Mary," Aimee replied. "We're the same age, you know. Both twenty-three this April. But Mary's been working forever. She started onstage when she was five years old. Her mother brought her down from Toronto, and little Gladys Smith, as she was called then, has been supporting her family ever since."

"Have you seen all her pictures?"

"All her features. The one- and two-reelers are too numerous to count. But take a guess – tell me how much you think Mary makes."

"How much she earns, you mean?"

"That's right." Mrs Cole's eyes blazed.

"I have no idea." Kitty hadn't encountered such devotion to an actress even among her school friends. And for a married lady of twenty-three, the passion certainly seemed, well, unexpected.

"Give it a try," Aimee cajoled.

"A hundred dollars a week?" It was a wild guess. Kitty knew that society reporters made fifty, and they were the highest paid in the business, so she took that number and doubled it.

"Try two thousand." Aimee sounded giddy, as though she'd just been handed that sum in cash.

"That's astounding," Kitty replied. "Every week?"

"Yes."

"But that's more than a hundred thousand dollars a year!" Kitty couldn't believe any woman could command such a salary. It was a heady figure.

"And the best part is that Mary started just like everyone else," Aimee said. "Five dollars a day, which doubled to ten, and then, when the public began to recognize her, she signed with IMP for $175 a week. She switched to Majestic for $225, then signed with Zukor for $500" – she rattled off the numbers – "and last year, Mr Zukor raised her to a thousand a week, and this year, she got him to raise it again. In addition to her salary, she earns a percentage of all her pictures' profits, and he even pays her mother a stipend."

"That's quite something." Kitty was fascinated.

"I don't bring this up lightly," Aimee said as the kettle in the kitchen began to whistle. "I would have liked to try for a career in pictures. Even a quarter of what Mary earns would have been enough to support us, but Hunter wouldn't allow it."

The whistle grew louder and more insistent. "I know I look plain in person, but that changes in front of the camera." Aimee Cole stood. "I've been photographed plenty of times. But the Coles would rather have us be poor than for me to act in the 'movies.'" She hurried off to the kitchen.

Kitty wasn't surprised that a man from a family like Mr Cole's would stand in his wife's way. Like the Vanderwell family, honor was probably all that was left to them. But poor Aimee Cole. Marriage and work didn't sit well together. Kitty had been to a symposium at Barnard College some months ago where, barring the motion-picture producer Madame Alice Guy-Blaché, all the career women who spoke had been unmarried. Dr Katharine Bement Davis, the city's commissioner of corrections; Dean Virginia Gildersleeve of Barnard; the journalist, Miss Ida Tarbell. All spinsters.

Mrs Cole returned with tea on a tray, and Kitty took advantage of the break to change the subject. "Mrs Cole?" she began.

"Aimee."

"Aimee," Kitty said, relenting. "Would you mind if I asked you a delicate question about the evening Mr Cole died?"

"So that's why you're here." Aimee gave a small laugh as she stirred a spoonful of sugar into Kitty's cup. "Of course. Ask away."

"There is one small matter." Kitty picked up her cup and took a sip. "It seems that a member of the staff noticed you were missing from the children's tables for a short while."

Aimee stiffened. "Was I?"

"That's what he said."

"You spoke to him yourself?"

"No, I didn't. But a reliable source" – she was about to say "Hotchkiss" but checked herself in time – "told me."

99

"Thank you for your concern, Miss Weeks." Aimee Cole stared at her Dresden figurines. "It was, as you say, just a trivial matter." She paused, and then said, "I'm a vain thing, and despite your kind efforts, the stain on my dress continued to trouble me. I slipped away for a few moments to give it another rinse. You can check with the attendant, if you like." She smiled. "I'm sure she'll vouch for me."

"I'm glad to hear that." As if in sympathy for what had happened to Mrs Cole that day, Kitty's hand shook, and tea spilled on her blouse. "Silly me." Her laugh sounded unsteady.

She looked down to see the splash spread like ink in water on the white fabric.

"Don't worry." Aimee led her to the bathroom.

Kitty locked the door behind her. She held on to the sides of the porcelain sink and lowered her head. What was happening to her? Was it guilt over questioning the widow, or the strong tea on an empty stomach? Whatever the case, she felt wretched.

Kitty stared into the mirror. A hollow-eyed stranger stared back.

She opened the door to the medicine cabinet. Her reflection gave way to rows of bottles and jars, tooth powder, body powder, and various hair and body lotions. Nothing to soothe her nausea.

Hunter Cole's things lined the shelf above: shaving soap, a razor, witch hazel, a jar of hair pomade, and a black toiletries case.

"Are you all right, Miss Weeks?" Aimee called through the closed door. "Is there anything I can do for you?"

"I'll just be a minute." Kitty stood on tiptoe and pulled down the case of toiletries. She undid the clasps and peered inside: gauze, cotton balls, and a bottle of bitters. She reached for it and felt a hard bundle wrapped in chamois beneath her fingers.

Kitty pulled out the bundle and found herself staring at six glass vials filled with clear liquid, and a hypodermic syringe. There was no needle.

"Miss Weeks?" It was Aimee again.

Kitty's heart beat wildly. She had a moment in which to decide her next step. She dropped one of the vials into her skirt pocket, wrapped the rest away, took a swig of the bitters, and replaced the case in the cabinet. She rinsed the stain from her shirt, then dried her face and hands and joined Mrs Cole outside, her heart still pounding.

"I'm sorry to keep calling," Aimee apologized, "but you looked pale, and I was worried."

Kitty couldn't bear her own duplicity any longer and took leave of the widow.

"So soon?" Aimee seemed disappointed. She walked Kitty to the elevator.

"May I ask whether Mr Cole had been ill recently?" Kitty broached the question while they waited for the machine.

"No. Did you hear that somewhere?"

"I probably misunderstood." Kitty's hand rested against the tube in her skirt pocket. Could this be why Dr Albert wasn't listed in the telephone book?

Chapter Twelve

The Misses Dancey, Kitty's teachers from her Swiss boarding school, were a pair of British sisters with strict ideas about decency and decorum. Kitty knew that becoming a reporter would strain what she'd been taught and how she'd learned to conduct herself, but it wasn't until that moment in the Coles' apartment that the rules she followed unthinkingly for the most part were put to the test.

It was rude to snoop through other people's belongings. Then she stole Hunter Cole's vial. There was no other way to put it. She had taken the tube without asking his widow's permission.

The question was what to do now that she had it.

The liquid in Kitty's pocket seemed to get hotter with every step she took, as though it might burn a hole through the fabric. She could throw it away and pretend none of this ever happened, or she could take it to the chemist and find out what it contained.

Kitty felt awful. How would she feel if someone poked around in her medicine cabinet and took one of her potions to be analyzed? However, the truth of the matter was that she didn't have any secrets, she assured herself.

If she heeded the dictates of her conscience, she would never amount to much as a journalist. If she didn't, she might learn something worthwhile, but at what price?

Recently, the yellow papers – the ones that ran shocking headlines in order to sell the news – had been full of stories about Harry Thaw being a dope fiend. It was part of their bid to whet the public's appetite for his upcoming trial, which would take place shortly, almost a decade after the initial trial that had been covered so colorfully by the Sob Sisters: A poor, pretty girl comes to New York. A powerful architect takes advantage of her. Later, she marries the millionaire Thaw who, in a fit of jealousy, shoots the architect on the rooftop of his own creation, Madison Square Garden.

There were some clear similarities between the Thaw case and the Hunter Cole shooting but also obvious differences. For one, Hunter wasn't rich like Thaw, and it was he who had been murdered. And for another, Kitty hadn't heard anything about Aimee Cole having been taken advantage of. Then again, with Mrs Cole's past, anything was possible.

Kitty walked up Broadway, one of the few avenues that didn't follow the right-angled grid and instead cut across Manhattan on a diagonal. On the way home, she would pass Murray & Son pharmacy on Broadway and Seventieth.

Thaw's addiction to morphine and opium and who knew what other drugs fueled his violent and unpredictable behavior. Even though Kitty had no other evidence to support such a theory, given Hunter Cole's vials and syringe, dope addiction was a possibility worth considering. It might shed a completely different light on his murder.

Kitty passed the greengrocer and the stationery shop and paused in front of the pharmacist's. A bell tinkled as she opened the door.

"Good morning, Miss Weeks." Mr Murray Sr. poured a quantity of fine white powder onto a set of scales. "I'll be with you in a moment." He adjusted the counterweights, tipped the powder onto a sheet of wax paper, deftly divided it into seven equal portions with his scraper, and wrapped each portion into individual sachets.

"One a day after breakfast, dissolved in a glass of milk or water." He scooped the sachets into a brown paper bag, which he handed to his customer, a portly, middle-aged woman.

"Thank you, Mr Murray. My heartburn has been giving me no end of trouble."

"That's what I'm here for, madam." The pharmacist turned to Kitty. "How can I help you today, Miss Weeks?"

In addition to medicinal preparations, his shop carried a variety of household supplies, soaps and beauty remedies, and Kitty often stopped by to pick up one thing or another.

Kitty made up a list as quickly as she could. "I'll take phenyl, Albi-Denta tooth soap, cough syrup and some Aspirin."

"Good, good. Anything else?" He repeated the names of the items one by one, and from the storeroom at the back, unseen hands tossed them out to him.

"Do you have something for freckles? Not for me – it's Grace again."

"You tell that girl of yours that preparations with arsenic won't do her any good."

"I've tried, Mr Murray. I've tried."

"This just came in." He scanned the shelves and pulled down a small bottle. "White Lily Face Wash." The pharmacist put on his glasses and read from the label: "'Guaranteed to brighten the skin and smooth out wrinkles, roughness, freckles and imperfections. Free of lead, arsenic, and mercury.' It'll run you ninety-five cents for four ounces."

"That's fine. What's this?" She glanced at her purchases and picked up a tiny sealed package marked with a cross and the word *Bayer* in bold letters.

He laughed. "The company doesn't want us dispensing the Aspirin powder anymore, so now they make their own pills. It comes directly from their factory so that you can be sure you're purchasing the real thing."

"I trust you, Mr Murray. Oh, there is one other matter." Kitty reached into her pocket. "I found this in my medicine chest, and the label seems to have fallen off." She placed the vial on the counter. "For the life of me, I can't remember what it is. I was hoping that you might be able to tell me."

The druggist held the container up to the light. "This is good quality," he said, tapping the glass. "Top quality, as a matter of fact. Very sturdy. Did you happen to purchase it in Europe?"

"I'm not sure. Why?"

"Oh, it's nothing," the old man replied. "I was just curious. We really don't see this type of thing here."

He tugged at the stopper and a shining globule of the liquid fell on the back of his hand as the cork came free with a jerk. Kitty watched as he brought the drop to his nose and inhaled deeply. Then he put out his tongue and licked his hand.

Kitty gasped.

"Don't you worry about me, Miss Weeks." The pharmacist seemed amused. "Belladonna, arsenic, sulfur, lead – you name it, I've tasted it, and nothing has gone wrong with me yet." He patted his belly with satisfaction. "I think I know what you have here. The scientific name for it is dihydrogen monoxide."

"What is that?" It sounded fearsome.

"Di-hy-dro-gen mon-ox-ide," the pharmacist repeated, clearly enunciating each syllable. "Water, Miss Weeks," he chortled, pleased with his little joke. "It's just water. H_2O. Whoever sold it seems to have cheated you." He was about to tip out the contents when Kitty stopped him.

"Please don't!"

Puzzled, he returned the vial, and she tucked it away inside her purse. "I'd like to hold on to this as a reminder not to be so foolish."

She picked up her packages and left the shop disappointed by Mr Murray's verdict.

Hunter Cole could have had no reason to store test tubes of *water* in his toiletries case. Either he had been misled about what the vials contained, or – and she thought this highly unlikely – the pharmacist didn't know his business.

Chapter Thirteen

"Capability!" Julian Weeks yelled for Kitty as she emerged from her bedroom the next morning, still in her nightgown and robe since she didn't have to go to work. She had hidden the dratted vial in her bureau drawer (out of sight, out of mind, she thought) and woken up early, eager to find out what the *Sentinel* had printed about the stable hand who allegedly murdered Hunter Cole; she then planned to begin her study of *The American Girl*.

But Mr Weeks had other ideas. "Are you awake? Come to my study."

She padded in to find him sitting at his desk, scowling and tossing his paperweight from one hand to the other.

"Have I done something wrong, Papa?" Kitty felt a frisson of anxiety. Perhaps he'd guessed that she had been in his study the other day.

"I'm not pleased," he said finally.

"Why, Papa?"

"Take a look at this." He pushed an envelope across the desk.

Kitty picked it up and removed two, two-by-two-inch square photographs. A hatless, expressionless man and young woman stared blankly into the camera. "That's you and me?" she said after a moment. "I almost didn't recognize us."

"Exactly." Mr Weeks slammed the paperweight on his desk. "What's the point of it, then?"

Kitty sighed.

"And in addition to that infernal photograph, which is no identification as far as I'm concerned, they want me to complete this." He handed her a document. "The other side."

She flipped it over. It was the passport form that Prentiss had partially completed. The second half required a written description of the applicant's physical features.

"Who's going to vouch for you?" Kitty glanced at the Proof of Identity section; the witness had to be an American citizen known to the applicant for several years. "One of your lawyers?"

"I'll find someone." Mr Weeks handed her a pen. "All right, let's begin."

"You want to do this now?" Kitty hadn't even had a sip of tea.

"Let's get it over with. What's the first one, stature? That's easy. Six feet." He picked up the paperweight again and rolled it between his hands as he waited for her to fill in the blank. "Next."

"Forehead."

"Forehead?"

"That's right."

"What do they care about my forehead?"

"What do you want me to fill in?" Kitty said. "Broad? High? Noble?"

"That's not funny. Just keep it simple."

"All right, broad. Now, eyes."

"Brown."

"Nose."

"Ha! Broken."

"Really? I would have said crooked."

"Broken," he repeated. "In a brawl."

"I had no idea."

"Well, yes. What's next?" He leaned forward. "Mouth? Let's put medium."

"Chin?" Kitty said.

"Square."

"All right. And I'll put hair – black. Complexion – olive. And face – square again? I'm afraid I'm not very good at this."

"You're better than I am."

Kitty finished writing and blotted the sheet.

"Thanks for your help." He sounded grudging.

"You're welcome." She returned the paper and stood.

"It's all a meaningless charade," he muttered under his breath and then asked, "By the way, did I tell you a business acquaintance will be joining us for dinner tonight?"

"No, you didn't." They rarely had guests.

"Sorry about that. Will you see to the menu?"

Kitty went to speak to Mrs Codd and then to breakfast. The morning's copy of the *Sentinel* lay folded beside her place with a prominent headline:

BERLIN SHUNS LIABILITY FOR
LUSITANIA SINKING, OFFERS
ALTERNATE PROPOSALS FOR THE
SAFETY OF AMERICANS.

How much longer would the president and German officials go back and forth on the subject, Kitty wondered before turning to the inside of the paper. The story she was looking for, "Country Club Shooter Arrested," appeared below the fold on page seven.

> Marcus Lupone, a twenty-one-year-old stable hand and recent arrival to New York City from Sicily, was found in a shed by the banks of the Connecticut River where he had been hiding since early Tuesday morning, following the shooting death of Mr Hunter Cole at the Sleepy Hollow Country Club.
>
> Prior to his employment at the country club, Mr Lupone had worked at the Aqueduct Racetrack, which was where, police say, he first became acquainted with the victim. It is believed that he was fired from the racetrack for colluding with bookmakers and that he managed to secure his position at the country club by providing the management with forged letters of reference as well as a false name – Lipton. He also shaved off his mustache in order to avoid being identified, but while walking about the grounds, Mr Cole recognized him nonetheless and this, in turn, led to their fatal encounter during the July Fourth fireworks.

Kitty recollected spotting the Coles strolling near the stables before the party began; she read on to learn that the police had questioned Lupone when they arrived at the club after the shooting and that he fled the scene only afterward. Because of the recent mishap at the jail in Mineola – where Mr Morgan's attacker had committed suicide – Lupone would be held in custody at the infamous Tombs prison in Manhattan.

Mr Weeks joined Kitty at breakfast. "Aren't you going to work?" He took his seat at the head of the table.

"Not today. I'm interviewing Miss Anne Morgan on Monday, so I have the day off to prepare."

He shook out his napkin. "*The* Miss Anne Morgan?"

Kitty nodded.

"My, my." His grin had a touch of amusement to it. "You are moving up in the world."

She reached for the caddy and spread a pat of butter on her toast. Something about the police's case against the stable hand troubled her.

On the surface, it all sounded reasonable enough – false identity, discovery, altercation – but Flanagan seemed to be pushing the Sicilian angle as though the facts alone weren't sufficient. He concluded his article with a quote from the commissioner of corrections, Dr Katharine Bement Davis, who said that over half of those confined in the murder cells at the Tombs had Italian names. "'I have been in Italy,' Dr Davis said, 'and especially, I have been in Sicily. Sicilians bring with them their own primitive ideas of vengeance when they migrate to this country.'"

Marcus Lupone probably didn't have very many friends here, Kitty thought, taking a bite of toast. More than likely, his English wasn't good. Perhaps, once he realized that Mr Cole had been murdered and the police would be questioning everyone, he panicked and fled. He understood that he would be an obvious suspect. But to the police, his act of self-preservation would only make him seem that much more suspicious.

Grace came in with a message for Mr Weeks. "Rao says the Packard has to be taken to the mechanic this morning, sir."

"What's the matter?"

"He didn't tell me, sir. At least, he said something about the oil, but I didn't understand."

"I see." Julian Weeks let out a deep breath and turned to Kitty. "I hate to ask, but would you drive me downtown?"

"What time do you need to be there?" she said.

"By ten."

That meant she wouldn't be able to start reading until eleven at the earliest.

"You don't have to wait," Mr Weeks said. "You can drop me off and come straight back."

Normally, she would have been happy to oblige him, but still she hesitated.

"This isn't a request, Capability." His tone was sharp. "I have a meeting to attend."

"Of course." Kitty pushed back her chair. His needs came first.

Chapter Fourteen

The Bearcat wouldn't start. It sputtered to life when Kitty turned on the electric ignition and then went dead in a couple of seconds.

"What's the matter now?" Mr Weeks drummed his fingers impatiently against the leather seat.

Kitty stepped out of the car, removed her gloves, and lifted the hood. "Just some leaves." She pulled them out and dusted off her hands.

This time, the engine roared. Kitty made sure her hat was securely fastened with her silk scarf and stepped on the gas. With a lurch, the vehicle surged forward.

Wind on her cheeks, she sped past other automobiles on West End Avenue. Ladies used to be relegated to electric motors since they were slower, cleaner and safer, but no longer. These days, almost everyone drove gasoline-fueled cars. The Bearcat had no sides or doors and no top, just two leather chairs, the driver's controls, and a jaunty round monocle windscreen behind the hood. Kitty loved the sensation of being in control of such a powerful machine and the thrill of being completely exposed to the elements.

Julian Weeks held his hat in his lap and his cigar clamped between his white teeth. Stronger, braver men might have quaked at some of his daughter's maneuvers.

She swerved around a horse-drawn cart and raced past a tram coming around the bend, its bells clanging. Through it all, she maintained good form, sitting confidently upright in her seat, neither looking stiff nor slouching behind the wheel, as her instructor, Mr Berriman, had informed her that "certain classes of motorists" were wont to do.

While motor-vehicle owners didn't have to pass a test to operate their vehicle, Kitty knew the rules: She must not drive while intoxicated. She should stop after an accident. She must signal with her hand before making a turn and should remain within the speed limit or else face a penalty of up to one hundred dollars.

"Who are you meeting today?" she asked her father after several blocks.

"Someone from out of town."

Julian Weeks didn't seem in a particularly talkative mood. Kitty didn't mind since she enjoyed just being in his company and besides, she needed to have her wits about her to negotiate the chaos that came with driving through Manhattan on a weekday morning. Mr Weeks's destination, the Edelweiss Café on the southern tip of Manhattan, obliged them to drive through some of the most congested parts of the city and negotiate shoppers with packages, rushing businessmen, and peddlers pushing carts, not to mention other motorcars and autobuses.

The right-angled grid gave way to the city's original winding paths, now paved over and flanked by commercial buildings like the Morgan Bank and the US Sub-Treasury as the Bearcat neared Mr Weeks's destination. Wall Street, so called because it had once been the site of a wall built by early settlers to defend themselves from the natives, was now the nation's – if not the world's – financial hub. The sun barely penetrated the valleys where pedestrians and motorcars inched along on narrow roads, hardly suited to their present heavy use.

Kitty pulled up at the corner of the block where the café was located and let her father out.

"Thanks, Capability." He patted her shoulder and stepped out of the vehicle. She watched him disappear into the sea of businessmen on the sidewalk.

It was all men, Kitty realized as she re-tied her head scarf. Men in suits, men with sleeves rolled up, men hurrying along as though civilization depended on their efforts, and men loitering – like those two fellows in dark suits with newspapers under their arms who hurriedly looked away when she noticed them staring at her.

There wasn't another woman in sight. All at once, Kitty felt vulnerable and ill at ease in her bright yellow motorcar. She switched on the engine and drove past the café, then turned right at the end of the street and right again, thinking she would be headed home. Instead, within a few blocks, it became clear that she had no idea where she was going.

A sense of panic threatened to overwhelm her, and she slammed her palm against the steering wheel. That was what came from doing a favor. Kitty hated losing her bearings and had no internal compass. It appeared that she only managed as well as she did because of the city's grid. Take away her usual markers and she was lost.

She didn't slow down to read the signs on the lamp-posts. She turned right, then left, then right again. Nothing looked familiar. The eerie sounds of an Oriental violin led her to believe she might be close to Chinatown and the police headquarters.

She drove past a group of men gathered on the sidewalk. One grabbed his crotch and called out something crude. Kitty stepped on the gas, made a sharp turn, and escaped down a quiet street. She allowed the motor to coast while she caught her breath. New York had never seemed so ominous.

Something at the end of the road caught her eye. Of its own accord, the Bearcat rolled forward.

A covered stone bridge floated above the street. It spanned the distance between a redbrick building and a forbidding structure with turrets on top and slit-like windows. Kitty had seen this view depicted in postcards: this must be the infamous Bridge of Sighs connecting the criminal courts to the Tombs prison.

Kitty's hands clenched around the wheel. These thick walls right in the middle of Manhattan held thousands of prisoners, condemned men and women packed into cold, damp cells without adequate sunlight or ventilation. She'd heard horrible stories about the place. That it had been built on the site of the old Collect Pond, which was once Manhattan's source of fresh water and later became so polluted from the waste of nearby abattoirs and tanneries that it had to be filled in. That the prison's foundations started to sink into the sludge from the moment construction began, and that vestiges of the old waterways still trickled beneath it, leading inmates to claim that the entire building swayed in sympathy with the East River.

A whistle's sudden blast nearly deafened Kitty.

"Didn't you hear me, madam?" an irate policeman barked. "Move on. There's no sightseeing permitted here."

"I'm sorry." Kitty hadn't realized she'd been gawking. "Am I correct that this is the Tombs?"

"That's right." He folded his arms across his chest. "Murderers, thieves, the worst of the worst. They're all holed up in there." He nodded with satisfaction. "It's no place for a young lady like yourself."

It was no place, Kitty thought, for the stable hand Marcus Lupone either. "Do they bring inmates over in the mornings?"

"At all hours."

"I think I may have a friend inside."

"You may?" The policeman seemed skeptical.

"I do." Kitty had read stories of wives going into the prison to see their husbands, mothers delivering food to their sons. "Are visitors allowed inside?"

"Ye-es," the policeman said hesitantly.

"Could I go to see him?"

The policeman looked at her with incredulity. "You're sure you'd want to go in there?"

"Should I be afraid?"

"No, no. It's perfectly safe for the rest of us. Who is it that's inside anyway?"

"His name is Lupone."

The officer shook his head. "Never heard of him, but park your vehicle over there" – he pointed to a vacant area – "and follow me."

"Ah—" Kitty had asked about visiting out of curiosity. She hadn't expected to succeed.

"You want to come back tomorrow? The place is packed on Saturdays."

"I see."

"Just leave your car right there." He chuckled. "I promise no one will steal it."

Kitty turned off the engine and followed him to the prison like a sleepwalker. She gave the guard at the front desk her name, stated the purpose of her visit – to see Mr Lupone – and signed her name and time and date of entry in a thick ledger.

The policeman left her, and she waited on a wooden bench, beginning to regret her impulsive decision. What would she say to Hunter Cole's alleged killer? Since he didn't know her from Adam, how would he react? Would they bring her to his cell?

Two guards led a shuffling prisoner by, his shackles clanking on the floor. His face was bruised and battered.

Kitty stood. This was too much. Had she lost her mind? She should leave this minute.

"This way, please." A bored-looking guard with a circle of keys hanging from his belt beckoned.

"Oh dear," Kitty said.

"Scared?"

She nodded.

He laughed. "They're just criminals."

She followed the man down a gloomy, mildewy hall. She heard footsteps, prisoners' voices. She could be killed in here – or worse. And no one would know.

They turned the corner and came to a row of doors. The guard unlocked one and motioned for Kitty to step over the threshold.

"I should go inside?"

"I'll be with you."

She didn't like the look on his face. "Where is Mr Lupone?"

"He's on his way."

"I prefer to wait outside until he arrives."

"Suit yourself."

Kitty drew herself up straight. "I'm a reporter with the *New York Sentinel*."

The guard smirked. "And they let you in?"

"Yes, they did." Kitty hoped she sounded firm.

Lupone soon arrived, escorted by another guard, his hands cuffed behind him. "Who is this?" he asked in thickly accented English. A mop of dark curly hair fell over his forehead.

"Why don't you both wait outside?" Kitty told his guard. "I'd like to speak to Mr Lupone on my own."

The guard snickered. "Very pretty for your first visitor, Marcus. Don't pretend you don't know her."

Bruises darkened the stable hand's neck and one side of his face. The guard pushed the door open. A single lightbulb hung from an electric wire above two chairs and a table.

Lupone lowered himself into one. The door closed behind them. "Who are you?" he said.

"I'm here from the newspapers," Kitty replied. "I'd like to help you."

"I no do anything, lady," Lupone said. "I no shoot anyone. You help get me free."

"Can you tell me what happened the evening Mr Cole was shot, Mr Lupone?" Kitty couldn't believe how composed she sounded. Just like a professional.

"I take everyone out of stables like Mr Cole say."

"He *asked* you to take the other lads out?"

"*Si.*"

"When? That afternoon?"

"No, no. A few days before. I meet him outside, and he say, 'Marcus, on Monday, at the party, take all the lads to see the fireworks.'"

"Did he tell you why he wanted everyone out?" Kitty had conjectured correctly. Hunter Cole hadn't just strolled down there; he'd had a plan. A plan to meet someone. His killer, no doubt. He may have been concerned about the meeting, which was why he'd brought the pistol to Mrs Basshor's do.

Lupone shook his head. "Mr Cole tell me nothing."

"But you weren't surprised to see him at the club on the day of Mrs Basshor's party?" If Lupone was telling the truth, the police's case against him no longer made sense.

"Of course, no. I know he was coming."

"Did you tell the police?"

"They no believe me! But why I kill Mr Cole? He a very nice man."

It was the first time Kitty heard anyone say that. "Do you have proof that Mr Cole met you before the party? Did anyone see you talking to him?"

"I no think so."

Kitty believed him. "But you were working at the club under false pretenses."

Lupone looked confused.

"You made up a false name when you worked at the club."

"Sure. I try to be English, but I no kill anyone." He leaned toward her. "*Signorina*, you find me a lawyer."

"I'll try," Kitty said. "I'm just a reporter." She knew it was a weak excuse when a man's life was on the line.

"I understand." Lupone's handsome face turned fierce. "You only want to speak to me for story."

Embarrassed and ashamed, Kitty had no reply.

"Guard," he called. "Guard!"

The door swung open.

"I finished." He rose to his feet.

"So fast?" The jailer winked.

Kitty felt dirty from the way he leered at her. Lupone's guard led him one way, and the other man led Kitty toward the entry hall. Before they reached it, he turned and held out his hand.

He expected a tip. Kitty gave him a dollar. Anything to get out. The hand didn't budge. She put in another.

Minutes later, Kitty was back on the street. She felt inexpressibly relieved to have made it out of the prison in one piece and didn't blame the stable hand for feeling used.

She asked a passerby for directions and started the Bearcat. She would make it up to Lupone. She wouldn't be able to hire him a lawyer, but she could find the evidence to prove his innocence.

Chapter Fifteen

Back at the apartment, Mrs Codd was busy preparing dinner, and Grace had set the table for their guest. Kitty said she'd take a sandwich in her rooms for lunch and hurried off to shower. She scrubbed her body and washed her hair and then soaked in the tub until she felt she had released every last bit of grime from the prison. She cleaned inside her ears and brushed her teeth. Then she changed into a comfortable robe and ate her sandwich while Grace brushed her hair. It was nearly three o'clock. Kitty had a few hours left before their visitor arrived. Her father hadn't yet returned.

She sat at the desk in the bedroom that she had converted into a private workroom for herself and began to read. Anne Morgan opened her first chapter, titled "Her Education," with a question:

> How can the girl of America be prepared and prepare herself for all that life will bring to her? How can her secret garden best be planted and watered, so that its soil may bring forth an ever-growing beauty of blossom and fulfillment, and its shady walks and running brooks bring rest and inspiration to the weary traveler along the road of life?

By way of an answer, Miss Morgan turned to her own experience of the American girl abroad – a type she'd had ample opportunity to witness in action, she said, pointing out that it was sometimes possible to make accurate deductions about a whole class based upon the careful observation of a few "isolated specimens."

> It has interested me exceedingly to observe the American girl who lives abroad, insignificant numerically though she is, and to note that notwithstanding her marvelous adaptability to her surroundings she is still the American Girl, unlike any other girl in the world.

Kitty liked the "notwithstanding her marvelous adaptability" point – it reminded her of herself, both in New York and in Switzerland. She read on, ready to be bowled over by Miss Morgan's insight and candor.

> No intelligent person can fail to remark how the qualities, both desirable and unfortunate, which make her unique, are, after all, American qualities.

Yes! But what were those qualities? Kitty hoped Miss Morgan would enlighten her readers.

> For generations, now, current literature has been filled with descriptions of the American girl. We find her in English novels as a wild, undisciplined creature, with a desire

for every luxury and a corresponding objection to any personal restraint. Germany and France present her to the world as an unsexed primitive force with an appendage of dollars, which should unquestionably be used to reinstate financially some old and historic name.

Kitty smiled. No doubt the author spoke from personal experience. On his death, her father, the first J. P. Morgan, had left her three million dollars. It was a staggering amount to bequeath to an unmarried daughter, especially when his married daughters had received so much less. (The current J. P. Morgan, Miss Morgan's brother, had received the lion's share of his father's fortune.)

Kitty continued reading:

The internationalism of the American girl is far in excess of that of any other nationality. Intermarriages always have existed and always will exist, but never, since the days of the barbarian invasions, has one country supplied so many instances.

A good point – Consuelo Vanderbilt, Jennie Jerome, there were so many examples – but it still wasn't the answer Kitty needed.

America is a country where, to its own undoing, individualism has reigned supreme. The time has come when forces of group conscience and group consciousness must be

> drawn up in hostile array against the doctrine of individual egotism. The American girl who seeks to avoid the inevitable conflict by looking to European sanctuary is indeed deceived. She longs for the finish and the beauty of the old order... She fails to realize that it lies in her own hands to bring that same beauty into her own surroundings.

Kitty shifted in her chair. When would Miss Morgan answer her own excellent question? What were the qualities, good and bad, that constituted the hallmark of an American girl?

Kitty flipped through the pages. Modern educators allow children to follow their own whims, they insist that the child must have complete freedom, so the girl "will rush with spasmodic enthusiasm into the mood of the moment."

Miss Morgan went on to discuss immigration and the need to teach foreigners to understand the responsibilities of American freedom.

Kitty heard her father enter the apartment.

"Capability," he called, "are you ready for this evening?"

She scanned through to the end of the chapter. While she agreed with many of Miss Morgan's shrewd observations, Kitty couldn't find a central thesis. And she couldn't see an answer to what made the American girl unique.

–

Kitty changed into a red gown and matched it with garnet-and-gold drop earrings and a garnet bracelet. She checked Grace's table setting and then joined her father in the living room.

"You look lovely." Mr Weeks nodded his approval.

"Thanks." She smoothed her hair.

"I think you will like Mr Maitland. He's Canadian. The smartest fellow I've met in a long time."

Coming from Julian Weeks, who was particular about the company he kept, that was quite a compliment.

Their visitor arrived soon enough. He had buttery skin like a baby and must have weighed over two hundred fifty pounds. He could have been as old as forty or fifty, or perhaps as young as his mid-thirties. It was hard for Kitty to tell. His size and his flair – he tied his cravat with the élan of a Frenchman – made him seem ageless.

His twinkling blue eyes followed Kitty as she served drinks. He was quite the conversationalist and described – of all things – how the bubonic plague spread through China.

"A Chinese trapper contracted the disease through contact with the tarbagan, a furry creature native to Mongolia," he said. "Once infected and back in Harbin, he transmitted it to anyone who happened to be near him during his coughing fits. What amazes me is that that's all it took. All one needs is a single spark to start a fire – and one sick man can contaminate an entire nation."

Kitty poured herself a glass of sherry and listened intently as her father and his guest spoke about a variety of topics, from the Panama-Pacific International Exposition in San Francisco, to Viennese art and architecture, to last July's murder of the Austrian archduke that precipitated the war in Europe.

"It was only because of a series of errors and unlikely coincidences that the Serbian gang's ringleader, Gavrilo Princip, managed to do in Franz Ferdinand," Mr Maitland declared, his deep voice rumbling.

Julian Weeks held his drink loosely in one hand, legs crossed at the knee.

"The archduke and duchess rode in their motorcade alongside the Appel Quay."

Kitty pictured the scene – the duke in his military garb with medals at his chest, his adoring wife in her white dress and ornate hat, both waving to the crowds they passed.

"The first plotter threw a bomb, which landed on a car behind his target," Mr Maitland continued. "The fool panicked and threw himself into the river, but the summer's sun had reduced it to a trickle, and so it was no trouble for the police to catch him.

"At that point, all should have been settled, everyone should have been safe, but in the confusion that ensued, the leader, Princip, ducked into a nearby coffeehouse. The motorcade changed its route, but somehow the archduke's driver hadn't been informed of the decision. He drove up a side street, following the original itinerary, when a general who was accompanying the royal couple ordered him to stop and turn the car around. But the street was too narrow, so all the chauffeur could do was to drive in reverse. Can you believe it? The heir to the Austrian Empire being driven backward down a narrow street after an attempt on his life had been botched just minutes ago!"

Kitty knew the outcome of the shooting – who didn't? – but hadn't heard this version of how it unfolded.

"In the coffeehouse nearby, Princip heard noises and stepped out to see what was happening. He couldn't believe his eyes. His targets were just feet away, crawling along like tortoises in their open car. He didn't hesitate. He raised his pistol, took aim and fired. The archduke and duchess fell. At such close range, there was no chance of their survival."

"Do you think the war might have been avoided if the archduke hadn't been killed?" Kitty asked.

"He was a fool to visit on one of the holiest days in Serbia, a fool to visit while tensions in their empire ran so high, but no. I think anything could have set Europe off last summer. German, Russia, England and France, all had been building up their weapons and armies and jumped on the opportunity to discharge them. If not the archduke's murder, they would have found some other pretext. And now each side has lost too much to call the whole thing off and admit that the war has been an unmitigated disaster."

Grace knocked on the door to the living room and looked in. Someone had telephoned for Mr Weeks.

"At this hour?" He didn't seem pleased.

"He said it was urgent, sir."

Julian Weeks excused himself to take the call, leaving her alone with his guest.

"Your father tells me you plan to become a journalist, Miss Weeks." The big man took a sip of his drink and stared at her so intently that Kitty didn't know where to look.

"I hope so." She smoothed the folds of her gown. "Right now, I work for the Ladies' Page of the *New York Sentinel*."

"I own shares in a paper in Canada, the *Star-Journal* – it's a daily. The editors there tell me that female reporters, thanks to their tact and intuition, catch stories that the men miss."

"You should tell that to our publisher." Kitty kept her tone light. "He doesn't allow women to step foot inside the newsroom."

"Well, I'll leave that for him to discover, but I'm sure both he and you are aware that your sex are the most powerful force behind any newspaper."

"How is that the case?"

"It's quite simple. Advertising brings in more revenue than subscriptions or direct sales. The most frequent advertisers are the department stores and other merchants whose clientele is primarily female. I assume that the situation is only more pronounced here in the United States."

"Why are women's stories confined to a single page then?"

"Because most newspapers are still obliged to report the news, by which I mean politics and foreign affairs," Maitland replied. "And I don't believe female readers care for that kind of information… May I be forward with you, Miss Weeks?" The big man set down his glass.

Kitty nodded.

"I'd like to invite you to accompany me to the Cloisters Museum before I return to Toronto. It opened last year and I haven't yet had a chance to visit."

Kitty opened her mouth and shut it again.

"What's that you say, Maitland?" Julian Weeks returned to the room.

"I just invited Miss Weeks to join me on a trip to the Cloisters Museum – that is if you don't object. You're welcome to join us," the big man said.

"I don't care for that sort of thing, but I don't mind if Capability goes." He turned to Kitty. "It's getting late. Would you check on dinner, my dear?"

Relieved not to have to reply at once to Mr Maitland's offer, Kitty excused herself. She wondered about his intentions. Given the difference in their ages, he couldn't possibly think—

She fiddled with her bracelet, then looked in on Mrs Codd. All burners were on, and dinner would be ready soon.

She and Grace made a final examination of the dining table. The corners of the starched damask tablecloth hovered a few inches above the floor, each cover had been set with geometric precision, the starched napkins seemed to float on the plates, and the polished silver reflected the light from the candles placed on either side of the centerpiece.

Mr Maitland and Mr Weeks joined Kitty in a few minutes, and then Grace brought out course after course in leisurely succession. Mr Maitland ate heartily and maintained a steady stream of conversation throughout the meal. If he had any particular interest in Kitty, he hid it well.

She left the two men to their cigars and brandy after dessert and had a cup of coffee in the pantry while Grace washed and dried the dishes and put them away in the cabinet.

"I've never seen anyone eat so much," the maid exclaimed.

"He has quite an appetite," Kitty agreed.

Grace giggled. "I pity his wife."

"I don't think he's married," Kitty said, surprised by the sharpness in her own tone.

It was close to midnight when Mr Maitland left. Kitty had already said her goodbyes and was in bed when she heard the front door close.

She lay under the covers, mulling over the day: Mr Maitland, Miss Morgan's book, her visit to the prison. As she drifted to sleep, one question nagged at her: What to do about Lupone's revelation that he had known that Mr Cole would be at the stables.

–

"Maitland seems to have taken a shine to you," Mr Weeks said when Kitty joined him at breakfast the following morning. "I didn't expect him to invite you to the museum. Not that I'm worried, of course." He sipped his coffee. "I don't expect you to have any interest in a man like him."

"What kind of man is he?"

"You know. Older. And so large. I'm sure it causes health problems."

"He's a fascinating speaker."

"That he is, that he is."

Kitty helped herself to a slice of toast and changed the subject. "So what do the papers have to say about Germany's latest response to President Wilson's proposals on the *Lusitania*?"

Mr Weeks picked up his copy of the *Times*. "They've printed the reply in its entirety. Would you like me to read it to you?"

"Just the gist," Kitty said.

Julian Weeks began:

"Berlin, July 9, 9 p.m. via London, July 10, 2:37 a.m. The text of the German reply to the American Note is as follows: On November 3, 1914, England declared the North Sea a war area, and by planting poorly anchored mines and by the stoppage and capture of vessels, made passage extremely dangerous and difficult... Long before the beginning of submarine war England practically intercepted neutral shipping to Germany. On November 14, the English Premier declared it was one of England's primary tasks to prevent food for the German population from reaching Germany through neutral ports. Since March 1—"

"I get the gist." Kitty laughed. "Not the full text."

"The gist is that Germany won't back down. They insist that Britain's actions have left them no other choice than to retaliate with submarines in order to be able to feed their people. Do you need Rao today?"

Kitty had decided to visit the country club and ask some questions on Lupone's behalf. "I thought I might go shopping at Altman's. But I can drive myself."

"All right." He returned to the paper. "This is really quite amazing," he murmured to himself.

"I should be back by three."

"Don't forget we have the concert this evening."

"Which concert?"

"At Carnegie Hall." Mr Weeks enjoyed music and often bought tickets for performances without checking with Kitty first.

"Oh." That would cut into her time with *The American Girl*, but the longer it took to find any exonerating evidence, the less inclined the police would be to believe her. And while she was at the club, Kitty thought she may as well look into Mrs Cole's whereabouts during the fireworks.

"Leaving so soon?" Julian Weeks asked as Kitty stood.

"I'd like to get an early start."

Her father frowned, puzzled. "What time does Altman's open on Saturday?"

"I'm not sure." To distract him, she added, "By the way, is Mr Maitland a friend or business acquaintance?"

"A bit of both, I suppose. We might embark on a venture together."

"That's nice." She pushed in her chair. "What kind of venture?"

"Ah." He nodded. "If it turns out right, it could be very good."

—

Kitty studied the map and wrote out directions. She dressed for the day, called for her car, and drove to northern Manhattan, then on to the Bronx, past the Botanical Gardens, Fordham University, and Van Cortlandt Park. Fortunately, there were fewer streets here so fewer choices and fewer opportunities to lose her way.

She stopped once to have the car filled with gasoline, and then pulled up outside the Sleepy Hollow Country Club where a sign that she hadn't noticed previously informed visitors that the club was *Private Property* and *Trespassers Will Be Prosecuted*.

As if that would dissuade a criminal, Kitty thought, parking her car outside. She pushed in the gate and entered on foot.

With her parasol open, she roamed across the lawns as nonchalantly as though her father were a member. No one stopped her.

Kitty wandered over to the rear patio where a few elderly sorts with nothing else to do on a Saturday morning sipped tea or leafed through magazines and newspapers. Some of them may have looked up as she went inside, but no one asked any questions. She made her way to the ladies' room, only to discover that the woman on duty that morning wasn't the one who had been there on the evening of the murder.

Kitty washed her hands. "You weren't here for Mrs Basshor's party on Monday, were you?" she said to the attendant who waited for her with a towel.

"No, ma'am. I'm only here on the weekends. Is there something that I can help you with?"

"Would you happen to know the name of the attendant who worked here that day? I think I may have lost my comb and was wondering if she found it."

The woman opened a cupboard and brought out a wicker basket for Kitty to inspect. "We keep all lost and found items here."

Kitty rummaged through the contents. "I'm afraid I don't see it. When will – what did you say her name is again?"

The attendant blinked. "It's O'Malley."

"That's right – O'Malley. And when will she be back?"

"On Monday. She works during the week."

"Of course, yes."

"If you give me your name, madam, I can ask her to keep an eye out for it."

Kitty had the feeling that the attendant sensed that something wasn't right, that she was neither a member nor a member's guest. She picked up her purse and dropped a few coins into the bowl. "That's quite all right. I'll be back again soon and ask her myself."

She hurried through the clubhouse and back out onto the patio. The sun was out, the trees rustled in the breeze, and the majestic Hudson River shimmered in the distance. Kitty recalled the scene at Mrs Basshor's party. There must have been at least a hundred people out on this patio and on the lawns. A hundred guests, plus waitstaff and grounds staff, and kitchen staff and chauffeurs at the entrance. Any one of them could have murdered Hunter Cole.

When he was shot was clear: during the fireworks. Where was at the stables, how was with his own gun. The only questions that remained were why and by whom.

As far as Kitty was concerned, those questions hadn't been properly answered.

A horse-drawn cart clopped briskly down the driveway toward the front gate. A driver holding the reins urged the animal on; beside him, a gentleman clutched his hat and doctor's bag while the cart bounced up and down over the gravel. From where she stood, Kitty couldn't make out what was in the back, except that a large tarpaulin covered the mound.

Kitty walked on. A girl's voice called, "Love thirty," as she passed the tennis courts. The speaker wore a long white skirt, her shirtsleeves rolled to her elbows. She tossed a white ball into the air and smacked it across the net with her wooden racquet.

A young man in sharply creased white trousers lunged to return the ball. He hit it back, but it shot over the fence, and Kitty, who had it firmly in her sights, caught it in midair. The ball slipped from her hands, and she ran to pick it up again and tossed it back.

"Thanks," the man called.

"Fifteen thirty," the girl said, and play resumed.

She could have been that carefree girl. Kitty's chest tightened as she neared the stone stables. The yellow-brick building looked lovely with the summer sun hitting its tiled roof, and colorful pansies in planters hung from wrought iron hooks.

The police had their man, Kitty reminded herself. No one had asked her to come here – not even Lupone, trapped in prison.

Whatever the outcome of her visit, it would be on her own head. There would be no going back. She had already done much more than she ought to, with her trip to the Tombs.

She took a deep breath, put her hand against one of the heavy wooden doors and pushed it open.

Chapter Sixteen

A dusty shaft of light filtered through a single window at the back of the barn and formed a puddle of brightness along the aisle between the two rows of stalls.

"*I'm on my way-way-way, To Mandalay-lay-lay...*" A young boy with knobby knees and a reedy voice sang and swayed in the circle of light, dancing with his broom.

"*Oh, let me live and love for aye, on that island far away.*" His eyes were closed, so he didn't notice Kitty watching. "*I'm sen-ti-mental – for my Ori-ent-al love, so sweet and gentle—*"

"Excuse me," Kitty interrupted, hating to break the moment.

The little lad swung around to face her just as a burly fellow in overalls emerged from the darkness of a stall, grooming brush in hand.

"G'morning, miss." He touched his cap. "Back to work, Turnip," he said to the boy. "And quit the warbling."

Kitty stepped forward gingerly, not wanting to tread on the spot where Hunter's body had lain. She had thought she remembered the area exactly, but now she wasn't sure, since all traces of the tragedy had been cleaned away. The place looked just like an ordinary stable ready for business.

"I was passing and thought I'd check in on the horses," she said.

"Are you an owner, ma'am?" The groom wiped his brow with the back of his sleeve. "Beg your pardon for asking, but only owners are allowed inside these days."

"New rule?" She tried to seem unconcerned.

"Don't know if you heard, but there was a murder on the premises."

"Ah, yes." Kitty nodded. "I was there. I'm a friend of Mrs Basshor's."

Groom and boy exchanged nervous looks.

"Is something wrong?" Kitty asked.

The boy opened his mouth to speak, but the man silenced him with a glare. "I told you to get back to work, Turnip." His calloused hand reached out to stroke a velvety nose that poked out from a stall. "One of our animals fell ill and had to be seen to by the vet."

"Was that him in his cart I just saw?"

"That's right," he replied. "You're fine, girl. Just fine," he murmured to the horse he was petting and fed her a carrot.

"That must be hard after all that's happened. I heard that they caught the fellow who did it. He worked here?"

The stable hand stiffened. "He did."

"Was he a foreigner?" If the stable hands held any grudges against Lupone or thought he was guilty, her question might prompt them to talk.

"We guessed that, didn't we, Turnip?" the older man replied. "From his accent. Still, he wasn't a bad sort. Kept to himself."

"You must have noticed something." Kitty tried to probe. "Didn't you hear or see anything suspicious?"

"Well…" The groom took off his cap, scratched his head, and put it back on. "Actually, no. He was a hard worker. Went away on his days off but always came back on time. We never had any trouble." Behind him, Turnip's head bobbed up and down in agreement.

"There wasn't anything suspicious about him at all? Did he know Mr Cole from his previous employment?"

"That's what they're telling us. That Mr Cole recognized him, and he would have lost his job—"

"Madam!" The door burst open and a man in a blue pin-striped suit rushed in. "Madam," he said again, out of breath. For a while, it seemed to be the only word he could manage. "I'm Phillips, the club secretary," he added finally. "And you are?"

Kitty froze. "Miss Lodge." The only name she could think of on the spur of the moment was Elaine *Dodge*, the character played by Pearl White.

"She's a friend of Mrs Basshor's," the groom offered.

"Well, Miss Lodge," said the club secretary, "I must inform you that only owners are allowed into the stables at this time and that all guests must be properly signed in at the front desk and be in a member's company for the duration of their visit. Is Mrs Basshor expecting you? I don't believe I've seen her this morning."

"I'm afraid she isn't." Kitty didn't think it wise to lie any more than necessary.

The boy started to whistle.

"Stop that," Phillips said. He turned to Kitty. "I regret to tell you then—"

"That I must leave the premises." She finished his sentence. "I know. I was in the vicinity and thought I'd stop in to see how things are going."

He bowed and held the door open for her. She passed through. "In the future, madam, please feel free to drive right up to the front. One of our porters will park your vehicle, and you are welcome to wait in the reception area until Mrs Basshor is able to meet you."

Kitty felt three pairs of eyes following her as she made her way to her car. She walked a good fifty yards before she turned back to the stables.

"I'm sorry," she said to the secretary, who didn't seem too pleased to see her again. "May I take your boy to help me? Something got caught under my chassis and made the most terrible racket all the way over here. I thought he might be able to slide underneath and take a look."

"That's fine." He nudged Turnip. "Go on."

The boy hurried behind Kitty, and as soon as they were out of earshot of his superiors, he slid his hands into his pockets and started singing again: "*Sister Susie's sewing shirts for soldiers...*" It was another hit tune but faster and catchier than his previous choice.

"Such skill at sewing shirts our shy young sister Susie shows,
Some soldiers send epistles, say they'd sooner sleep in thistles
Than the saucy, soft, short shirts for soldiers sister Susie sews."

"That's excellent, Turnip." Kitty laughed at the tongue twister. "I wouldn't be able to manage it myself."

"I know you," the boy said. "You're not Miss Lodge. You're that lady from the papers, aren't ya?"

Kitty had the grace to blush.

"I was there the night Mr Cole was killed. I saw you. You went all woozy and Lewis brought you a stool."

"That's right."

"So what brings you back to our neck of the woods?" He seemed terribly confident for such a little fellow.

"I have some questions," Kitty said.

"It's gonna cost you, y'know. Five dollars, if you want to know what I know." He walked half a step behind her.

"Five dollars?" That was a lot of money. "What *do* you know?" she asked.

They approached the Bearcat.

"I know," the boy replied, "that if this is your car, you can afford it."

Kitty stifled a smile and pointed to the vehicle. "Slide under – they're watching us. Don't worry though. I'll pay you."

She stood beside the car with her back to the stables. "What can you tell me about Lupone?"

"Well, he was the one who said we should all go out to see the fireworks. Joe – the man you saw inside – wasn't feeling too good, but he dragged him out as well. Said it was a chance none of us should miss."

"I see." That matched what Lupone had told her. "And he was with you the entire time?"

The boy paused, and then said, "I can't be sure, but I think so. That's what we all said to the police anyhow."

"What's that – that he was with you, or that he wasn't?"

"That we thought he was but couldn't be sure. The coppers told us we were just sticking up for him. But that's not true. Lipton – I mean Lupone" – he corrected himself – "was one of us, but none of us would lie if we really thought he killed someone."

"And he disappeared later that evening?"

"That's right. After talking to the cops like the rest of us."

Kitty put five single dollar bills on the running board, and a second later, they disappeared. "Tell me, have you heard anything about Lupone speaking to Mr Cole a few days before he was murdered?"

Turnip peered out from under the car. "No." Noticing her disappointment, he added, "You want to know something for free?"

"I wouldn't call it free. I just paid you!"

"Do you want to know or not?"

"I'm all ears."

"It's about Breedlove, Mrs Basshor's pony. That's the one that took ill this morning. They put him down and carted him off before you could say Jack's your brother."

"What's wrong with that?" Kitty tied on her hat. The boy was just talking for the sake of talking now.

"It's just that they told us he stepped on a nail and was starting with tetanus, but I know that's not true." He looked aggrieved. "I sweep the stalls myself. There aren't any nails lying about."

Kitty agreed. The place seemed spotless for a barn. But Mrs Basshor's pony's sickness had nothing to do with her.

"I think we're all set." She climbed into the car and waved at the club secretary who still watched her from the door to the stables. "They'll wonder what's taking you so long."

Turnip slid out from under the chassis. "Did you see the look on Mr Phillips's face? He must be terrified that if word spreads about Breedlove, all the owners will take away their animals. Two deaths in one week."

"Two?" Kitty looked down at the boy.

"Mr Cole and the pony."

"That's right." Kitty turned on the engine and drove away. Two deaths in one week. A man and a horse.

She shook her head. There couldn't be a connection.

Chapter Seventeen

"What do you think?" An hour and a half later, Kitty told Amanda what she had learned.

Amanda examined her reflection in the mirror and wrinkled her nose. "Too feminine." She returned the swatch of Liberty's fabric to the Altman's salesgirl. Then she said to Kitty, "How can Hunter's death have anything to do with a horse being put down?"

"I know."

"You're confused and clutching at straws." They strolled toward a bank of elevators.

Kitty hadn't told her friend about her trip to the Tombs. Amanda had been shocked enough that she drove up to the country club by herself. "You'll get a reputation," she had warned.

"Where to, miss?" The elevator operator held open the door.

"World bazaar," Kitty replied. At Altman's department store, she was on home turf. She knew the giant emporium, which occupied an entire city block, like the back of her hand. The trick was in understanding the logic to how the store displayed its merchandise: impulse purchases, like cosmetics, gloves, notions, small wares and also men's apparel, were placed on the street level; ladies' ready-to-wear, millinery, lingerie, mourning and other specialty items occupied the middle floors; the topmost levels sold items that warranted a special trip, like home goods or the world bazaar; and groceries and discounted wares were buried in the basement.

"I'm glad we're here." Amanda linked her arm through Kitty's as they stepped out into a pavilion of colorful stalls. "And I'm glad Mama said I could join you."

"I am too." Kitty had wanted to run her thoughts by someone and besides, she had to buy at least a couple of items, or else her father would never believe that she had spent her entire day shopping.

–

Kitty returned home by three as promised. She planned to bathe and then study for a couple of hours before the concert. The telephone rang as soon as Kitty put down her parcels.

Grace picked up the line. "It's for you, Miss Kitty," she said after a moment.

Kitty pressed the instrument against her ear.

"Miss Weeks?" It was Mrs Basshor's secretary. "I must speak to you. This is urgent."

"How did you find my number, Mr Hotchkiss?"

"I asked the operator. You're the only Weeks on the west side of Manhattan, so I thought it must be you."

Kitty checked her watch. "I don't have much time, Mr Hotchkiss."

"Please, Miss Weeks."

She could sense the anxiety in his voice. "Go ahead."

"Did you talk to Mrs Cole?"

"I did, and she told me that she went to the powder room for a few moments during the fireworks."

"I see. And you didn't happen to say anything about me? That it was I who told you that she went missing?"

"No, I did not." Time was ticking away. Kitty wished the secretary would stop beating about the bush.

"I think she found out somehow." He sounded distressed. "She suggested as much when I saw her at Mr Cole's funeral. I accompanied Mrs Basshor to Connecticut."

"Well, I can assure you that I never said anything."

"I appreciate it, Miss Weeks."

Kitty heard Mrs Basshor calling in the background. "Hotchkiss," she trilled in an insistent tone. "Hotchkiss."

"I'm finished," Hotchkiss whispered. "Finished."

"I don't understand, Mr Hotchkiss. Did Mrs Basshor find out that you came to see me? Will you lose your job?"

"It's much worse than that." The line went dead.

The secretary's woes weren't her problem, Kitty told herself as she hurried back to her rooms. She asked Grace to bring in a cup of tea and raced through chapter 2, "Her Responsibilities."

"The girl must be a link in the chain of life... A woman's appeal...is supposed to be an emotional appeal. Let us accept the fact and glory in it. Let us train our girl's quick instincts and emotional reaction to be the biggest and best force in the community..."

Kitty scribbled notes furiously. There was much to discuss here.

"The eighteenth century brought to the world a deeper and better understanding of the rights of man; the nineteenth century has carried the message on; but it remains for the twentieth century to develop a new interpretation of the *duties*" – Kitty paid special attention to the phrase – "*rather than the rights of woman.*"

She began the third chapter, "Her Recreation," in which Miss Morgan described "developing the limited, class-conscious, or group-conscious girl into the socially conscious woman" and discussed the work of the National Vacation Committee, one of the branches of the Woman's Department of the National Civic Federation, in meeting the recreational needs of self-supporting women and girls. Kitty was halfway through the passage detailing how a fund had been created to help city girls rest from the stresses and strains of their everyday life when Grace knocked on the door.

"Mr Weeks wants to know when you will be ready, Miss Kitty."

Kitty left her pencil in the book to mark her page. She would have liked to finish the section today. She washed her face, did her hair, and changed into a pearl-gray dress with lace around the neck and at the cuffs. Then she joined her father for a light supper before Rao drove them to the concert.

–

Carnegie Hall thronged with New York's finest. In a recent bit of busywork for Miss Busby, Kitty had counted the number of families who provided foreign addresses to the Summer Social Register, and compared the figure to the same time last year. In 1914, nine hundred families had left for Europe by May; this year, only two hundred had gone away by the beginning of June and by the looks of it, the rest were here this evening.

On her way up to her seat, Kitty caught a glimpse of Mrs Basshor in conversation with her friends, Poppy Clements with a man Kitty assumed was her husband, and other faces that looked familiar but she couldn't name – she must have seen them in the papers.

Kitty and Mr Weeks took their places; she unfolded her mother-of-pearl opera glasses and scanned the crowd. Unlike her father, Kitty didn't care too much for classical performances and would much rather spend the concert watching people.

She spotted Amanda in a box diagonally opposite. Amanda wore a pretty sea-foam-blue gown, Mrs Vanderwell was dressed in dark brown with a string of pearls around her neck, and Mr Vanderwell sat beside them staring vacantly off into space and fanning himself with a program.

Kitty watched Amanda laugh and flirt with the two young men in the row behind her. She envied and admired the expert way in which her friend seemed to deflect their comments and managed being the center of attention. Kitty found that she became tongue-tied on the rare occasions when she was introduced to an eligible bachelor. The supreme self-confidence of the New York City man unnerved her, as well as his assumption that the world revolved around Manhattan, with a few forays to Harvard or Yale, Groton or Andover. She never knew what to say, and the harder she tried, the more stilted she sounded.

The orchestra started to tune up, and the lights dimmed. Kitty put away her glasses and glanced at the program: Mozart's Symphony No. 40 in G Minor, followed by Haydn's Concerto in D Major for Violoncello and Orchestra, then an intermission.

She wished she could have brought along Miss Morgan's book and read while they played, but even if the light had been sufficient, that wasn't the proper thing to do. She would have to sit through it all. She closed her eyes and dozed off. It had been a long day.

Mr Weeks nudged her awake when the pieces ended. "Tired?" he said.

She smiled. "Who knew that shopping could be so exhausting?" She followed her father out, glad to stretch her legs.

"I say." A business associate approached Mr Weeks.

"I didn't expect to see you here, Schweitzer," Julian Weeks replied and introduced the man to Kitty. "Are we settled, then?"

"Good to go, Mr Weeks."

Kitty felt someone jolt her arm.

"I beg your pardon."

She found herself staring into friendly brown eyes framed by a pleasant face.

For a moment, Kitty thought she might have seen the man before, but she couldn't put her finger on the occasion.

"I hope you're all right," he said.

It had been just the slightest of bumps. "I'm fine, thank you."

He smiled, nodded and moved on. Kitty wouldn't have minded prolonging their conversation, but she didn't know how, and clearly, he wasn't good at small talk either, or he had no interest in her.

She turned to watch him from the corner of her eye – he spoke to a friend, a stocky older man, then he seemed to glance her way. She instinctively avoided his gaze and pretended to be absorbed in a flyer from the previous night's show.

"What Miss Addams Learned about Peace in the War-Torn Nations – Hear It from the Eminent Emissary First-Hand!" the flyer said.

A woman behind Kitty spoke a few words in German. Kitty glanced over her shoulder. The speaker was a buxom, raven-haired beauty with sapphires cascading from her ears. When Kitty searched for him again, the personable young man had disappeared.

"*Er müsste längst da sein.*" He must be late, the woman said to her companion.

Kitty couldn't help listening in to the conversation. The woman had a piercing voice and hearing German spoken aloud brought back a rush of nostalgia for her days in Switzerland.

"*Es ist eine lange Reise aus Washington,*" the woman's companion replied. "*Vielleicht hat Herr Doktor Albert seine Plan geändert.*"

Kitty caught her breath. Did the man just say that Herr Doctor Albert might have changed his mind because it was a long trip from Washington?

The woman asked him to check at the ticket booth downstairs.

"*Ja gerne,*" he replied.

"I'll be right back," Kitty said to her startled father and his business associate, who were deep in conversation. She followed the German-speaking gentleman.

She kept her eyes trained on the back of his head, determined not to lose him. He wore black tails just like every other man in the place, and she hadn't seen his face.

He made his way to the central staircase; Kitty noticed the pleasant-looking young man heading downstairs as well, a few paces behind him.

"Capability!" Amanda emerged out of nowhere with a girlfriend on either arm. "I've been looking for you."

"I'll be right back – I left something at the front door." Kitty couldn't afford to stop, but Amanda and her friends barred the way.

"Not so fast." Amanda smiled. "Not before I've introduced you to Miss Hibben and Miss Nicholls."

Kitty had no choice except to curtsy.

"Miss Hibben and Miss Nicholls will be joining me at the YWCA training." Amanda turned to her friends. "I'm trying to convince Miss Weeks to join us too."

"Please excuse me." The foreign gentleman had disappeared from Kitty's sights. She edged past the ladies and raced down the staircase, not caring what they or anyone else might think of her.

She reached the bottom of the stairwell, out of breath, but the foyer was empty. There was no one near the ticket booth, and even the pleasant-faced young man had vanished.

Chapter Eighteen

Sunday morning brought extras with the news: cartoons, fashions, reviews, and queries. Kitty set aside "Doings and Sayings in the Real Estate World" and "Riverside Regatta Well-Patronized" and smiled at an advertisement in Apartments and Automobiles: "The Tires That Fell Off Looked like Goodyear Tires – at First." She browsed through the photograph pages, which featured the lavish interiors of the New Bankers Club of America at 120 Broadway that had completed its renovations to the tune of six hundred thousand dollars, an amazing sum of money.

"Where did you run off to during the intermission last night?" Mr Weeks asked, neatly cracking the top from his soft-boiled egg.

"I lost my handkerchief."

"Must have been a pretty important handkerchief."

"Grace embroidered it for me." Kitty quickly finished her cereal. "I'd better get back to work."

"Preparing for the Morgan interview?"

"Yes." She took the napkin from her lap and dropped it onto the table. "By the way, is it true that Mr Morgan loaned the British government one hundred million dollars to support its war efforts?"

"His bank did. Why do you ask?"

"I'd like to understand why he supports England."

"The family has connections there. Morgan spent years running the bank's London branch while his father dominated the American business scene."

Kitty returned to her rooms and finished "Her Recreation" before continuing on to "Her Future," Anne Morgan's final chapter.

Miss Morgan began feistily, observing that "the problem now facing the American girl is her utter inability to realize that her future can only be a logical development of her present."

A few pages later, she declared that the average girl has "the tools of reading, writing, and arithmetic… placed in her hands with such blunted edges that they are of little value, and the basic qualities of accuracy, concentration, thoroughness and ambition are conspicuous by their absence."

Industry could only be improved when employer and employee worked side by side to reach a common end, "thus bringing about an additional financial return as well as a larger opportunity for development of the individual."

Kitty wondered what Miss Morgan's brother would make of that proposition.

Although eight million American women had entered industry, Miss Morgan claimed that girls still believed that "woman's duty is not to work, but simply to exist until such time as she can find someone who will work for her and support her parasitic existence. The harder her struggle the more she considers marriage as an ultimate goal where she can rest from her labors."

Too true, Kitty thought. Then again, not everyone had the freedom and courage to buck expectations and remain unmarried like Miss Morgan and her cohort.

Grace looked in. "Mr Weeks asks if you'll join him in the study."

"In a little while," Kitty replied. She reached the end of the chapter and then jotted down questions based on her notes. She would review and memorize them, but first, she took a break and went to see her father.

"Are you done?" he said. "How was it?"

"Stranger than I expected."

"In what way?"

"I agree with much of what Miss Morgan says, and then I find some of her points strange. For instance, she says that girls should have the courage to remold the circumstances in which we find ourselves, rather than seeking different problems elsewhere. And that we should have self-control and self-discipline so that we can take our place in the general scheme of the universe."

"A little self-control and self-discipline never hurt anyone," Julian Weeks said with a smile.

"She's forty-one and unmarried, Papa. She's traveled all over the world and does whatever she wants, and yet she advises girls to embrace the domestic feeling."

"And that's what you object to?"

"I don't see how she can make such a strong case for domestic life when she hasn't followed that path."

"There are some women," he replied, choosing his words with care, "who prefer to fulfill their domestic obligations in the company of other women."

"Do you mean the Versailles Triumvirate?"

"That's right." It was the term the press used to refer to Miss Morgan's living arrangement in France, where she had kept home with the theatrical agent Miss Elisabeth Marbury and Miss Elsie de Wolfe, now a well-known interior decorator.

"If she can live a carefree life, why do the rest of us have to settle down and marry?"

"You don't want to marry?"

"That's not the point."

"The point is that she has millions at her disposal in the bank, and most women don't."

"That's not fair," Kitty said.

"To whom?"

Kitty sprang to Anne Morgan's defense. "To her, as a matter of fact. She didn't have to write this book, and she didn't have to dedicate herself to public service."

"You could be right." Julian Weeks picked up his papers.

The telephone rang, and Mr Weeks picked it up. "It's for you, Capability," he said. "Amanda Vanderwell."

"Really?" Mrs Vanderwell never allowed Amanda to chat on the phone on Sundays. She thought it went against the spirit of the Sabbath.

"Is everything all right, Amanda?" Kitty said, speaking into the mouthpiece.

"You'd better sit down. You're not going to believe this."

"What is it? Are you engaged?"

"Hardly." Her friend's voice was dry. "Remember Hotchkiss, Mrs Basshor's secretary?"

"Of course, I spoke to him yesterday."

"Well, one of Mama's friends called this morning. It seems that Hotchkiss has gone and killed himself."

Chapter Nineteen

"Excuse me, Amanda." Kitty turned to her father. "Do you mind if I take this outside?"

He noticed her stunned expression. "What's wrong, Capability?"

"I'll tell you in a minute." She went to the foyer, picked up the receiver and heard him hang up his line. "Are you sure?" she said to her friend.

"Certain as the day I was born. He didn't come to work this morning. So of course Bessie Basshor was distressed."

"He works seven days a week?"

"It seems so. Anyhow, she sent her chauffeur to his place in the Bronx. He had to break down the door and found Hotchkiss lying in the bathtub. The poor fellow was in his dress clothes, his shoes on and everything. He had slit his wrists. Apparently" – Amanda's voice shook – "the water was red with his blood."

"Oh my goodness." Kitty pulled up a chair and sat down. "Have the police been called? Do they know why he did it?"

"I think they have. I wanted to telephone you earlier, but I didn't get a chance. Bessie's fallen to pieces, so Mama has gone over, which is why I've been able to reach you. Do you think there could have been foul play?"

"Foul play?" Kitty struggled to make sense of things. What had Hotchkiss been so upset about when they spoke yesterday?

Amanda asked, "Maybe he knew who killed Hunter?"

"They're saying the stable hand shot Mr Cole."

"Well, that can't be it then."

"Thank you for telling me, Amanda." Kitty hung up the line.

Throughout the day, she recalled snippets of her interactions with the secretary: how flustered he had seemed at the party, the gossipy manner in which he filled her in on all the guests. Meeting him in the silver-papered foyer to Mrs Basshor's apartment. His conversation with her at the *Sentinel*. And finally, their telephone conversation yesterday.

Why hadn't she paid more attention? She had been so preoccupied about preparing for her interview that she couldn't recall exactly what he'd said.

He had told her that he was finished. What did that mean? Was it significant that he whispered it just as Mrs Basshor called his name?

She pictured him fully clothed and floating in the bathtub in his own blood and screwed her eyes shut to drive away the image.

Had he left a note? Did he suspect that Mrs Basshor might fire him? What could be worse than that?

The first thing that popped into Kitty's mind was that Mrs Basshor had killed Hunter Cole and that the secretary was trying to protect his mistress. But she dismissed the thought at once. Someone would have noticed if the hostess had gone missing.

Kitty stared distractedly into her closet and finally chose a white pleated dress paired with a bolero-style velvet jacket to wear the next morning. She wrote down her questions and memorized key paragraphs and phrases from Anne Morgan's book.

Tomorrow's interview had lost some of its luster.

She arrived at the *Sentinel* the following day less rested and more agitated than she ought to have been, but Miss Busby didn't seem to notice.

"Turn around. One more time." She put Kitty through her paces, scrutinizing her apprentice like a *maître de ballet* examining his prima ballerina.

"I like it." She nodded in approval at Kitty's choice of outfit. "Attractive yet no-nonsense. Just the right balance." She unscrewed her bottle and downed a spoonful of Rowland's.

They went over Kitty's notes, with Miss Busby muttering under her breath and making corrections. "I don't know about suffrage," she said, pausing at one of Kitty's notes. "It's controversial." Then she changed her mind. "Feel her out. If she's willing to reply, you can try asking."

They spent half an hour practicing Kitty's entrance and delivery. How she must talk and present herself. What to do if she forgot a question – ask for a glass of water. "Don't panic. It will come back to you," Miss Busby said. "And in the meantime, you will be surprised how much people talk to fill in the silence."

The clock on the editor's desk showed it was half past nine. "Are you ready?"

"I am now." Kitty felt like she was on the way to the gallows.

"Remember that you're from the *Sentinel*." Miss Busby clapped her on the back. "Hold your head high."

She accompanied Kitty downstairs and hailed her a cab. Just as Kitty was about to climb in, the editor reached into her purse and handed her a dollar for the fare.

"Thank you, Miss Busby," Kitty said.

The cab merged into the traffic.

Fifteen minutes later, it pulled up at the corner of Park Avenue and Sixty-Second Street beside a five-story marble-and-brick building with a mansard roof and pillared facade still partially covered by scaffolding. The Colony Club was a ladies-only establishment, of which Miss Morgan was a founding member. Kitty had heard that in order to join, one had to be either fabulously wealthy or fabulously accomplished.

"Are you Miss Weeks?" A businesslike woman hurried down the stairs. "I'm Daisy Rogers, Miss Morgan's secretary. Unfortunately, Miss Morgan has been detained, but I can give you a tour of our new premises while you wait."

Kitty eagerly accepted the offer.

"Mind your step," Miss Rogers said as they entered a vast circular entrance hall. She gestured to a door to the right and smiled. "A kennel purpose-built for our members' dogs. They will be cared for here, while their mistresses are within."

Four arches opened onto different sections of the facility. One was a members-only sitting room paneled with wood flown in from London.

"We're a bit of an experiment," Miss Rogers said. "This is the first clubhouse in America – in the world perhaps – built especially for ladies. There are those who wonder why we need so much more space, but we had no choice, really. The old location on Madison just wasn't large enough to accommodate everyone. All thirteen floors here—"

Kitty couldn't hide her surprise. From the outside, it seemed there were just five or six.

"I know." The secretary seemed pleased. "Appearances can be deceiving. We have thirteen levels inside – each catering to our members' needs and desires."

Wide-eyed, Kitty followed the secretary into a one-and-a-half-story ballroom, complete with a retractable stage at one end and a balcony for the orchestra at the other. Above it was a seventy-foot lounge, a suite of card rooms, public and private dining rooms, and private dressing rooms for members who didn't wish to stay overnight.

"Do you happen to know how the club was founded?"

"No." Kitty shook her head, overwhelmed not solely by the opulence – that was commonplace – but by the fact that all this had been built as a female-only enclave.

"About ten years ago," Miss Rogers told her, taking the stairs up, "Mrs J. Borden Harriman wanted to come to the city for a few days to run errands. The problem was that she had nowhere to stay. The Harrimans were renting in Newport while their town house was being renovated, and Mr Harriman didn't approve of ladies taking a room at a hotel by themselves. Mrs Harriman realized then and there that what was required was a women's club, a place where ladies could spend the night, have parcels delivered, make telephone calls, and receive guests. She applied to Miss Morgan, and Mr Pierpont Morgan put up the first ten thousand dollars on the condition that they find nine others to contribute equal sums. That bought the place on

Madison Avenue. And now, ten years later, we've grown to need a million-dollar building."

They passed two floors of sleeping and sitting rooms en route to a gymnasium equipped with the latest equipment. Members could book private rooms for manicures, hairdressing, or individual sessions with fitness instructors; they could play a game of squash at the squash courts, then step into the express elevator – which Kitty and Miss Rogers did – and drop down six floors to arrive at the edge of a sparkling underground marble swimming pool. It was the deepest indoor pool in the city, Miss Rogers said, at sixty feet long and twenty feet wide. Another section was devoted to special treatments usually found only in the best health spas in Europe.

The door to the elevator opened, and a messenger looked in to tell them that Miss Morgan had arrived. Kitty and Miss Rogers went back upstairs to wait for her on the third floor loggia, where a flock of pink flamingos, painted by the muralist Robert Chanler, soared across a vaulted ceiling. Live macaws and a marble fountain designed by Mrs Harry Payne Whitney would complete the scenery closer to opening day, Miss Rogers whispered.

"Do you know what one of the members said to me the other day?" The secretary stood at attention. Sensing her anticipation, Kitty began to feel nervous once again.

"She told me," Miss Rogers went on, "that it wasn't the facilities that mattered to her. What she liked best about the club was being able to telephone her husband at the eleventh hour and tell him that *she* wouldn't be coming home for dinner."

A set of double doors swung open, and a crisp voice called, "I'll see you later, Elsie." Moments later, a surprisingly tall, broad-shouldered woman strode forward to greet Kitty.

"Nice to meet you, Miss Weeks." Anne Morgan shook Kitty's hand with a firm grip.

She wore her short hair swept away from her forehead. Dark eyebrows framed a no-nonsense gaze. She wore four strings of pearls around her neck. Only the wide Peter Pan collar of her blouse softened her appearance.

"So, Miss Weeks." She spoke in clipped, patrician tones. "What do you think of our little place?"

"It's wonderful," Kitty replied breathlessly.

Miss Morgan pulled up a chair around one of the pretty white-painted, wrought iron tables. "And my book, what do you think of that?"

"I enjoyed it, but I do have questions."

"As it should be." Miss Morgan laughed. "Fire away!"

"Well." Kitty wasn't prepared to begin with such little preamble. "May I have a glass of water?"

"Of course. Daisy." She shot a glance at her secretary. Miss Rogers slipped away. Contrary to Miss Busby's advice, Miss Morgan said nothing to fill in the silence and instead waited for Kitty to begin.

Kitty forced herself to breathe. She smiled and dove in with one of the first questions on her list. "May I ask what prompted you to write this book?"

"You may ask me anything. That's why we're here." Miss Morgan launched into an answer about her interest in bettering working women's lives.

Miss Rogers arrived with two glasses of water on a tray. Kitty gulped hers down and moved on to a different question that she and Miss Busby had prepared. Miss Morgan's reply sounded practiced, as though she had given a similar response many times before.

This didn't feel like the easy give-and-take of a conversation. Kitty found it difficult to focus; even Miss Morgan seemed slightly bored.

She decided to shake things up a bit. "What are your views on suffrage, Miss Morgan?"

The philanthropist's eyes narrowed. "I'm not against suffrage," she said after a moment. "I am simply not interested in the topic. I believe many things are more immediately necessary, such as the economic welfare of women. And once suffrage comes – and I believe it will – we must regard it not as a right but as a duty. With greater freedom comes greater responsibility – that I believe to my core."

Kitty nodded. Finally, they might be getting somewhere. "I think our readers would like to know," she said, "why, when men are encouraged to do and see so much, you suggest that girls focus more narrowly on their domestic and local responsibilities?" Her question wasn't one from the list that Miss Busby had vetted.

Miss Morgan paused to think, and Kitty worried she might have spoken too boldly.

"Excellent question," Anne Morgan replied finally as she adjusted her pearls. "Men and women are fundamentally different creatures, with different abilities and different temperaments. To me, equality of the sexes in no sense means similarity. For women to move forward, we must embrace our difference from men. For most girls – working women who come from families struggling to make ends meet – the best way to improve their lot is by improving the condition of their communities."

"But what if a girl isn't interested in public service?" Kitty persisted. "Must she give up her own ambitions in order to serve the greater good?"

"Let's make this more concrete," Miss Morgan proposed. "I take it that you plan to be a journalist?"

Kitty nodded.

"My great friend Ida Tarbell writes for magazines and newspapers."

"I know of Miss Tarbell," Kitty said.

"Of course you do. Her investigation into the monopolistic activities of Mr John D. Rockefeller and the Standard Oil Company opened the public's eyes and resulted in the government taking decisive action. I bring up this example not to point fingers but to illustrate my conviction: any vocation, if pursued courageously and with a pure heart and honest motives, will bring about a betterment of one's community. It's just that it's more realistic for most women to limit their scope of activities, whereas a smaller group benefits from having a freer rein."

Kitty liked Miss Morgan's turn of phrase and hoped she'd be able to remember it.

"My book has been written for girls who must work to make ends meet," Miss Morgan continued, taking a sip of water. "They don't have the luxury of choosing between professions. I have long been an advocate for a living wage for both men and women. Only when she can support her family can a woman realize her true potential."

She looked Kitty in the eye. "I have the same attitude toward suffrage. I want to prepare women so that they may be able to make proper use of suffrage when it comes."

Kitty took the bit between her teeth. Neither her questions nor Miss Busby's questions would do. She had to treat Miss Morgan as a person in order to breathe some life into this interview and get behind the public persona.

"May I ask how Mr Morgan is faring?"

"He has been released from his sickbed, thank you. He will spend the next month or so recuperating on the *Corsair*. That's my father's yacht." Miss Morgan smiled to herself. "My father and I used to sail all over Europe together. We even hosted the kaiser on board once, if you can believe it."

That was exactly the kind of thing that would fascinate their readers.

"You met the kaiser in person, Miss Morgan?"

"Only for a short while, but yes, I did."

"May I ask what he was like?"

Kitty had wondered about the man behind the pointy, upturned mustaches. The man who everyone said had single-handedly started the war.

Anne Morgan thought for a moment, and Daisy Rogers stepped forward as though to intervene.

"That's all right, Daisy," Miss Morgan told her secretary. "She means well and after all, I have met Germany's emperor."

Kitty realized that with Jack Morgan so firmly on Britain's side, any comment, positive or negative, made by his sister might be misconstrued.

"You see," Miss Morgan said, "his Prussian stiffness might seem comical to us, but like anyone born into a position of great power, the kaiser has a difficult part to play. Men jump to his command. He must choose his words with care. But he is an impulsive individual."

Miss Rogers coughed discreetly in the background.

"Daisy is worried that I might say something foolish" – Miss Morgan laughed – "so don't quote me on this. I don't believe that fellow who took a shot at Jack had anything to do with the kaiser or the German government. If Berlin had wanted to finish my brother off, they would have sent someone far more competent than that half-cracked professor."

Daisy Rogers tapped her watch.

"I suppose it's time for us to finish," Miss Morgan said.

"May I ask just one more question?" Kitty couldn't leave without getting her answer. "In the first chapter of your book, you say that the qualities that make the American girl abroad unique are truly American qualities, but unless I missed it, you don't specify what they are. Can you tell our readers now?"

Miss Morgan threw her head back and laughed. "Very good."

"I beg your pardon?"

"You see, Miss Weeks." She leaned forward in her chair, dark eyes flashing. "If you don't find it in my writings, then your readers must look in the mirror and discover the truth for themselves."

–

On the taxicab ride back to the office, Kitty scribbled a quick outline of her conversation so she wouldn't forget. She walked into the *Sentinel* surprised to see it looking so much the same when she felt so altered. She couldn't have said in what way; she just felt that spending three quarters of an hour in the company of a woman of Miss

Morgan's stature had somehow left its mark. She felt elevated, special, ready to leave her own mark perhaps.

Jeannie Williams pounced on Kitty when she entered the hen coop. "How did it go, Miss Weeks? I wish I could have been there."

Miss Busby materialized beside Jeannie's desk before Kitty could reply. "What are you girls chattering on about? You should know better, Jeannie. You were supposed to send Miss Weeks in to me right away."

She caught Kitty by the elbow and steered her to her alcove, but not before Jeannie pointed furiously to a half-typed sheet in her machine and mouthed *sotto voce*, "You have to see this."

"Start at the beginning," Miss Busby told Kitty, sitting her down. "Don't leave out a single detail."

Kitty opened her mouth to speak and realized she wasn't yet ready to describe the meeting. She needed a few moments of peace and quiet first. A few moments to digest it. "Would you mind if I get a bite to eat before we start, Miss Busby?" she asked.

"Of course, of course." The editor could afford to be magnanimous. "Interviews can make you ravenous. Go on to the cafeteria. I'll be waiting."

Kitty thought she might take a moment in the basement but had to walk back through the hen coop to get there.

"Miss Weeks." Jeannie beckoned her over.

"I'll be back soon," Kitty said. "We can talk after I finish with Miss Busby."

"I think you'll want to see this." Jeannie turned the wheel on the carriage and pulled out a typewritten page, which she handed to Kitty.

Kitty took a look. "In a letter written before he killed himself," it began, "Mr Lucian Hotchkiss, secretary to Mrs Elizabeth Basshor of Park Avenue, confessed to murdering Mr Hunter Cole, a guest at his employer's annual Fourth of July gala."

Chapter Twenty

Kitty tore up the stairs to the City Desk. As usual, the men were huddled behind their glass barricade. She tapped on the glass and mouthed Mr Flanagan's name. The door wasn't locked. What, she wondered, would they do if she barged in? Call for help? Scream and jump on their chairs as though they'd seen a rat? The thought of the reporters panicking like ladies diverted her as she waited for Mr Flanagan to make an appearance.

"Back again, Miss Weeks?" His thick black mane gleamed under the overhead light bulbs.

"I read about Mr Hotchkiss's confession."

"Ah, did Miss Williams show it to you? Last I heard, her job consisted of typing up stories, not broadcasting them to whomever she chooses."

Kitty ignored his comment; she had no interest in arguing over Jeannie's actions. "The story said that not only had Mr Hotchkiss confessed to *killing* Mr Cole, but that he also had been *stealing* from Mrs Basshor at the party and Mr Cole caught him in the act."

"That sounds about correct."

"It just *sounds* correct, Mr Flanagan?"

The reporter took a step toward her. "I think you're forgetting who you are, Miss Weeks."

"Hotchkiss wouldn't have stolen from her," Kitty said. "He was devoted to Mrs Basshor."

"Stranger things have happened."

"But did they, in this case?"

"Look here, Miss Weeks. The secretary told his employer that she would be paying one sum for the fireworks, and then he paid those Chinamen quite a bit less so that he could pocket the difference."

Kitty recalled those gold cuff links. She wouldn't have expected Hotchkiss's salary to pay for them. "The men were Japanese," she said. "From Yokohama."

"That hardly changes the fact that the secretary would have gotten away with his trickery if Mr Cole hadn't overheard their conversation."

"Is that what he wrote in his suicide letter?"

"That's what the police gathered from it."

"Do they know what happened?"

"Mr Cole arranged to meet the secretary in the stables, and there's no doubt about what happened after that."

"But Mr Lupone told me—" Kitty stopped herself.

"Yes. What did Mr Lupone tell you?" Flanagan flipped open his penknife. "I was wondering when you would get to that."

Kitty stood stock-still; she had no reply.

"You think I didn't know you went to the prison?" He leisurely cleaned under his nails with the blade. "You signed your name in the ledger, Miss Weeks."

Kitty's cheeks flamed. "Mr Lupone told me that Mr Cole arranged with him a few days beforehand to make sure the stables were clear."

"Does he have any witnesses, any evidence to prove it?"

She shook her head.

"And still, you believed him." The penknife closed with a click. "The good or bad news, depending on how you view it, is that Mr Lupone will be released this afternoon. And Mr Hotchkiss, who went on in his letter to beg Mrs Basshor's forgiveness for who he was and what he had done, will officially be listed as Mr Cole's killer. Since he's dead, he can't be prosecuted for the crime, but at least justice will have been done."

"Did Mr Hotchkiss explicitly confess to shooting Hunter Cole?" Kitty couldn't picture him pulling the trigger.

"Men," Flanagan said, his voice rising, "do not commit suicide because they've stolen a few hundred dollars, but they might kill themselves over a more serious crime, even if it happened by accident."

"I see," Kitty said. "Well, thank you for explaining it to me." She turned to leave.

"One question, Miss Weeks. How did you manage to get into the Tombs?"

"I asked," Kitty said.

"That's it?"

"Just about."

He made a rumbling sound in his throat. "Why is it that, preposterous as it sounds, I believe you?"

Kitty passed Jeannie's desk on her way back to Miss Busby.

"What did he say, Miss Weeks? Was he angry that I showed you the article?"

"You probably shouldn't do that again, but it's all right, I think."

"So the secretary did it?"

"That's how it appears."

Kitty returned to the alcove and began reviewing her notes with Miss Busby. The editor didn't seem too concerned that the interview had veered away from the prewritten questions. About twenty minutes into their discussion, she told Kitty to go down to the morgue and bring the file on Miss Morgan so that they could add some background information to the write-up.

"Where were you on Friday?" Mr Musser asked Kitty when she requested the file.

"I took the day off to prepare for my interview with Miss Morgan. That's why we need the extra material."

"Finally, a subject worthy of your talents. Did you know that she received an award this year from the National Institute of Social Sciences for making public service her private vocation?"

"I did not."

"See, you should come to me first." He smiled beneath his mustache. "Besides, I was looking for you."

"Anything in particular?"

He called to one of his boys, who went off to the back to unearth the file. "I think I know your Dr Albert."

She took a step back. "You do?"

He stroked his chin, clearly enjoying the effect he had produced. "Well, it's as though you had asked me about a Mr Wilson, and I say, sure, I know someone by that name: he lives in a big white house in Washington on Pennsylvania Avenue."

"Go on, Mr Musser. Please don't keep me in suspense."

"He's a diplomat," Musser said.

"Really?"

173

"He's Germany's commercial attaché to the United States, as a matter of fact. His full name is Dr Heinrich Friedrich Albert."

"That's a nice coincidence, Mr Musser." The old man's filing-cabinet brain produced little marvels. "But I'm not looking for a diplomat. Dr Albert is a physician. Mrs Clements told me so."

"Ach." The archivist shrugged his shoulders. "I tried."

"You did. Thank you." She took the file on Miss Morgan and walked toward the elevators, sifting through the stories, many of which had to do with Miss Morgan's years in France and the well-known guests that she, Miss Marbury, and Miss de Wolfe entertained.

She pressed the button and waited for the elevator, but when the door opened, she realized that she was missing something.

"Go ahead without me," she told the operator. She dashed back to Mr Musser's counter. "People keep jumping to conclusions based on incomplete information," Kitty said to the baffled archivist. "The police think Hotchkiss shot Mr Cole because he begged Mrs Basshor's forgiveness and then killed himself; Mrs Clements assumed Dr Albert must be a physician because of the word *doctor* and Mr Cole's remark that he had been seeing him regularly and never felt better."

"That is generally how it works with physicians," Mr Musser said.

"On the other hand," Kitty went on, "he didn't tell Mrs Clements what illness he suffered from, and when she questioned him later, he denied being sick. His wife also told me he was fit as a fiddle…" Kitty's thoughts began to race. "The Coles needed money. What does a commercial attaché do?"

"Dr Albert, you mean? Well, during peacetime, his responsibilities would include promoting trade between Germany and America. But now that his country is at war, his main duty must be to purchase all necessary war materials and ship them home."

"Does Germany need horses?"

"I'm sure they do. They need everything."

"Well, could Mr Cole have been buying them for him?" That might shed light on his visit to the stables.

"He could have been." Mr Musser considered the idea. "Yes, Britain has contracted with the Morgan bank to handle all their American purchases. As far as I know, Germany has no such counterpart here. Maybe they rely on individual contractors."

From the little she knew of Hunter Cole, Kitty could imagine that he might have liked to hobnob with diplomats and have a hand in wartime business, whether for the Allies or the Germans. It might have fed his sense of self-importance, and Berlin no doubt paid well for any assistance. Could that be why Hunter Cole told Mrs Clements that he "never felt better"?

"There is just one problem," Musser said.

"What is that?"

"Jimmy, get me the Albert file," Musser called. "Albert comma Dr Heinrich Friedrich."

The file appeared a few minutes later.

"Look at this." Mr Musser opened it and handed Kitty the two articles it contained.

Both stories dated from the start of the year, and both had to do with the *Wilhelmina*, a shipping vessel that Dr

Albert had chartered and that the English navy seized and detained in port.

"I don't understand," Kitty said.

"Read it carefully."

Kitty did. The *Wilhelmina* had American registry and had been transporting grains to Hamburg. After capturing the ship, Britain had quarantined the cargo on the grounds that the English courts had ruled foodstuffs bound for enemy nations to be contraband.

American shippers protested, but the British government stood behind the decision. They paid the shipper's invoice price for the grains and issued a warning that henceforth any such cargo bound for Germany was liable to be seized without compensation.

"Don't you see?" Musser said. "If they can't get food across, do you think England will allow them to transport horses?"

"There's only one way to find out." Kitty recalled her wild-goose chase at the concert. "And I think Dr Albert might be in New York."

"Quite possible. He keeps an office at the Hamburg-American Line downtown. On Broadway, you know." He frowned. "You're not thinking of going, are you?"

"Why not?"

"He's a diplomat," Musser sputtered. "Second only to Ambassador von Bernstorff. What do you think you're going to say him?"

"I'll ask whether he knew Mr Hunter Cole."

"And if he did, what of it?"

"If Mr Cole was working for the Germans, that might explain why he was shot. It would make more sense than some ridiculous story about a secretary stealing from Mrs Basshor and being found out, and so on and so forth."

Kitty stared at the Anne Morgan file during the ride back upstairs. Impressive though Miss Morgan might be, Kitty knew which story meant more to her.

One could go into journalism to educate and inform, or to uncover the truth. This was Kitty's chance to do the latter. It would come at a high price – abandoning the Anne Morgan piece and disappointing Miss Busby – but the interview wasn't timely, and one day here or there wouldn't make a difference. In a murder case, however, things moved fast. Who knew where Dr Albert might be tomorrow?

Kitty hurried into the hen coop and handed Jeannie the file from the morgue. "Would you please see that Miss Busby gets this?"

She went out to the street to hail a cab. She had given the Ladies' Page editor everything she needed to write the article that her heart desired.

Kitty jumped into the taxi that screeched to a halt by the curb. Now it was her turn.

Chapter Twenty One

Colorful posters advertising travel to exotic destinations filled the plate-glass windows at the Hamburg-American Line's street-level ticket office, just south of Rector Street at 45 Broadway. *Around the World – 110 Days – SS Victoria Luise – Departures from New York and San Francisco – $650 and Up. Cruise to Panama with onboard dance instructors trained by Vernon and Irene Castle.*

Kitty caught a glimpse of her reflection in the glass – and that of two men watching her. She swung around. There was no one there except the usual pedestrians hurrying along. She blinked. Had she imagined it? No matter. She took a deep breath and pushed her way inside via a brass revolving door.

Inside, the single attendant behind a row of black-marble-topped counters stifled a yawn. A plaster cherub gazed down from its perch on a ceiling, surveying the luxurious but empty ticket office. An intricate model of an ocean liner stood in a glass case in the center of the spacious waiting area. Kitty recalled hearing somewhere that most of the Line's sailings had been suspended since the previous autumn.

"*Guten Tag,*" she said. "*Ich bin hier, um Herrn Doktor Albert zu treffen.*" She could easily be mistaken for a native speaker.

The attendant looked up, startled by the newcomer. "*Herr Doktor Albert?*"

"*Ja.*"

The woman shook her head and said that there was no one by that name there.

"*Ich heiße Fräulein Wochs,*" Kitty made up a name for herself on the spur of the moment. She asked whether the attendant was certain that Dr Albert didn't have an office in the building.

The Hamburg-American employee eyed her up and down, taking in the white dress with the bolero jacket, the silk purse, and the expensive hat. "*Hat Frau Held Sie geschickt?*"

Kitty had no idea who Frau Held might be, but she answered yes, that was indeed who had sent her.

The woman picked up her telephone, waited for a moment, then hung up the line.

No one was answering on the other end, she said, but Fraulein Wochs could go upstairs. She would find Dr Albert in Room 74, on the seventh floor. She apologized for her caution earlier. One could never be too careful these days.

Kitty took the elevator upstairs, and the operator pointed her in the right direction. The hall was eerily quiet for a commercial building on a weekday afternoon.

She knocked on the door to Room 74. No one replied.

She heard voices within and knocked again. Still, no answer.

Kitty twisted the handle and eased the door open.

Someone was being reprimanded in an inside room. "*I* take the train, Hiliken, and you *take a cab*? Do you want Ambassador von Bernstorff to hear about this? You know a full accounting of all expenses will be sent to Washington and then on to Berlin."

"*Guten Tag*," Kitty said loudly. The room before her was evidently a front office and contained nothing more than a desk with a chair and a telephone.

A flustered man in a pince-nez peered out from behind a connecting door. "*Kann ich ihnen behilflich sein?*" Could he help her?

Kitty replied that she had come to see Dr Albert. Like the attendant downstairs, she allowed him to think she was a fellow countrywoman.

The man inquired whether she had made an appointment.

"*Nein.*" Kitty smiled and dropped a curtsy. Like a coquette, she looked at him from below her lashes.

"*Warten Sie, Bitte.*" He took her name and disappeared inside.

While Kitty waited, she peered at a framed map hanging from the wall. Colored in pink, the tiny island of Großbritannien and its dominions – Canada, Australia, New Zealand and India, parts of East Asia and Africa – covered most of the habitable world. Giant *Russland* and its territories loomed large over the rest of Europe, while *Deutsches Reich* – the proud state of Imperial Germany – only exerted its influence over a tiny sliver of Asia, a small patch of western Africa, and the island of Madagascar.

With a few simple blocks of color, the map summed up yet another cause for Europe's conflict. Germany hungered for more territory to feel on par with its powerful neighbors.

An aristocratic gentleman emerged from the adjoining chamber, bowed and introduced himself. "*Ich bin Doktor Heinrich Friedrich Albert.*"

He must have been in his midfifties, Kitty thought. His watchful eyes had a slightly downward cast, and his neatly trimmed gray mustache ended at the sides of his lips. "You wanted to see me?" He radiated quiet confidence.

Kitty forced a smile. "*Ja, gerne.*" Now that she had succeeded in meeting him, it was time to come clean and tell him exactly who she was and why she had come to see him. She sensed that he'd be able to detect a liar.

He invited her into his office and took his seat behind a fine mahogany desk. "*Sie heißen Wochs?*" He sounded skeptical.

Behind him, in a stiff, high-collared military uniform, Kaiser Wilhelm II gazed toward the heavens, his waxed mustaches also pointing upward.

"I'm Miss Weeks, actually," Kitty replied, switching to English. "I work for the *New York Sentinel.*"

"You are American?"

"Yes."

"You speak my language without any accent." His face betrayed no emotion.

"I studied in Switzerland for ten years," Kitty said. "Afterward, I traveled through Europe for several months in the company of a chaperone from Karlsruhe."

"I see." He sat back in his chair. "And is Weeks a common name?"

The question puzzled Kitty, but she replied, "It's not an uncommon name, but I wouldn't say that it is too common either."

He nodded, apparently satisfied. "So how can I help you? And why the subterfuge?"

Kitty blushed. "I wasn't sure whether they'd let me in… I have a bit of an odd question." He didn't flinch, so she continued. "I wonder – may I ask whether by any chance the name Hunter Cole means something to you?"

The diplomat sniffed. He removed his hands from the desk, his actions unhurried and measured. He opened his mouth to speak when his secretary knocked on the door and looked in to say that they should leave for his next appointment.

Dr Albert rose to his feet. "You will excuse me, please."

"This is very important," Kitty said. "Could you please give me just one more moment?"

The diplomat checked his pocket watch. "Very well, you can walk with me." He reassured his secretary: "*Das geht in Ordnung, Hiliken.*"

The secretary glared at Kitty as they rode downstairs in the elevator. They walked out on the street, crossed Broadway, and continued westward on foot.

Kitty struggled to keep pace with Dr Albert's long strides; other pedestrians swerved to make way for him since the diplomat didn't deviate from his course.

"Who is this Mr Cole?" he asked once they'd reached a quieter corner and waited for a break in the traffic to cross. "And why do you think he has anything to do with me?"

"Hunter Cole was shot last week at the Sleepy Hollow Country Club, sir," Kitty replied. "One of his friends said that he spoke about knowing a Dr Albert, which is why we're making inquiries."

"There must be plenty of Dr Alberts in this great city," the German remarked and stepped into the street. Kitty and Hiliken followed.

"I've called every Dr Albert in the telephone book," Kitty said, "but none of them knew Mr Cole. Then my colleague mentioned you, and I thought I would come and check in person. We don't want to print anything inaccurate."

"That is commendable. Much better than most of the other newspapers. I must assure you though: I have nothing to do with this Hunter Cole. I've never heard of him."

Kitty told herself she had done her best and she wouldn't learn anything else from a man whose profession it was to manage relationships and keep secrets. She ought to get back to the office and try to patch things up with Miss Busby.

"Allow me to show you something," the diplomat said. Seagulls circled the blue skies overhead; a flea-bitten dog strolled past them. They had reached the docks.

"Herr Doktor." A well-built Negro ran over to the diplomat.

"Not now." Hiliken steered him away.

With almost a thousand miles of waterfront as measured around the piers, New York's ports surpassed those of London, Hamburg and Liverpool in foreign trade. Kitty had read in *King's Views of New York*, a popular photographic guide to the city, that almost six thousand crafts traversed these waters each day, and three thousand immigrants daily landed at the barge office.

She followed the attaché past sailors and stevedores. Foremen barked orders in all languages and accents that made it hard to detect whether they were speaking English. Men of every color – white, black and the shades in between – loaded and unloaded massive pallets, hauled carts, or lounged in the shade smoking cigarettes.

Kitty ignored a couple of low whistles. She sensed the eyes staring at her. Even in the diplomat's company and the bright light of a Monday afternoon in summer, she began to feel afraid.

Dr Albert came to a halt. He stood in the shadow of a vessel taller than a four-story building. "What you should know as a reporter is that there are sixty-six ships of German and Austrian registry valued at over thirty-three million dollars currently being held in American ports. All these craft have been forbidden from sailing since the war broke out last August. My country has a problem: if the United States enters the war on the side of the Allies, not only do all sixty-six vessels automatically become American property, but they can be converted into warships and used against us."

"But that won't happen, will it?" Kitty said, wondering what grounded ships had to do with Hunter Cole. "We're neutral."

"For the moment, yes. But pressure to enter the war is mounting." The diplomat gave a short laugh. "Your press has incited the feelings of the public against Germany. Especially in the wake of the *Lusitania* sinking, they don't shy away from hurling the most foul insults. They call us beasts, baby killers, barbarians."

He tapped his cane on the ground for emphasis. "None of this is true. Germany has given the world Bach and Beethoven, Kant and Goethe. We are the most civilized nation on earth. Right now, however, we are simply fighting for our survival."

Kitty looked up at the gigantic black hull looming over them. When she first heard the news about the *Lusitania* sinking, she had tried to imagine the experience of the passengers as their ship went under, but her mind hadn't been able to comprehend it. For her, boarding a boat to cross the Atlantic was an act of faith in itself. Once she took that step and believed that such a huge hunk of metal could cross the ocean, then it seemed perfectly normal to be one of two or three thousand people dining and dancing above water a mile or two deep.

To have that security ripped from you in a mere eighteen minutes, to have the world under your feet tilt by a full ninety degrees, to have the china fall from your hands and chandeliers crash and slide down the floor, to have water fill your lungs – if that didn't constitute terror, she didn't know what did.

"Were you aware that my embassy printed a warning in the papers right before the *Lusitania* sailed?" Dr Albert asked. "We reminded travelers that a state of war exists between Germany and her allies and Great Britain and her allies, and that the zone of war includes the water around the British Isles. We clearly stated that anyone sailing in a British vessel through the war zone does so at his own risk. The *Lusitania* was secretly loaded with ammunition for the British, which is why she sank so quickly after a single torpedo hit."

"Why are you telling me all this?" Kitty said. "I came to you to inquire about Mr Cole."

"A third of Americans, a good thirty-two million citizens, are in fact born in other nations," Dr Albert went on. "Nearly ten million of those come from Germany and the countries of the Central Powers. Millions more Irish support us because of their grievances against England. The president is correct to espouse neutrality: the United States will be ripped apart along ethnic lines if it takes sides. Your streets will erupt in riots. But your country's desire to remain neutral is matched neither by its trade practices nor its domestic actions."

"Dr Albert," Kitty interrupted. She didn't want to hear any more. All she wanted was to return to the *Sentinel*.

"Still," he continued, "they're shutting down German papers, closing our churches, harassing our leader, and it is not wise to speak my language in public. A certain politician has even gone so far as to suggest that German reservists will hang from every lamppost in America if we attempt to bring them home to fight on behalf of the Fatherland." He thought for a moment.

"To return to your question: Have I met this man Hunter Cole? Upon further consideration, I realize that I have. Mr Cole came to me with a business proposition – as do many others – and I turned it down. I don't believe we met again. If you like, you may check the date book at the office in which Hiliken records each and every meeting I attend, no matter how insignificant."

"Thank you, Dr Albert," Kitty said, astounded by his candor.

"But would I wish you to report even that single encounter in your paper?" he continued. "Never. Because I know that what will happen next is that some scoundrel – not you, I can tell that you mean well – who catches hold of the story will find a way to insinuate that my government had a hand in Mr Cole's murder. Everything that goes wrong these days" – he fixed Kitty with a steady gaze – "seems to be our fault, laid at our doorstep."

His color was high, and Kitty thanked him for his frankness. "It was not my intention to cause you any distress," she added in German.

"That's quite all right." He gave a short bow. "I'm happy to explain and to have found a sympathetic listener."

"May I ask one final question? Do you recall what sort of business proposal Mr Cole made to you?"

Dr Albert seemed distracted. "It might have been about bandages. You can go back to the office with Hiliken and check. I really don't remember."

"That won't be necessary. Thank you for your time."

"Very well, Fraulein." He bowed again. "Good luck to you." He went to attend to his business, while Hiliken, who had reappeared toward the end of their conversation, escorted Kitty to the gate.

"Would you like me to find you a taxi?" he asked when they reached the street.

"No, thank you." Something about the man made Kitty's skin crawl. "I'm sure I'll find one on Broadway." She took her leave of him and hurried off down the lonely side street back toward the bustle near the Hamburg-American Line offices.

How strange of the diplomat to confide in her, she thought. He did have a point though – even if he had met innocently with Mr Cole, that meeting was liable to be misconstrued. Had they only met once? That seemed to be the key question. Didn't Hunter Cole tell Poppy Clements that he met Dr Albert regularly? Could he have been exaggerating? Kitty could imagine Mr Cole overstating his connection to the German diplomat to make himself seem important. He had seemed like a man full of bluff and bluster.

A tap on her shoulder made her heart jump from her skin. She swung around to face a stocky fellow.

"Are you Capability Weeks?"

"I beg your pardon?" She assumed her most haughty demeanor.

"I'm Agent Booth from the United States Secret Service." He flashed a badge. "This is my colleague, Agent Soames." He nodded toward the young man at his shoulder.

What a coincidence, Kitty thought. He was the same young man who bumped into her at Carnegie Hall.

"What is this about?" she asked.

"You will come with us, please." It wasn't a request.

"Is something the matter?"

The stocky agent replied, "We have to ask you some questions about Mr Julian Weeks, your father."

Chapter Twenty Two

"I'm expected back at the *New York Sentinel* in fifteen minutes," Kitty said, fear gripping her. "They'll be waiting for me."

The agents didn't respond and instead led Kitty to a nearby dive, a greasy joint that reeked of boiled mutton and beer. They headed for a table behind a group of sailors telling bawdy jokes to a couple of women.

The older, stocky agent, Booth, ordered three glasses of water from a passing waitress.

"That's all?" the waitress said with annoyance.

"We won't be long." He showed her his badge.

"Oh, I'm sorry. Yes, sir." She disappeared.

"All right then." The agent turned to Kitty. "Let's start with first things first. What were you doing at the Hamburg-American?"

Kitty gasped. "How did you know I was there?" The laughter from the next table made it hard to concentrate. "Have you been following me?"

"We ask the questions, Miss Weeks," Booth replied.

Kitty's mind raced. How could they know where she'd been? Had they seen her with Dr Albert? Surely it wasn't a crime to converse with a diplomat from a foreign country. Could Hiliken have telephoned to report her? But no – it was her father they were interested in.

Kitty explained about Mrs Basshor's party, the shooting, and Hunter Cole's mention of a Dr Albert. Throughout, Agent Booth listened impassively, his arms folded across his barrel chest, while Agent Soames didn't look at her once. He had his pad open and took notes as she spoke.

"I don't know where I'm going with this," Kitty finished sheepishly. "Mrs Basshor's secretary confessed to the crime, so that's that. I suppose there were just a few loose ends nagging at me."

"And what did Dr Albert have to say to your question about whether or not he knew Mr Cole?" Booth and Soames exchanged glances.

Kitty felt she had implicitly given the diplomat her word not to repeat what he had told her, but she couldn't lie to the representatives of the Treasury Department.

"He said he might have, but if he did, it didn't lead to anything," she replied. "He said I could check his daybook at the office to confirm, but I believe him."

Agent Soames kept scribbling. If their positions had been reversed, she would have had to memorize all this information rather than writing it down, Kitty thought.

"Why," Booth went on, "did you drop off Mr Julian Weeks at the Edelweiss Café? Who was he meeting and for what purpose?"

Kitty's hands flew to her mouth. "You've been spying on us! How long has this been going on?"

Silence. Or, at least, silence from the agents. The diner resounded with joke-telling and raucous laughter. The disgruntled waitress thumped three glasses of water onto the table so hard that some of it spilled.

"This makes no sense." Kitty's eyes filled with angry tears. She wiped them away with the back of her hand. "You must have the wrong person."

"Did you or did you not drop off Mr Weeks at around ten a.m. on Friday, July 9?" Booth said.

"Yes, I did."

"Why?"

"Our chauffeur had to bring the other car to the mechanic's for an inspection. My father doesn't drive and didn't want to ride in a taxi." She took some satisfaction from her answer.

Booth continued, unperturbed. "Who was Mr Weeks meeting there and for what purpose?"

"I have no idea."

"I see." The big man didn't sound convinced. "You're sure?"

She shrugged. "He said it was someone from out of town."

"And that's it?"

"That's it." The disbelief showed on his face, so she added, "If you met my father, you would know. He doesn't tell me anything." She waited a moment. "May I ask you something?"

Booth gave a grudging nod.

"Has he broken the law?"

Soames finally spoke. "You can help us prove that he hasn't."

Kitty wanted to ask whether Soames had bumped into her on purpose. "How can I do that?"

Booth said, "Tell us whom Mr Weeks met at the café and why."

"I just told you I don't know."

"You're his daughter," Booth replied, unmoved. "I'm sure you can cajole it out of him."

"You'd be helping your father and us, Miss Weeks," Soames added. "Your actions would count in his favor."

Kitty began to feel cornered.

"We're from the Secret Service." Booth leaned in, his beefy face just inches from hers. "We'll get what we need whether or not you help, but unlike you, we won't have a light touch." Pockmarks scarred his cheeks. "The stain of being under government investigation doesn't wash away easily. Once we start asking questions, everyone will find out."

"I see—"

"So give us what we need and we'll leave you in peace. Just remember, you can't breathe a word to anyone. This is strictly government business."

—

It was too late to go back to work at this point, and Kitty was in no mood to face Miss Busby. All she wanted was to speak to her father. She would find out the information somehow and then the two Secret Service men would leave them alone. There was something about the agents that frightened Kitty: the older one seemed like a bully; the younger one – he spoke well and he was nice-looking, she had to give him that. But he was too reserved: his smile didn't reach his eyes.

She found it odd that they didn't want anyone to know about their conversation, but for the moment, at least, she had to trust them. She wished she had someone to whom she could turn for advice, but she had no one, and even if she did, what could she say when she had been forbidden to breathe a word about it to anyone?

She returned home shaken from the encounter, hoping to find her father in his study sipping a whiskey so she could engage him in a nice little chat. Instead, he had left her a note saying he would be out to dinner with Maitland.

Kitty handed Grace her hat and purse.

"I have to check something," she said to the maid before opening the door to the study.

A pair of milky white eyes stared at her from the darkness. Kitty took a deep breath and turned on the lamp. How she hated that infernal sculpture.

She wasn't betraying her father, she told herself. She was helping him. If she found any information that was even the slightest bit incriminating, she wouldn't hesitate to warn him.

She found his leather-bound notebook in the second drawer of his desk and leafed through the thick cotton pages, smiling fondly at the sight of his spidery handwriting. In contrast to Julian Weeks's imposing physical presence – the sculpted head, the strong arms, which caught her when she jumped off trees in her childhood – his script resembled that of an elderly man's.

Kitty traced the shaky letters with her finger. From the authors on his shelves – Adam Smith, Rousseau, Gibbons – one would never guess that he had taught himself to read and write. He'd mastered the former with no apparent difficulty. The writing, well… As the Misses Danceys said, that required practice, practice, and more practice. Julian Weeks came from humble beginnings and, unlike Kitty, hadn't had years of leisure to perfect his penmanship.

What he didn't have himself, he had given her: a good education and every conceivable luxury.

Kitty began to read, ignoring her twinges of guilt. She would tell the men from the Treasury Department what they needed to know, and then they would vanish without her father or any of their acquaintances being the wiser.

Most of the diary was blank. On weekdays, he simply wrote *club*, *home*, or sometimes *mtg* followed by a brief note.

He recorded details about his Sunday outings with Kitty, however. Kitty was touched to see the entries, which ranged from *Botanic Gdns* to *F.T. Park* to *Chinatown* with an exclamation mark. He'd even noted the items that they'd ordered from the restaurant on Mott Street: *Duck soup; fried squid in cracker dust, 79¢; Chinese noodles, 50¢.*

He had jotted down the ferry timings for the day they drove to Jersey City. Kitty recalled how surprised she had been to discover that they could cross the Hudson by train or take their car across on a boat, but that no bridge connected New Jersey to Manhattan.

Here and there, Kitty saw his lawyer mentioned, and in late June, Mr Maitland's name popped up. For Friday, July 9, the morning Mr Weeks went to the Edelweiss Café, he had written the address and *H.S. + 1.*

Kitty replaced the diary in his drawer, switched off the lamp and closed the door to the study behind her. *H.S.*

She didn't know of anyone by those initials. In fact, save for his lawyer, doctor, and a handful of other business colleagues, she didn't know the names of any of her father's friends. He so rarely mentioned them. And who was the plus one?

Chapter Twenty Three

Kitty arrived at the hen coop the next morning steeled for the worst. An uneasy night's sleep only intensified her sense of dread at facing her boss.

"How is Miss Busby?" she asked Jeannie as she passed by the typist's desk.

"Not pleased," Jeannie replied, her round face pinched with concern. "She sent me out three times to look for you. Why didn't you tell anyone you were leaving?"

"I hardly know myself." Kitty put down her things and began the long march to the editor's office. She found Miss Busby buried behind ominous headlines:

> PRESIDENT MAY DELAY REPLY TO
> BERLIN BY A WEEK. PRESENT
> ATTITUDE IS ONE OF
> DELIBERATION.

"I'm so sorry about yesterday." Kitty came in and sat down.

Helena Busby lowered her paper. She didn't respond for a moment. Then a single tear trickled down her withered cheek and splashed onto the news. Her hand trembled as she unscrewed her bottle of Rowland's.

Miss Busby looked worn out. The older woman had no personal photographs on her desk, no family or friends that Kitty had heard her speak of. Beneath the president's portrait hung a faded clipping from the '90s, which Kitty had once read. It described the new type of "bachelorette girl." "She paddles her own canoe, works for a living, and *chooses* to make her own way in the world."

Kitty had assumed that the piece referred to the kind of life Miss Busby lead or, at least, to the life that she dreamed of.

She tried to imagine her editor young and carefree, with stars in her eyes. Had Miss Busby wanted to write breaking news or travel the world like Nellie Bly? Then twenty, thirty, maybe even forty years later, the once-fresh girl reporter finds herself chained to her desk, stuck in an airless alcove, and all for what?

Miss Busby tilted the bottle over her spoon, but only a drop came out. She rummaged in her drawer for another but found it was empty too.

"Hundreds of girls would kill to be in your shoes." She tossed both bottles into the waste bin.

"I'm so sorry, Miss Busby," Kitty repeated. She meant every word. She would give anything for a second chance.

"Do you know what Mr Bennett says about female journalists?" Miss Busby asked.

Mr Bennett wasn't a colleague – he was the English author Arnold Bennett, and Miss Busby considered his *Journalism for Women* her bible.

"He says we are unreliable as a class. He says that it is not surprising that the young woman who is accustomed to remark gaily, 'Only five minutes late this morning, Father,' confident that a frown or a hard word will end the affair, should carry into business the laxities so long permitted to her around the hearth," the editor went on.

"I've coddled you. That's the problem. You don't know what it's like to have to start from nothing. To have to scratch and fight for every inch of opportunity."

Kitty stared at the papers on the editor's desk, contrite.

"I've met all kinds of girls in the course of my work." Helena Busby rose to her feet and continued, like an orator addressing crowds. "There's the sprightly type who martyrs herself because she must work with other women whose dullness and primness jar on her vivacities; the girl who feels insulted because men don't accord her the deference to which she is accustomed; the woman who says, 'I forgot to do so and so, I'm so sorry,' and stands like a spoiled child expectant of forgiveness…"

The beanpole frame thrummed with emotion. "In men destined for business or a profession, carelessness is harshly discouraged at an early age. In women, who usually are not destined for *anything whatever*, it enjoys a merry life."

Kitty wondered whether she should call for help, but what would she say was the matter? That Miss Busby was quoting Mr Bennett almost word for word?

"In journalism, as perhaps in no other profession, success depends wholly upon the loyal cooperation, the perfect reliability of a number of people," the editor said. "Some are great, and some are small, but none are *irresponsible*."

"Won't you sit down, Miss Busby?" Kitty suggested. "Let me get you something to drink."

"A vast number of women engaged in journalism secretly regard it as a delightful game." Spittle collected at the corner of the thin lips. "On no other assumption can the attitude of many women journalists toward their work be explained. My final words as I leave you on the threshold of an office are these" – she gasped – "journalism is not a game, and in journalism there are no excuses."

And like a tree hacked at exactly the right angle, Miss Busby toppled forward.

–

Mr Hewitt addressed the stunned typists an hour after the doctor came to take the Ladies' Page editor away, summarizing the medical diagnosis. "The female constitution cannot withstand the pressure of working at a newspaper year after year for eight- to ten-hour days. I hope for your own sakes that you will all someday marry."

He nodded at Kitty. "Come with me, Miss Weeks."

Kitty followed him down the hall to his office. She couldn't bring herself to look Miss Busby's superior in the eye.

"This is why we insisted that she take on an apprentice," he said, settling into his seat behind his desk. "Still, she didn't exactly keep you busy, did she? No. She held on to the reins too tightly."

He rummaged through his papers. "You needn't worry though. Mr Eichendorff will make sure that she's sent to a sanitarium. She went to one upstate a couple of years ago. Came back in fine fettle. But enough talk; we have a Ladies' Page to publish."

He cleaned his glasses with his kerchief. "Did you bring me her proofs?"

Kitty handed them over. She had overheard whispers between Mr Hewitt and the doctor. The physician had said something about displaced ovaries and a collapsed uterus, the effects of working too hard and not having borne children. The strain on Miss Busby's system had also been exacerbated by neurasthenia, a complete depletion of the nerves, the doctor had added.

Mr Hewitt wrinkled his nose while he scanned the pages that Kitty had given him. "In the words of the late, great Horace Greeley, the only way to succeed in this business is to eat ink and sleep on newsprint. Miss Busby certainly did that. No one could accuse her of shirking. Yes, it seems we have a head start on this week, and there are more than enough advertisements and announcements to fill in any blank spaces. What matters most" – he glanced at Kitty over his glasses – "is that the Morgan interview be top-notch. It's to be the centerpiece of Saturday's edition. Get a draft done by this afternoon, and we'll review it."

"Yes, Mr Hewitt."

"Call the compositor," Mr Hewitt continued, "and let him know that I'll speak to him at five. I expect you to be present to take notes. Now that Miss Busby is gone, you will take over some of her responsibilities. Who knows? This might even lead to a promotion for you… That will be all."

Kitty turned to leave. She couldn't believe that she hadn't been reprimanded, and that moreover, she might benefit from Miss Busby's collapse. "Yes, Mr Hewitt."

She returned to her desk. All the typists were back at work as though nothing had happened. Kitty retrieved her notes from the Anne Morgan interview. Somehow, the sight of her scribbles reminded her of Agent Soames and his note-taking. She pushed away the attendant anxiety that the thought brought up and focused on the task at hand.

In no time at all, Kitty found herself immersed in the world of the Colony Club. She could see the ballroom, the underground swimming pool, and the loggia with its mural of pink flamingos. She recalled Miss Morgan's flashing dark eyes, her clipped speech, and the string of pearls – and Kitty's writing flowed, as though Miss Busby herself guided her hand.

She reviewed the draft when she finished, corrected the grammar, and removed any trace of unnecessary gush or shrillness – Mr Arnold Bennett disapproved of superlatives, overpunctuation, trite expressions and wordiness. She prepared a fresh copy and brought it to the Weekend Supplement editor in his office.

"You called the compositor?"

"Yes, Mr Hewitt."

"All right, come back and see me at five. I'll have read this by then."

And then Kitty remembered – she had to meet the agents first thing tomorrow and so couldn't stay late today. "I'm afraid I can't, Mr Hewitt."

"Can't what, Miss Weeks?"

"Stay past five." She needed time to speak to her father.

"I beg your pardon?"

"I have to be home for dinner this evening."

The editor held up his hand. "Don't give me any excuses. I have no interest in your domestic affairs. As far as I'm concerned, the choice is simple: either you give your work one hundred percent, or you don't."

Kitty remained silent.

"All right, send that girl" – he snapped his fingers – "Janie Williams to see me."

"You mean Jeannie Williams, Mr Hewitt?"

"That's correct."

"Will that be all, Mr Hewitt?"

He nodded. "You're free to leave."

Kitty told herself she couldn't expect anything else under the circumstances. Hopefully, he would feel better once he had read her interview.

Chapter Twenty Four

Rao drove Kitty home and let her out in front of the New Century. She half expected to find the Secret Service agents staring from across West End Avenue, but all she noticed was a crumpled ball of newsprint blowing down the scorching sidewalk like tumbleweed.

The doorman greeted her at the front of the apartment house. "There's a letter for you, Miss Weeks." He tipped his hat. "Two men dropped it off." He reached into his pocket.

Kitty took the unmarked envelope and made her way past the display of cut gladioli in the vestibule. She didn't open the letter while she rode upstairs in the elevator.

"You're back at last," Mr Weeks called from his study when Kitty came in through the foyer. "You've been having some late evenings."

She slipped the letter into her purse and handed her gloves and scarf to Grace. "I was only late yesterday, sir."

"I'm sorry Maitland and I couldn't join you for dinner."

"That's quite all right." Kitty peeked into his room. "Do you mind if I freshen up? I'll be back in a minute."

"Of course." He resumed reading his papers.

Once in the safety of her bedroom, Kitty removed the envelope from her purse and extracted a small sheet of notepaper.

"Riverside Park tomorrow, 8:30 a.m. sharp," it said. It was signed "R. Booth. US Treasury Dept."

Kitty tore the note into tiny strips and tossed them into her wastebasket, then changed into an evening dress and joined Mr Weeks in his study.

"Will you have a drink?" he asked. She nodded and he poured her two fingers of black-currant cordial, which he diluted with a spray of fizzy water and a cube of ice.

He served himself a tumbler of bourbon, pulled back the curtains, and opened the windows. "Much better, don't you think?" He loosened his collar and dropped into his favorite armchair, crossing one leg over the other. "I read in the papers that Mrs Basshor's secretary confessed to shooting Mr Cole, and that the stable hand was set free. You must be pretty happy."

"Ah." Kitty didn't want to get into that.

"What's the matter?" He swirled the amber drink in his glass. "Aren't you pleased? I thought you believed that that fellow, Lupone, was innocent."

"I don't think it matters what I believe."

"Come now, don't go feeling sorry for yourself. What has always baffled me," he went on cheerily, "is why people with a lot of money put those with less of it in charge of paying their bills."

"I beg your pardon?"

"Wasn't the secretary cheating Mrs Basshor?"

"That's what the papers said." Kitty took a sip of her drink.

"It seems as though he would have gotten away with it since those Japanese were on their way back to Yokohama and had no idea what they were missing. It's just his bad luck that Cole found him out."

"And Mr Cole's bad luck too. He was killed for his efforts."

Julian Weeks shrugged. "He shouldn't have gone around meddling in other people's business."

"You think that's a fair outcome?"

"Not exactly—"

"Hotchkiss told me he owed everything to Mrs Basshor, but I didn't think he was talking about money."

"It's always about money, my dear." Mr Weeks laughed.

Kitty gathered her courage. "May I ask you a question?"

"Go ahead."

"Why don't you tell me anything about your business?"

"Which business?" He seemed legitimately confused. "I have my hand in several pots."

She tried to sound casual. "Well, for instance, why did you go to the Edelweiss Café on Friday? You told me you had to meet someone from out of town. Who was it?"

"Why the sudden curiosity, Capability? I had to meet the colleague of a colleague, that's all."

"Can you give me a name?"

"A name means nothing. You don't know him. I hardly know him myself."

"Why won't you tell me anything about yourself?" The words came out much more forcefully than Kitty had intended. Her questions, she realized, were as much to satisfy her own curiosity as to provide the agents with answers.

"Whom I met at the café has nothing to do with you. But you're right, I have kept you in the dark, so allow me to tell you this: my lawyers have a copy of my will and my life insurance policies, and when I'm gone, everything I have will be yours."

Kitty could have screamed, but she forced herself to keep calm. "That's not why I asked."

He checked the time on his pocket watch. "You know, I should have dinner at the club this evening. Forgive me, Capability." He put down his glass and stood, his expression maddeningly opaque. "I'll see you at breakfast."

Chapter Twenty Five

"How can I be sure that you're with the Secret Service?" Kitty said to the two agents. They stood near the entrance to Riverside Park with the wind rustling through the trees and the skies a bright summery blue.

"Our badges should be proof enough, Miss Weeks," Soames replied, "but if you'd like additional assurance, you might telephone the Treasury Department's office at the Customs House downtown." He dropped his formal manner. "But I promise, we're not lying to you."

"What do you have for us, Miss Weeks?" Booth stepped forward.

Kitty had so little information to report that she didn't think she could hurt anyone by answering. "My father told me nothing, but I did check in his daybook, and all it says for the day he went to the café is 'H.S. + 1.'"

Kitty noticed Soames watching her. "Am I free to go now?"

"Not so fast." Booth held up his hand. "We can guess who 'H.S.' is – Hugo Schweitzer, a German chemist with whom Mr Weeks has been doing some business."

Schweitzer. Kitty wondered why that name sounded familiar. "Well, I'm glad I could be of use." She turned as though to leave, but Booth wasn't finished.

"Have you heard Mr Weeks mention the word 'phenol,'" he said, "or seen it in any of his documents?"

Kitty stopped in her tracks. "Household cleaners don't really concern my father, Agent Booth."

"I'm not talking about *phenyl*, Miss Weeks, although you are correct that phenol is used in its manufacture. In fact, phenol is used to make a variety of domestic products, everything from phonograph records to disinfectants. It is also used in the manufacture of trinitrophenol, a powerful explosive that both sides are using to deadly effect in the war."

Soames stared at the ground.

"Maybe you've heard it called TNP or picric acid," Booth said.

"I've not heard of it by any name, Mr Booth," Kitty replied angrily.

"Well," he went on, "in the past, we imported all the phenol we needed from England at 10 cents a pound. Now, a year later, it costs $1.25 for the same amount, and even if you're willing to pay, it's almost impossible to get ahold of."

Kitty's chest started to feel tight.

"There aren't many players in the phenol business these days." Boats drifted along the Hudson behind Booth. "We know all the key names, where they buy their phenol and who they sell to. Only one newcomer remains a mystery. Mr Julian Weeks. We don't know where he gets it, and we'd like to know what he's doing with it."

"My father has no use for phenol," Kitty said. But her denial was reflexive and not heartfelt.

"He's been buying significant quantities of the stuff."

"How do you know?"

"I'm afraid we can't tell you."

"Where does he store it?"

"Again, that's confidential."

"Well, if the price has gone up more than ten times over the past year, I'm sure it's a good investment," Kitty said.

"You can invest in gold or stocks, but you don't invest in phenol, Miss Weeks. At least not at the present moment."

"You think this has to do with whomever he met at the café."

The agents didn't reply.

"He's not some anarchist!" she said. Although he could perhaps be a war profiteer. "Look." She faced both men. "This is beyond me. You must speak directly to my father."

Booth pulled a paper from his jacket. "Does this look familiar?" He handed it to Kitty.

The words danced in front of Kitty's eyes. "This is my father's passport application. Where did you get it?"

Booth flipped the paper over. "Do you recognize this signature?"

Kitty shook her head.

"It belongs to the man who Mr Weeks chose to vouch for his identity. We know him well because he signs on behalf of Krauts trying to return home with falsified documents."

"What are you saying, Agent Booth?" Kitty was furious.

"Julian Weeks has no birth certificate, no proof for what he's written here. The Bureau of Citizenship will scrutinize his claim. And I don't have to tell you, an unmarried daughter's nationality follows that of her father's."

"All right. Enough, Booth." Soames stepped in.

Kitty blinked away tears.

"Help us, and we'll make all of this go away." Booth folded the form and replaced it in his pocket.

"I'm sure there's a reasonable explanation for Mr Weeks's lack of documentation," Soames added.

"You mean, he's not a German spy." Kitty stood still. This was ridiculous. Just because her father didn't have proof of his birth didn't mean he was lying. He may have lived abroad most of his life, but that didn't make him any less American than the two men standing in front of her. And just because they had badges and worked for the government didn't mean that they could threaten her, a wealthy, well-brought-up young woman.

Then it hit her. Something else must be going on.

"Why me?" Kitty said finally. "I've been wondering why you need to go through me to get to him. Why you followed *me* to the Hamburg-American building when it's my father you're interested in."

Both agents stiffened.

"But I'm beginning to suspect that you're not interested in either one of us."

Their faces went blank.

"The only way you could have known that I went to the Hamburg-American," she continued, testing her theory as she spoke, "is if you'd been waiting for me outside the *Sentinel* all morning. But why would you do that? No, you knew I went downtown because you were there already. It's not me or my father you've been following... It's Dr Albert."

"That's not true," Booth said. But his voice and manner lacked conviction.

"You followed Dr Albert and me to the docks," Kitty continued. "Two out of the three times that you've seen either my father or me – at the Edelweiss Café, at Carnegie Hall, and at the docks – there has been another man present. *Dr Albert* was expected at the concert, Dr Albert was certainly at the docks, and now I think" – she worked it out as she went along – "that Dr Albert was the '+ 1' at the meeting with my father and the German chemist, Schweitzer."

Soames tapped his foot. Booth exhaled deeply. "That's ridiculous."

"You've been suggesting that my father is selling phenol to the Germans," Kitty said. "But since we're neutral, that can't be against the law. So what is against the law then – and what are you both trying so hard to hide by approaching me and not him?"

No reply.

"You don't really think my father is doing something criminal or you wouldn't be talking to me. After all, you can hardly expect me to incriminate him." Kitty hoped to get a response – any response – so she could see the situation with more clarity.

"You're right, Miss Weeks. Our approach has been unorthodox," Soames replied. "These are unusual times. We're faced with unusual threats," he continued, ignoring Booth glaring at him. "And we're responding as best we can. I will tell you this – if word got out that we were shadowing Dr Albert—"

"Which we are not," Booth butted in.

"—it would be considered a gross violation of protocol and cause an international incident," Soames finished. "Dr Albert is the official representative of a nation with which the United States has no quarrel. He's a respected guest on our soil. And the Secret Service only acts in accordance with the president's orders."

"Fine," Kitty said. "If you were indeed shadowing me and not Dr Albert, tell me where I was before I arrived at the Hamburg-American on Monday."

"We caught up with you late," Booth said.

"Where?"

"At the *Sentinel*."

"And how did you know you'd find me there?"

"We took a chance."

"You don't take a chance on anything. That's codswallop."

"Enough." Booth looked furious. "Mr Julian Weeks has made false claims to the federal government. He could face jail time if the matter was brought to the right individual's attention. So you will do as we say, Miss Weeks." He patted the form in his pocket.

"I work for a newspaper, and I will tell everyone about this." Kitty's boldness amazed her.

"And who would believe you? A Ladies' Page reporter's word against that of two agents from the Treasury Department? We're in charge here," Booth continued as a girl with a pink ribbon in her hair rolled a hoop past them. "You tell us what your father is doing with all that phenol, and we'll do our best to help him with his troubles."

Kitty watched the hoop spin as the girl maneuvered it with her stick. That was her life, Kitty thought – she would have to keep moving if she didn't want to fall.

–

To distract herself, Kitty browsed through the papers on the drive to the *Sentinel*. But the headlines, which she once would have skimmed over, now took on a new significance:

> WILSON SAYS HE WILL ACT
> PROMPTLY AFTER DECIDING
> REPLY TO GERMANY; AMERICAN
> COMMENT DISTURBS BERLIN.

Echoing the theme, a newsboy on the corner shouted: "President Plans to Return to Capital. Talks of New Warning to Germans!"

Kitty wanted to scream with frustration. Had the president ordered the Secret Service to spy on a German diplomat? Was the country, much as it might not want to, sliding into war, as Dr Albert himself predicted? How was her father mixed up in it? Kitty thumped her fist against her thigh. And why was he *lying* on official documents? It wasn't a crime to supply the Germans with phenol, but thinking of him as someone who profited from death and destruction was scarce consolation.

Never before had she been so glad to step inside the *Sentinel*. Never had she been more relieved to see that clock or the mosaic decorating the floor. At least here, for the most part, life remained predictable.

She rode up in the elevator, eager to resume her duties. She neared her desk and noticed that Jeannie's place was empty; the typist was sitting in Kitty's seat.

Jeannie didn't hear Kitty approach over the din of the machines.

"I hope you approve," Kitty said.

Startled, the other girl dropped her pencil. "Oh, Miss Weeks!" A crimson stain spread across Jeannie's cheeks. "You took me by surprise. Mr Hewitt said I should check the Anne Morgan interview."

"And how does it stack up? Are there very many errors?" Kitty couldn't control the bite in her tone, but Jeannie didn't seem to notice.

"You write so clearly, Miss Weeks," she said. "What a treat it must have been to visit the Colony Club and speak to Miss Morgan."

"May I?" Kitty moved to hang her purse on the back of her chair.

"Mr Hewitt said you should speak to him," Jeannie replied.

Could Jeannie have moved because she, Kitty, was being promoted to Miss Busby's position? That didn't seem likely.

She knocked on the Weekend Supplement editor's door.

"I suppose you're wondering why Miss Williams is in your place," he said when Kitty came in. "She's a surprise, that girl." The editor removed his glasses, fogged them with his breath, and gave them a quick polish with his handkerchief before returning them to his nose. "Much more competent than I expected. Stayed until eight last night without my having to ask and was back at seven thirty this morning."

"Miss Williams is a hard worker," Kitty agreed. She couldn't compete with that kind of dedication, but still, she had other skills to offer.

"You will be happy to know that I spoke to Miss Busby's physician, and he told me that she would need plenty of rest, as well as complete peace and quiet for the next four to six weeks in order to recover. In the meantime, I will take over as Ladies' Page editor."

"Yes, Mr Hewitt."

"As such," he went on, "I require an assistant who is able to work long hours on short notice."

"I understand, Mr Hewitt." Kitty noticed that he hadn't invited her to pull up a chair.

"You see, I warned Miss Busby when she hired her apprentice to pick a workhorse and not a thoroughbred, but she wouldn't listen. And she's paid the price. Thoroughbreds look pretty, and they do a few things well, but they're fussy. They don't stand up to everyday use. You may as well know that Miss Williams applied for your position when it was announced."

"I see," Kitty said. No one had told her that. Not Miss Busby, not Jeannie, nor any of the other girls.

"She was my first choice, but Miss Busby rejected her. She said that you had something none of the other applicants possessed."

"May I ask what?" Kitty hoped to hear something complimentary, like intelligence or eloquence, but right now, she'd settle for good penmanship or a mastery of grammar.

"Miss Busby told me that she wanted someone with class, someone who dressed well and spoke well. It didn't trouble her that you had never worked before, either at a newspaper or anywhere else."

Kitty staggered as though she'd been punched. How could she have flattered herself that Miss Busby had seen some latent merit in her, some untapped potential?

"It's not my fault," she protested. "Miss Busby didn't allow me to do any heavy lifting. It's only recently that she gave me any freedom—"

"That's exactly my point." The editor sounded firm. "This isn't about you or your talents – such as they may be. It's about work. Hard work, day-to-day work. The ability to churn out paragraphs day after day on any subject, for any reason.

"I'm afraid I don't have much patience for thorough-breds. I have enough on my plate as it is, and what I need is a workhorse. Miss Busby is free to hire you back once she returns."

"Please, Mr Hewitt," Kitty begged. "Give me one more chance." She didn't offer any excuses since she didn't think he would care to hear them.

The editor pulled a stack of files toward him. "I suggest, Miss Weeks, that you think long and hard about whether you are suited to our profession. I think you're unhappy because humble Miss Williams has displaced you. After some time, you will realize that today was a blessing in disguise. And if you don't" – he opened one of the folders – "well, that's not my problem."

Kitty returned to her desk – or, rather, Jeannie's desk. "Did you know about this?" she demanded.

"I'm sorry, Miss Weeks." Jeannie stood to allow Kitty to collect her things. "If I thought that it would end like this, I would never have agreed to help yesterday." She sounded contrite, but her wisp of a smile revealed the pride she felt in her promotion.

Kitty swept her few personal items into her purse: a pen, a rabbit's foot good-luck charm from a school friend, and a pocket dictionary.

"I hope you can forgive me," Jeannie said. Kitty's Anne Morgan interview sat on the desk, neatly corrected in red ink.

"Good luck, Miss Williams." Kitty hurried away before she said something she might regret.

She had been ousted by Jeannie Williams, a girl she hadn't even perceived to be a threat. She had been found lacking, not because she had disobeyed Miss Busby and gone off on her own, but because she didn't work hard enough or – and perhaps this was the same thing – for enough hours in the day. Miss Busby had hired her not because of what she could do, but because of her breeding.

None of the typists batted an eyelid as Kitty left the hen coop. As she made her way through the cavernous hall for the last time, it seemed that the music from their machines swelled to a crescendo.

It was her send-off, Kitty thought, trying to stifle any feeling of self-pity: a screeching symphony of metal against metal that produced nothing but line after line of black type against white paper, each and every day.

Chapter Twenty Six

Kitty couldn't believe that all her efforts had been for nothing: her meeting with Mrs Stepan, the interview with Anne Morgan, the months of drudgery leading up to it. None of it mattered, and worse still, Mr Hewitt believed that she wasn't cut out to be a journalist.

A newspaper boy shouted, "Harry Thaw to Know His Fate Tonight!" Streetcars clanged noisily. Elevated trains clattered in the distance. Whoever said that New York was a great city had blundered. It was mayhem, a place where a million and a half souls feverishly pursued their business without regard for any niceties.

Kitty walked back home. There was no need to take a cab, because she wasn't in a hurry. She recalled the questions Miss Busby had posed to her when she came in to apply for the position as her assistant. They had been lifted straight from *Journalism for Women*, although Kitty hadn't realized that at the time.

"Are you seriously addicted to reading the newspapers?" Miss Busby had said. "Does the thought frequently occur to you, apropos of incidents witnessed, that this would make fine copy for a story? Do you have the reputation among your friends for being an excellent letter writer?"

Kitty had replied yes to each question. She read the newspapers – not necessarily the political stories, but those with human interest.

"Quite right." Miss Busby had nodded.

"And I do see things I would like to know more about." Kitty had several questions about the city and how society functioned. "And I think my friends enjoy my letters."

In retrospect, her answers hadn't been terribly compelling, but Miss Busby hired her nonetheless. Of course she had – she didn't require an apprentice reporter. She had wanted someone with the social graces to enter any living room in town, and Kitty fit the bill exactly.

She had been a fool, Kitty thought. Naive and vain. So self-centered that she couldn't see that Jeannie's goodwill toward her might not have been entirely disinterested.

Kitty stopped herself. The past was the past. She would do better next time – and there *would* be a next time. If not at the *Sentinel*, then elsewhere.

The doorman at the New Century tipped his hat as Kitty entered, dusty and perspiring.

"Good morning, Miss Weeks."

"I hope you don't have anything for me, George." She managed a smile.

"No, ma'am, nothing today."

The cool foyer, which usually felt like a sanctuary from the busy streets now felt like a hotel – some luxurious but temporary accommodation from which her trunks would be shipped off to the next destination.

She rode up in the brass-trimmed elevator. Grace opened the front door when she rang the bell.

"You're back early, Miss Kitty." The maid took Kitty's purse and gloves.

The telephone rang in the foyer, and Kitty picked it up.

"I'm coming to get you," the voice on the other end of the line said.

"What?" Kitty's grip on the receiver tightened.

"Say 'I beg your pardon,' silly girl."

"Oh, Amanda. It's you." Kitty relaxed.

"Of course it's me. Who else could it be? I hope you haven't forgotten today."

"What is today, Bastille Day?"

"It is that." Amanda paused. "It's also the first day of the YWCA training. You promised me you'd come, Capability. I told all my friends that you would be there."

"What time is it at?"

"Four o'clock. I'll pick you up. By the way, Mama wants me to ask you a favor."

"I don't think I'm in a position to do anyone a favor at the moment." Normally, Kitty would have jumped at the chance to oblige snooty Mrs Vanderwell.

"You can pay a visit to Mrs Basshor," Amanda said. "Poor Bessie has been reduced to a puddle of jelly over the business with Hotchkiss, and Mama thought it might help to have someone from the outside hear her out. You can tell the old dear that you will write a story about it. You don't have to actually do anything – just tell her you might. I hink Bessie would like to feel that someone cares. That someone is willing to listen to her side of things."

The words echoed Kitty's remark to Hotchkiss just eight days before. That she would help Mrs Basshor tell her side of the story. It didn't feel like eight days; too much had happened since then.

"I don't work for the paper anymore," Kitty said.

"You don't? No wonder you're home." A pause. "Well, just pretend that you do for one more day. And, Capability—"

"Yes?"

"You do realize that this gives you one less reason for turning me down."

"If I hadn't realized before, I do now, Amanda."

"See you at three thirty?"

"I'll be ready." Kitty hung up the telephone.

She went to her rooms and opened a black-lacquered Russian keepsake box, decorated with a painting of a young man on a horse jumping over the shining sun. It contained letters and cards from friends as well as the last letter her father had sent her. In the winter of '13, while Kitty was still on her European tour, Julian Weeks had written to tell her that as soon as he found a suitable place for them to stay in Manhattan, she would be joining him for good.

The remaining month of her trip had passed in a haze, overshadowed by visions of their future together. The last week of her Atlantic crossing aboard the *Aquitania* had seemed interminable. She had flirted with a handsome young man from Virginia, but her heart hadn't been in it. All she'd really wanted was to set foot on native soil and enjoy living with her one remaining parent. Their arrangement – him at his club, her at the *Sentinel* – might have continued until the day she married or the day one of them died if she remained a spinster.

Kitty put her father's letter back in the box. Instead, it would all come to an end because of the Secret Service men and their talk of phenol and falsified passport applications.

-

"More than three million soldiers have perished," the representative from the Red Cross told the audience of young women who were gathered on wooden benches, watching images flash across a cloth screen.

"I will enumerate the death toll for you: France has lost three hundred thousand men; Germany, a quarter of a million. Thirty thousand British troops have perished. Austria-Hungary has lost a million and a quarter, and Russia one and a half million."

On the screen, helmeted soldiers, their rifles at the ready, stood in twisting gullies of narrow trenches. At some unheard signal, they scrambled to the surface, fountains of dust erupting around them, and they fell like dominoes.

The image shifted to a scene of infantrymen, cavalry, and teams of horses pulling carts loaded with cannons marching down a country road as though to take the place of their fallen comrades.

"All told, that's five times the number who were killed during the entire Civil War," the woman from the Red Cross continued. "In the span of less than a year."

Kitty turned to look at Amanda, who seemed rapt in concentration. To kill more than three million men in a little under a year must require a tremendous amount of weaponry. If her father sold phenol to either side, he had a hand in the horrific death toll. She had always assumed that, like any decent man, Mr Weeks must be against war-profiteering. On the other hand – she hated to even think this – she could imagine him saying matter-of-factly that someone would make money from the war, so why shouldn't it be him?

The Red Cross representative, a no-nonsense woman with her hair pulled into a tight bun, had moved on to the subject of the injured and wounded.

Kitty couldn't bear to watch a nurse unwrap bandages from charred and oozing limbs. The images became worse: a soldier screamed in agony as a doctor sawed off his leg; another moved his hand away from the side of his head, revealing a hole in the place where his ear should have been. To Kitty's surprise, Amanda didn't flinch.

"Chlorine gas has been used to devastating effect," the Red Cross representative continued, "and has killed scores of soldiers as well as civilians."

The newsreel concluded with images of injured and crippled men recovering in a convalescent home, tended to by uniformed women in white caps.

"We need your help," the speaker said. "This is woman's work, and there is no one more suited to the task, but those planning to go abroad must be ready to remain calm and resourceful even under the most taxing conditions. You must be prepared to set aside all sentimental feelings and obey without question the orders of your superiors. If you are able to do all of this, then I can think of no better reward than the effect you will have on your patients."

A round of enthusiastic applause broke out. Amanda took Kitty's arm. "What do you think?"

The lights came back on, sparing Kitty from having to answer.

The representative from the Red Cross began to describe the training course. It would last five weeks, and graduates of the program would receive an official certificate signed by the president. They wouldn't become registered nurses, just nurse's aides, so they should give up all hopes of wearing the cap.

Laughter rippled through the room.

She went on to outline the course of study in further detail: mornings would be spent in lectures and demonstration, afternoons at hospitals. Fridays would be devoted to practicing invalid cookery and working on first-aid techniques using dummies.

"Registration forms can be found at the back of the room," the speaker said. "Feel free to check with me if you have any questions."

A trio of well-heeled girls came up to Amanda. Kitty recalled Miss Nicholls and Miss Hibben from the concert at Carnegie Hall, and Amanda introduced her to the third, Miss Amour.

"If the course is good enough for Miss Cleveland, it's good enough for me," Miss Amour said with a giggle, referring to the former president's daughter, who had become a nurse's aide.

"Mama says we can be placed with her friends, the Haywards, who have given over their country home entirely to the convalescing men," Miss Hibben added.

Miss Nicholls turned to Kitty. "So, will you be joining us, Miss Weeks?"

Four pairs of eyes stared at Kitty. Four young women, all about her age, all the cream of society, waited for her answer.

Kitty knew that, once made, the offer would not be repeated.

"Miss Weeks?" Miss Nicholls prompted.

Kitty's future flashed before her eyes: Arm in arm with Amanda. Working hard. Traveling to Europe. Accomplishing something worthwhile. Accepted as part of a set. And not just any set, the best one.

"I'm sorry. I can't." Not while so much was up in the air.

"You can't or you won't, Capability?" Amanda said, dismayed.

"I don't know."

Miss Hibben linked her arm through Amanda's. Miss Amour and Miss Nicholls curtsied. Four backs turned on Kitty. Only Amanda looked over her shoulder, and that was just for an instant.

Chapter Twenty Seven

"Aren't you going to work this morning?" Julian Weeks looked out from behind his paper. Kitty had joined him at breakfast later than usual.

She filled a glass with water and swallowed an Aspirin for her headache. "I am." If he could hide the truth, then so could she. After all, wasn't she his daughter?

"This is amusing." He sniffed and read, "'Austria-Hungary Protests Our Export of Arms to Britain and Her Allies; Says We Have Means of Exporting to All Alike.'"

"I don't see what's funny about that." She buttered her toast with such force that the slice broke in two.

"It's the Austrian foreign minister's language. You can tell he's terrified of upsetting us. Listen to how he dances around his complaint – on the one hand, he observes that the United States has been exporting war materials on a great scale to Britain and her allies, and that Austria and Germany have been almost entirely cut off from the American market. Then he says" – Mr Weeks quoted from the article – "'the question arises whether conditions as they have developed during the course of the war, certainly independently of the wish of the American government, are not of such a kind as in their effect to turn the Washington cabinet in a contrary direction from neutrality.'"

He turned to Kitty. "Can you decipher that?"

"I'm not sure that I care to." She brushed crumbs from her hands.

"What's the matter?"

"Nothing." Nothing, she thought, except that his actions had compromised them both. If she believed she might get a direct answer, Kitty would have spoken to him directly, but from experience, she knew she needed to be better informed, or else he would deflect her questions.

As if to underscore the point, his newspaper went back up, creating a wall of words between them.

Kitty finished her breakfast in silence, dressed for the day, and told her father she would take a cab to work. Instead, she walked toward Broadway.

"Miss Weeks!" She was halfway down the block when a voiced called her name. She turned around to see one of the Secret Service men running after her.

"Mr Soames."

"I have a message for you from Agent Booth. He'd like to meet tomorrow at nine o'clock."

"And what if I don't have any additional information?"

"Look, Miss Weeks." He took off his hat and ran a hand through his hair. "I'd have preferred to have done this some other way – but now that we're at this point, please, do both of us a favor. Give Agent Booth what he needs, and let us move on." His brown eyes looked sincere.

"I have no guarantee that you won't use what I tell you to hurt my father."

"How should I put this?" He looked away for a second, thinking. "What we're interested in is the phenol, Miss Weeks. Tell us about that, and I promise – unless Mr Weeks has committed some monstrous crime, which I'm sure he hasn't – I will personally make sure that any irregularities in his actions are treated with the utmost leniency."

Kitty hesitated.

"I've already told you more than I should," Agent Soames said, "so please believe me."

Kitty continued on to the public library. Unless there was some other highly profitable use for the compound, her father could only be selling phenol to the Germans. There was only one hitch to that guess – one that Mr Musser had pointed out when he and Kitty had discussed Hunter Cole and horses. Germany was finding it almost impossible to ship supplies across the Atlantic, so even if they bought the phenol, what would they do with it?

Kitty spoke to the librarian, Miss Evers, and asked for a book on the uses of various chemicals.

"Any chemical in particular that you're interested in, Miss Weeks?" The librarian seemed curious.

Kitty cleared her throat. "Phenol."

The woman's eyes widened. "I see. Just a moment."

She returned with a heavy volume. Kitty carried it away to a table. She opened *Common Chemical Compounds and Their Applications* and flipped through densely printed columns of text. The long strings of C's and H's and O's with tiny numbers dangling below, as if from a laundry line, looked like symbols from a foreign language. The Misses Dancey saw no reason to teach their charges chemistry or physics. When one of Kitty's classmates had pointed out Marie Curie's accomplishments, the older Miss Dancey had replied, "That's fine for her. She's Polish."

Kitty consulted the index at the back to find the chemical name for phenol – "C_6H_5OH, hydroxybenzene." There was a page number listed beside it.

Kitty read the full entry to herself. "Also known as carbolic acid…derived from coal tar…crystalline compound at room temperature." A list of uses followed. "Key ingredient in the manufacture of disinfectants and germicides. Also used in the manufacture of dyes, perfumes, carbolic soap, household cleaners, photographic chemicals, phonograph records, and in the production of salicylic acid…"

Although none of the uses seemed promising, Kitty copied down the list and returned the book to Miss Evers.

Who could she turn to for advice – Amanda? Mr Musser? Kitty groaned. She must telephone the old man and let him know that, for the present, she no longer worked at the *Sentinel*. She had left in such a hurry that she forgot to say goodbye.

She headed down Broadway and passed the Majestic, which was playing Pearl White's latest picture. Kitty wondered what Pearl would do in her shoes. How did the feisty heroines she portrayed respond to seemingly impossible situations?

She paid ten cents and bought herself a ticket. Since each episode of Miss White's serials lasted only about twenty minutes, she might as well take a look. If nothing else, a short break would do her good.

She settled into a seat between two schoolgirls playing hooky and a mother with young children. Usually, Kitty took Grace with her to the movies, but the audience at matinee shows, especially for Pearl's pictures, was mostly female. She need not worry about being molested in the darkness.

A colored slide advertising a new book appeared on the screen: "A Chicago Girl's Harrowing Adventure…Drugged in a Restaurant, She Barely Escapes! *THE GIRL WHO DISAPPEARED* by Clifford G. Roe. Published by the Uplift Press. $1.00 only." The Junior League House was next: "Absolutely fireproof hotel for unmarried women. Prices include three meals per day."

The Romance of Elaine began a few minutes later, following the production company Pathé's emblem, the proud French cockerel. Like all of Pearl's wildly successful serials, it was an adventure. Kitty had missed prior episodes, but it didn't take her too long to find her bearings. A title card introduced the audience to Elaine's nemesis, German secret agent and saboteur Marcus del Mar.

It hit too close to home, Kitty thought, and she watched with growing unease as del Mar and his female accomplice drugged the unsuspecting Elaine and spirited her away to a secluded cabin in the woods. When Elaine regained consciousness, she found herself bound and gagged in an empty room. She struggled free from her bonds and snuck out, but del Mar discovered that she had escaped and chased her through the forest.

Fortunately, Elaine found an abandoned canoe, jumped in and paddled away, but one of del Mar's well-aimed bullets shattered her only paddle.

A steep waterfall thundered in the distance, the current pulling Elaine toward it.

What would the desperate girl do?

Kitty sat on the edge of her seat.

In the nick of time, Elaine's admirer, Walter Jameson, who had been searching for her, tossed her a rope. Elaine caught hold of it and leaped to safety seconds before the canoe plunged into the abyss.

"To Be Continued..." A title card flashed on the screen while the audience, stunned for a moment, clapped and cheered.

Kitty rose and squeezed her way out of the theater; others remained to see the picture that followed.

She stepped out onto the street, blinking in the bright daylight. Unlike Elaine, she had no Walter Jameson to come to her rescue. She was on her own.

Chapter Twenty Eight

Kitty knew she was killing time. She didn't have a plan, and yet, she couldn't stand idle. One of the Misses Dancey's favorite mottoes was "When in doubt, do something. Activity pays dividends."

With Amanda's request in mind, she took a taxi to Mrs Basshor's apartment.

"Delphy Vanderwell told me you'd come if her daughter asked." The hostess's lips twisted into a smile. She lay bundled in a shawl on her chaise longue, the windows to her pale-yellow morning room tightly closed. "My world is smaller without Hotchkiss. I relied on him completely, but I didn't realize how much he meant to me until he was gone."

"May I be of assistance?" Kitty fanned herself with a magazine. She hoped Amanda would return the favor one day if it became necessary.

"You can tell those damned police fellows to believe me for a start," the hostess said. "Hotchkiss would never shoot anyone, let alone kill himself. He begged my forgiveness in his letter, but he knew I would have forgiven him for anything. What I can't stand is his absence."

"So Mr Hotchkiss wasn't stealing from you?"

"Of course he was. I knew it. And he knew that I knew." Elizabeth Basshor pulled herself up from her recumbent position. "I told the police that we never discussed what he did with my money. I looked the other way. Did you read the letter he wrote to me before he took his life?"

"Only the parts that were printed in the paper."

"That was garbage. And the police took away the original for evidence. But I remember it clearly, and nowhere did he confess to shooting Hunter. Nowhere."

"Why commit suicide then? I mean, if you knew he was stealing—"

"Exactly!" Life flooded back into Mrs Basshor's face. "He begged my forgiveness, but as I say, there was nothing to forgive. So I have to conclude that he was trying to tell me something that all of us have missed."

Kitty began to feel light-headed. It was either the heat or Mrs Basshor's wild guesses. She asked for some water.

The hostess tinkled a bell. "Do you keep a cook, Miss Weeks?"

"Yes."

"Does she do the marketing or someone else?"

"She does." Kitty wondered where Mrs Basshor was going with this.

"Then you must know what I'm talking about."

"I'm afraid I don't, Mrs Basshor."

"What do they teach you girls these days?"

The maid brought in water on a tray, and Kitty gratefully took a sip.

"In my day," the hostess said, "we had to draw, paint, play an instrument, sing, and dance, as well as run a house. Do you pay your cook well?"

"The going rate." Kitty wondered whether Mrs Basshor would come up with another of her personal ambushes. If so, this time she would be ready for it.

"There's a going rate for cooks who do the marketing, and a higher rate for ones who don't," Elizabeth Basshor said. "You are familiar with that arrangement?" She looked at Kitty in dismay. "No, I can see that you aren't. A cook who does the marketing charges less, because she takes a cut of whatever she buys for her mistress." She explained it as though to an imbecile.

Fairly certain that Mrs Codd did no such thing, Kitty replied with a touch of asperity, "I keep a running tab at the grocer's and pay in full at the end of each month."

"That's what you think." Mrs Basshor laughed. "Speak to your grocer, my dear. Ask him whether he's slipping your cook a couple of dollars each month. Not that he'll tell you anything. But that's the way things are done.

"I knew Hotchkiss was pocketing a portion of my expenses. That's par for the course. And when it came to the party, of course he would expect a bonus. So you see, if Mr Cole had threatened him about it, he wouldn't have been concerned. And certainly not concerned enough to murder Hunter and then take his own life. If your cook was pinching a bit from you when she did the groceries and I accused her, would she shoot me and then kill herself? Really."

"Put that way, it does make sense." Kitty's head spun. She had been lectured about phenol by Secret Service agents and now about how to pay one's cook by a society hostess.

"Can you do something about it then?" Mrs Basshor leaned forward eagerly. "I know what I said when you first came here, about your wanting to be a reporter and all. But you should ignore that. I was angry that you were doing what I had wanted to do and were getting away with it."

"You wanted to be a journalist?"

"Not exactly. But I did want to do something daring and provocative. I still do." Mrs Basshor fluffed her hair. "Anyhow, that's not the point. I'd like you to tell your readers my story."

"I no longer work for the paper, Mrs Basshor. They let me go," Kitty said.

"Who did – the beanpole?"

"Miss Busby has been taken ill. It was her supervisor."

"Well, that's ridiculous. You're very good. I'll have a word with Frieda Eichendorff, shall I?"

"Please, Mrs Basshor, don't say anything to anyone."

"Well, who will help me with what I want to say about Hotchkiss?"

"I'm afraid I can't help you there."

Mrs Basshor sighed. "The police, my lawyer and even my friends think I'm a fool… What will you do now?"

"I haven't formed a plan yet."

Mrs Basshor leaned back and placed an eye pillow over her face. "You shouldn't let one individual's actions stop you."

"What about everything you said about my not being able to get married?"

"Didn't I just tell you to forget it? When you're ready to settle down, come see me. And in the meantime, please help me clear my secretary's name."

–

Kitty reached a decision on the taxi ride back home: if she couldn't glean the information she needed from her father, she must try to extract it from one of his associates.

"Back so soon?" Mr Weeks called from his study.

Kitty handed Grace her purse and gloves. "It's one o'clock," she said as she went in.

"I suppose I've grown accustomed to the longer hours you've been keeping recently."

She drummed her fingers on the back of his sofa. "Would you mind telephoning Mr Maitland? I think it's a good day for an outing to the Cloisters. If he's free, I'd like to go."

"Wouldn't it be better if you went with a friend your own age?" Julian Weeks sounded baffled. "Maitland is entertaining but hardly a spring chicken."

"It's only a trip to a museum, Papa." The comparison amused Kitty, but she couldn't help resenting him for putting her in this position. If she knew more about his life, she wouldn't have to resort to such tricks.

"Should I accompany you?" Julian Weeks said. He seemed unsure about how to proceed.

"Please don't," Kitty replied at once, then added, "You've told me time and time again that you don't care for religious art."

–

Mr Maitland arrived in a chauffeur-driven limousine at three. Kitty and her father exchanged a glance before she climbed in.

"Are you sure you won't join us, Julian?" Mr Maitland asked.

To Kitty's relief, Mr Weeks waved them off.

The buildings on West End Avenue flashed past Kitty's window as the motorcar raced uptown. Kitty began to have misgivings. The Misses Dancey had warned their charges not to drive in automobiles with strange men after a discussion on how chauffeurs not only ignited motors, but also passions. The word *chauffeur*, after all, came from the French *chauffer* – to heat.

"Apparently, George Gray Barnard, the man behind the Cloisters' collection, bought many of his pieces from French peasants," Maitland said. "He paid as little as thirty francs for some."

"I had no idea. And this was recently?"

"Oh yes, within the last decade. He found farmers allowing their chickens to lay eggs on medieval platforms and supporting their vines on ancient columns. To my mind, that makes him not just a great collector but one of the best."

"Because he bought things cheaply?"

"Because" – Maitland turned to face her – "he saw beauty where others didn't."

Kitty shifted uncomfortably in her seat.

"He also acquired an arcade from the Abbey of Saint-Michel-de-Cuxa." Maitland resumed speaking like a lecturer. "No one thought much of it at first, but then the French government made quite a fuss about the arcade leaving the country. In hindsight, it's fortunate that it didn't remain on-site. If it had, it's quite likely that it might have been blown to smithereens by now. France isn't just losing thousands of men each day; she's also bleeding away her history."

Kitty struggled to find a way to broach the subject on her mind. Should she start with general questions? And if that weren't enough, Mr Maitland's talkativeness made it hard to get a word in edgewise.

"I'd like to create a museum in Canada someday," he told her. "One that will have my name on it." He chuckled. "I'm afraid I'm not self-effacing like Mr Barnard."

They arrived at a barnlike building overlooking the Harlem River at 699 Fort Washington Avenue. Maitland's chauffeur opened the door, and Kitty stepped out onto the street and, a few paces later, into a world of pious saints, demure Virgins, and gargoyles sticking out their tongues from cornices and capitals.

She followed Mr Maitland beneath ancient arches, between fluted stone pillars and past entire walls that had been transplanted from their original faraway sites to create a magical experience that resembled neither wandering through a museum nor a church, but something altogether different.

Mythical beasts leaped out from friezes, tenacious flora curled up columns, fantastical creatures – some human and some animal, some a combination of both – mocked Kitty's astonishment.

Maitland paused to examine a six-hundred-year-old Madonna and Child. Kitty stared at a frieze in which the devil, burning with glee, prodded a row of protesting sinners into the flames of hell.

They walked on to the main attraction – the cloisters, a tranquil courtyard bordered on all four sides by a covered walkway with a fountain at its center.

"Mr Maitland?"

"Yes?" His voice was hushed. "Did you know that hundreds of years ago, this is where monks prayed?"

"May I ask what kind of business you're doing with my father?"

Maitland turned away, but not before she noticed his look of distaste. "This is hardly an appropriate moment."

Kitty could have kicked herself. How could she have waited so long only to put the question so baldly?

He headed back inside. "I'm no fool," he said under his breath. "I had an inkling that you might not be interested in me personally, but I thought you might enjoy my company. I can see that I'm mistaken."

"I beg your pardon, Mr Maitland." She would love to start again. "I only asked—"

He raised a hand to silence her. "Because you think I'm leading your father astray? Julian warned me that might be the case and he said not to say anything to you for that very reason. But I'm not a Rasputin – I'm a businessman – and whatever decision Julian has made, he's made of his own free will. I don't *lead* anyone anywhere. He came to *me* with the proposal."

"What proposal, Mr Maitland?"

"Don't you know?"

"No."

"I see. You must speak to Julian then."

He gestured toward a section of the museum they hadn't visited. "I'm going to take a look over there. I'll meet you in a quarter of an hour."

Kitty took a seat on a bench beside a mother and daughter pair. All roads led to her father. She would have to find a way to broach the question with him.

The child tugged at her mother's skirt. "I want to go home! I don't like it here!"

"None of this is real. There's no need to be afraid," the mother said.

If only that were true, Kitty thought. The clock was ticking, and she hadn't made any progress.

Maitland returned, and he and Kitty climbed into the car in silence.

"Your father and I are going into the pharmaceutical business," he said after a while. "But it's complicated. That's the part that Julian doesn't like."

Kitty had no idea what he was talking about.

"I think you ought to understand that, unlike Canada, the United States upholds Bayer's patent."

"I'm sorry, Mr Maitland – who is Mr Bayer, and what does he have to do with my father?"

"Bayer is the company that manufactures Aspirin, Miss Weeks. But Aspirin is just an invented name for a chemical compound. Anyone can make it, and in other parts of the world, they do. However, Bayer currently has a monopoly on the American market.

"In two years, their patent will expire, and then we'll be able to sell our product here. We won't be able to call it Aspirin, of course – Bayer has trademarked that and spends a fortune on advertisements in the hopes that customers won't buy anything else."

"You and my father are making Aspirin?" Kitty said incredulously.

"ASA," Maitland replied, "short for acetylsalicylic acid, which is the same thing as Aspirin, but not the same name. And we're not making ASA in the United States, only in Canada – where it's legal."

"So why won't my father discuss it?"

"That's Julian for you. He gets nervous about details."

Kitty thought for a moment. "What did you say ASA stands for again?"

"Acetylsalicylic acid."

"That wouldn't happen to have anything to do with salicylic acid, would it?" Kitty vaguely remembered the word, or something like it, from her list.

"As a matter of fact, it does."

"And does my father supply you with the phenol to make it?"

Maitland's jaw dropped. "What do they teach you girls?"

"I read an article." Kitty waited for him to answer.

"Well, you're correct. Without Julian's supply, I'd have to close down my factory. In the short term, you see, it's much more lucrative to use phenol to make explosives."

A wide smile split across Kitty's cheeks. "Well, that's tremendous." And here she had been thinking her father sold the stuff to take lives, not save them.

"We stand to make a killing by '17," Maitland continued. "Everyone needs ASA, especially all those injured men coming out of the battlefront. Not to mention anyone with a garden-variety fever or headache."

"And your operation requires a large quantity of phenol?" All that remained was to check that her father sold his full supply to the Canadian.

"Yes, it does." Maitland stared at her in amazement. "I'm sorry. That word sounds strange coming from your lips."

It felt strange too, Kitty thought, and after tomorrow, she hoped never again to have to repeat it.

Chapter Twenty Nine

Nothing could dampen Kitty's ebullient mood when she entered the apartment.

"How was the outing?" Julian Weeks called. He sat in his study, chewing on the end of a Cuban cigar and tapping his foot in time to the lively rhythm of the Clef Club playing on the gramophone.

"It was lovely, just lovely." She perched on the arm of his settee.

"And Maitland didn't talk your ear off?"

Kitty took a deep breath. "He told me that you're working with him to manufacture ASA in Canada."

Julian Weeks's foot stilled. He put down his cigar, rose and lifted the needle from the phonograph record. The room went quiet.

"I hope you're not angry with him," Kitty said. "It was I who asked."

Julian Weeks poured himself a drink. "The world has become too complicated." He took a large swig. "It's all right for Maitland – he's Canadian – but I'm participating in the production of a drug that's still under patent in the United States."

"As far as I understand," Kitty said carefully, "he's neither producing nor selling it here. So your participation shouldn't be a problem."

"That's what my lawyer tells me." He sat back down, his mouth twisted in a grimace. "I'm an old-fashioned man, and I like to do business the old-fashioned way. Buy something cheap in one place, sell it for more elsewhere. I hate" – he almost spat out the word – "to depend on legal niceties that I must have interpreted for me by specialists."

One small matter troubled Kitty. "Why did you go to the Edelweiss Café?"

He looked puzzled. "Why do you keep going back to that?"

"I'm just curious. Does it have any connection to the phenol?"

"Who said anything about phenol?"

"Mr Maitland did." Kitty spoke quickly to cover up her slip.

"That man talks too much."

"Are you buying the phenol from Dr Albert?"

"Doctor who?"

"Ah." Kitty panicked. "Dr Albert," she repeated, as though the name was common knowledge.

Her father glared at her. "I've never heard of him. Who is he?"

"He…" Kitty scrambled for an answer. "He's in the papers. I wanted to check something with you, so I peeked into the restaurant and saw him there. I recognized his face from a photograph. I thought you knew."

"No, I don't know." He seemed honestly surprised.

"He's Dr Heinrich Friedrich Albert," Kitty said as nonchalantly as she could manage. "The German commercial attaché."

Julian Weeks's brow darkened. "Out," he thundered. "Right now. And close the door."

Kitty did as she was told but waited outside in the foyer. She heard him pick up the telephone and speak to the operator.

As quietly as she could, Kitty picked up the earpiece in the hall.

"Schweitzer," she heard him say.

"Good evening, Mr Weeks." The man at the other end of the line spoke with a thick accent. "What can I do for you today?"

"You can tell me the truth for starters—"

"I beg your pardon?"

"Who is this Dr Albert who can be recognized from his photograph in the papers? You told me that we would be meeting a colleague of yours from out of town. Now I find out he's Germany's commercial attaché?"

After a pause, the voice replied, "I apologize, Mr Weeks. It was not my intention to deceive you."

"But you did."

"You see, the problem is" – Schweitzer sounded nervous – "Dr Albert—"

"So I did meet this Dr Albert."

"Dr Albert," the other continued, "is very particular. He wanted to make sure that you could be trusted."

"That *I* could be trusted?" Kitty would have heard her father's bellow without the telephone. "Who is this man? What right does he have to vet me?"

"He's the one who is paying for the phenol, sir."

"Come again?"

"I can't afford to advance the money for the purchase of surplus phenol from Mr Edison's factories. As you know, they are one of the few firms in the United States capable of producing it – and they do so in order to be able to continue to manufacture their own gramophone records."

"Yes, yes. Go on."

"Dr Albert put up the money for the purchase and used me as an intermediary, since Mr Edison never would have sold to him. But since it has become almost impossible to send anything safely back to Germany, he, in turn, wanted me to find a buyer who could be guaranteed not to use it for the production of munitions that might fall into the enemy's hands. You see, I don't have much to do with it. I'm just the middle man."

"I gave you my word, Schweitzer. Pharmaceutical production in Canada, nothing else."

"And I told Herr Doktor that. But he insisted on meeting you in person. It was his idea that you should not know his identity."

"If I had," Kitty heard her father say, "I might have backed away."

"Now you know everything, sir. I promise there will be no further surprises."

"I hope not."

"Mr Weeks?"

"Yes."

"I'm sorry, may I ask you a question?"

"Make it quick, Schweitzer. I must say I'm not in the best of moods. I'm still tempted to call this entire business off."

"May I ask how you recognized the commercial attaché from his likeness in the papers? I inquire because Dr Albert goes to great lengths to avoid any kind of publicity. To the best of my knowledge, he has never been photographed."

Kitty helped herself to a handful of salted cashew nuts from the glass bowl in the living room. A few seconds later, she helped herself to some more. A pile of the latest issues of *Photoplay*, *Good Housekeeping*, and *Vogue* littered the sofa. It had been an hour since her father finished his telephone conversation, and she'd heard the front door slam behind him as he'd left the apartment.

She told herself that he would be back soon. Just a short while ago, she had doubted him, and now, what must he think of her?

Grace came in to ask whether Mr Weeks would be home in time for dinner.

"Of course he will," Kitty snapped, "and please make sure that Mrs Codd prepares his favorite chicken dish — the one with the apricots."

The telephone rang, and Kitty rushed to answer it. It was only Amanda, calling to thank her for visiting Mrs Basshor.

"I don't think I accomplished much," Kitty said. "But I appreciate your taking the trouble to telephone."

"That you went so soon after I asked is enough. Bessie Basshor called Mama and told her you were the first person who really listened to what she had to say and that you understood her." Amanda's voice cracked. "It seems you have a talent for newspaper work, Capability, and if that's what you want to do, then you should do it. Don't worry about what the rest of us might say. But you ought not to have made a fool of me at the YWCA. It only makes matters worse when you pretend that you haven't made up your mind."

Kitty didn't think it would help to explain that at one point, she hadn't been certain she would refuse and that her choices, at the moment, were far from clear-cut.

"I put myself out for you," Amanda said, "and you let me down in front of my friends. I can allow bygones to be bygones once, but if it happens again, people will ask why I keep giving a girl from the wrong side of town another chance. You know that kind of thing isn't important to me—"

"But it is important in your circle." Kitty didn't have the strength to argue. "I appreciate the warning, Amanda."

"I don't mean it that way. Just make up your mind, and everything will be all right."

Coming from a long line of Vanderwells, it was easy for Amanda to say everything would be fine. She didn't need to worry about proving herself or her family's lineage. Kitty excused herself and hung up the receiver. She couldn't bear to be cooped up any longer, so she asked Grace to call downstairs for the Bearcat.

It was past seven, and Kitty had never driven alone at this hour. She headed toward Forty-Sixth and Madison. She thought her father might be at the Ritz-Carlton with Mr Maitland, and she could bring him home. Or, if not (and Kitty didn't want to admit this to herself), she hoped that Mr Maitland would make her troubles go away, as he had done this afternoon.

Kitty's hands trembled on the wheel. Her father used to call her his little Violet and tossed her in the air when he came home to their shady bungalow with the garden of palm trees and bougainvillea. When she made a mistake or did something reckless, he would correct her with a few well-chosen words or a smack on the hand, but he never walked out in disgust. He only started to call her by her first name, Capability, when she stepped off the gangplank in New York. Everyone else called her Kitty while she was growing up.

What had happened? Did she really know anything about him? They must clear the air between them. It had been far too long since they'd had an honest and open conversation.

"You will find Mr Maitland in the Palm Court." The concierge replied to her query in hushed tones. If he thought it was unusual for a young lady to come in on her own, he didn't give it away in his manner or in his voice. "Would you like one of the bellboys to accompany you, madam?" he asked.

"That's quite all right." Kitty followed his directions and spotted Mr Maitland at the far end of the glass-covered court. He was deep in conversation with a lady in an ostrich-feather hat.

He said something, and his companion threw her head back and laughed. There was no sign of Mr Weeks, and Kitty turned to leave, but Maitland noticed her across the room and beckoned her over.

There was something about Mr Maitland, perhaps his size combined with his intelligence, that exerted its own gravitational force over Kitty. She found herself drawn toward him, weaving her way through a field of circular tables.

There were couples in conversation to the right and left of her and, all around, the clinking of crystal glasses and silver knives and forks.

Mr Maitland introduced her to Mrs Cordell, recently arrived from Biarritz. His friend said something pleasant and then excused herself; she had to make sure that her packages had arrived.

"So how can I help you?" He pulled a chair back for Kitty. "Don't tell me you have more questions about acetylsalicylic acid, or phenol, or some other chemical compound?" He smiled.

"I thought I might find my father here." Kitty glanced at the two glasses of wine, the half-eaten plate of mushrooms on toast bread, and Mrs Cordell's napkin tossed on the table.

"He wasn't home when you arrived?"

"He was."

"I see." Mr Maitland folded his arms across his chest. "Then I'm sure he will be back."

Mrs Cordell reappeared. "John," she called, "Lester's forgotten to deliver my music box."

Kitty stood. "I'm sorry to have disturbed your tête-à-tête." She felt stupid for not having recognized at once what she had interrupted. A man of the world, Mr Maitland evidently had an eye for women, and they for him. "I should be on my way."

She left the hotel and climbed into the Bearcat. She was better off by herself.

Chapter Thirty

"Where have you been?" Mr Weeks demanded from his study.

"I might ask you the same question." Kitty handed Grace her purse and gloves.

He had his back turned to her when she came in and then sat, having poured himself a tumbler of bourbon.

"Perhaps I made a mistake," he said. "Perhaps it was wrong of me to put you in a position where you had to ask my business colleague what I was doing. I still think of you as an eight-year-old, but I'm willing to change. Go on, ask me whatever you like, and I'll do my best to answer."

"Anything?" Kitty had expected a fight, not this laying down of arms.

"Within reason, yes." Mr Weeks allowed himself a smile. "I won't pretend that I've changed overnight. But I do see that we can't allow this state of affairs to continue indefinitely, or it could easily spin out of control."

"Can we turn on some music?"

"No, let's talk. That's what you want, isn't it?"

The clock in the corner struck the quarter hour and kept ticking, its pendulum swinging back and forth.

Kitty laughed guiltily. "I don't know where to begin." She smoothed her skirts. "Do you have any questions for me?"

"Ladies first."

"All right, who vouched for you on your passport?"

She could tell that the question surprised him. But to his credit, he didn't flinch and replied at once, "I paid a stranger ten dollars for the favor, which he's probably already drunk through."

"Why do you need someone you don't know to lie for you?"

Mr Weeks breathed in sharply. "I could tell you that it was the most expedient solution, but the truth is that I've spent years putting miles between myself and my past. I see no reason to undo that in order to satisfy some nitpicking requirement."

"What do you mean?" Kitty pressed him, eager for an answer. She had always suspected he was running away from something and that was why he never remained in one place for too long. She used to imagine him having committed some noble crime – killing a sailor in a barroom brawl, for instance, in order to protect a woman's honor.

"Did you do something wrong?" she said. His confession would explain his tight-lipped silence on certain subjects and his lack of childhood stories or mementos.

"No. Unless you consider it a misdemeanor to be orphaned." He cleared his throat. "Or perhaps my parents are still alive. I don't know who they are, so I can't be certain."

"But I thought—"

"I know what you thought, or rather, what I allowed you to think. But you should know what really happened. There were no parents who died when I was a boy and left me to be raised by uncaring relatives."

The image that Kitty had held in her mind for all these years dropped and shattered into a million pieces.

"I was abandoned on the doorstep of a crumbling convent when I was an infant and was raised by unforgiving nuns. My name was Peter then."

Peter? Kitty looked at him. *Peter?* She couldn't believe it. The words kept coming.

"We had three Peters, three Pauls, and five Gabriels, their favorite. Whenever they called a name, whichever ones of us had it had to come running. If you didn't run fast enough..." He shook his head at the memory. "Let's just say that their reed switch would help remind you to run faster. As far as I'm concerned, my story begins when I escaped and stowed away on a vessel sailing out of Baltimore."

At least she had heard this part before.

"Before then, I was no one. I became who I am on the ocean."

Kitty's wrenching relocation to Switzerland when she was eight hardly compared to his plight.

"I was about thirteen at the time. I'm not sure of my exact age, because no one knows it. When the ship's cook found me hiding behind a sack of potatoes and asked my name, I told him 'Julian,' after Caesar."

"Why?"

"I decided it was time for a change. Then I stole a look at the onion crate beside me and chose my surname in honor of Weeks & Co. Fresh Produce. Don't worry," he said, amused. "We may be named after root vegetables, but I don't feel sorry for myself, and you shouldn't either.

"The other boys weren't allowed to leave the confines of that cold, bleak place," he continued while Kitty hoped he had no more surprises. "I escaped, and I traveled the world. I don't know if you can understand what that means after the childhood I've given you, Capability, but for a boy like me – with nothing to look forward to – it was heaven on earth.

"And somehow, after starting without two pennies to rub together, I've managed to amass a tidy fortune. I've done business in Russia, China, Mongolia, and Malaya. I've crossed paths with Cossacks and petty potentates and Burmese traders, and I don't owe my success to anyone. So now you know why I don't have a birth certificate or some document showing whether my father is 'native' or 'naturalized.' I don't know if he was ever married to my mother – from the way the nuns treated me, I suspect not."

"You're a bastard," Kitty said.

"What does that word mean?" He shrugged. "In the end, it's his inner compass that gives a man his bearings. And for the first time in ages, I haven't followed mine—"

"By making that fellow sign for you on your application?"

"No." He seemed surprised by the question. "I'd do that again in a heartbeat. My past is no one's business except mine – and now yours. It's my venture with Maitland that bothers me. I swore that I'd never undertake a dealing that I didn't fully comprehend, and this business of transporting phenol across the border turns out to be much more complicated than I thought.

"It's not just the difference in laws between the United States and Canada – which I will admit troubled me. But also that I appear to be buying phenol from someone who took pains to conceal his identity from me."

He put down his tumbler and leaned forward in his seat. "How," he said to Kitty, "did you recognize Dr Albert?"

The world went still. Kitty could hear her own heartbeat. Two forks in the road in one day: the first, whether to join Amanda and her friends; the second, whether she should tell her father that *she'd* been concealing things from him for a while.

The clock struck the half hour, giving her a few seconds respite. In those seconds, Kitty realized, she would be making the most important decision of her adult life.

"The Secret Service," she said when the last chime died down.

"What?"

She started at the beginning – how the agents confronted her outside the docks and what they'd asked her to do. Mr Weeks frowned when she mentioned looking through his diary, but she didn't let that stop her and plunged ahead.

When she finished, she closed her eyes, ready for the ax to fall. But instead, he laughed.

"What's so funny?"

"You outsmarted them." He thumped his palm against his knee. "You discovered what they wanted to keep secret – American Secret Service men tailing a German diplomat. If it was printed in the paper tomorrow, no one would believe it."

Kitty recalled Soames's words. "They told me it would cause an international incident."

He nodded. "That sounds about correct."

"Why take the risk?" Kitty said. "If the result of being exposed for tailing Dr Albert could be so serious, why do it at all?"

Mr Weeks stared at her blankly.

The answer dawned on Kitty. "They must think he's up to something dangerous – the question is what?"

Chapter Thirty One

"Wake up, Miss Kitty." Grace drew back the curtains in Kitty's bedroom.

Kitty opened her eyes a crack. She had stayed up late the previous night, discussing Dr Albert with her father. Mr Weeks hadn't wanted to talk about his childhood any further – some things never changed – but was eager to speculate on the diplomat's relationship with Hunter Cole and whether that had played a part in Mr Cole's murder. Then, Kitty pointed out that – unless she had been completely mistaken, and she didn't think she was – until she mentioned Mr Cole's name, neither agent seemed to have heard of him. So if Dr Albert did have something to do with Hunter Cole's death, the connection must be obscure.

"It's almost eight o'clock," the maid said, offering Kitty her dressing gown.

Kitty groaned and jumped out of bed. Now that she had good news to share, she didn't want to be late to meet her new friends from the Treasury Department. To his great credit, throughout their conversation the previous evening, Mr Weeks hadn't once turned on Kitty. He never expressed dismay that she hadn't taken him into her confidence.

Grace fluffed the pillows and straightened the sheets while chattering on about the latest developments in the Harry Thaw case. "They let Mr Thaw go, Miss Kitty. They said he had spent enough time at the lunatic asylum and that he didn't need to be punished any more for shooting the man who stole his wife's honor."

Kitty wondered whether the result would have been different if women were allowed to serve on juries. Judging from Grace's fervent support of the millionaire playboy, probably not. But, in every photograph that Kitty had seen, Harry Thaw looked like a demented leprechaun. If she had any say in the matter, millionaire or not, Mr Thaw would remain behind bars.

Kitty sat at her dressing table while Grace combed her hair and pinned it into a chignon. "What do you think, Miss Kitty?"

Kitty glanced at her reflection. "Very nice, thank you, Grace." She looked older and wiser and felt stronger as well. It wasn't just the new hairstyle that made the difference. It felt liberating to be the daughter of a man without antecedents. It meant she could do as she pleased and that she too could be who she wanted.

Kitty stepped into her pale green skirt and slipped on the matching jacket with military-inspired cording on the edges. She fastened her earrings and joined her father in the dining room.

"You look lovely." Mr Weeks smiled. "My Athena. Ready to do battle."

"I hope that won't be necessary." Kitty laughed.

"Have you seen this morning's news? The pressure seems to be mounting." He pointed to the paper.

GERMAN AMBASSADOR ANXIOUS
TO SHOW THAT BERLIN IS OPEN
TO FURTHER COMMUNICATION
WITH PRESIDENT.

"I wonder how it will end." She took her place at his side.

Julian Weeks turned serious. "I could go with you to speak to those men."

"You're not supposed to know about them, remember?" She reached across her plate and squeezed his hand. "Besides, I can manage."

—

"Aspirin in Canada." Booth whistled when Kitty finished her story. "Well, I never." They met under clear skies in Riverside Park.

"ASA," Kitty corrected. "'Aspirin' would be illegal, and my father and Mr Maitland aren't breaking the law."

"At this point," Soames said, "I think we'd look the other way even if they were."

"So, can I have the passport, please?"

"We'll verify your claims, Miss Weeks." Booth tucked his newspaper under his arm. "If you're telling the truth, we'll see that Mr Weeks receives his papers."

"Then I'll expect them soon. Do you require any additional information from me, or are we all done?"

"Just one question," Booth replied. "How did you find out about the ASA?"

"I was keen to discover the truth for my own peace of mind," Kitty said, "so I persevered. It took a few tries."

Booth tipped his hat. "Thank you, Miss Weeks. By the way, you never met us, and none of this ever happened.

Come along, Soames." He headed for their car, but the younger agent lingered behind.

"I'm sorry we had to put you through so much trouble," he said. "It's not our usual way, Miss Weeks. The Secret Service doesn't usually strong-arm civilians. It's just that we're in a bit of a struggle—"

"With the Germans?"

He looked sheepish. "Actually, with the Justice Department."

Now it was Kitty's turn to be astonished. "I don't see—"

"Justice runs the Bureau of Investigation. Since the war broke out, we've been facing new threats and there's a bit of a battle going on between the Bureau and the Service about who will be in charge."

"So you're battling Justice?" Kitty said.

"When you put it that way, it sounds awful." Soames laughed.

"What are you two lovebirds going on about?" Booth yelled from up ahead.

"Tying up some loose ends," Soames called.

"May I ask *you* a question?" Kitty said. "Had you heard of Mr Cole before I mentioned him?"

"We hadn't, but I went over your story." Soames dusted his hat and put it back on. "While I couldn't find any evidence that Mr Cole had a connection to Dr Albert, I did learn that, before they married, Mrs Cole worked for one of Dr Albert's associates, a Mrs Martha Held. Mrs Held was at the concert where we first met. She was standing right beside you, in fact."

"The beautiful woman wearing sapphires?" It had to have been the same woman she'd heard speaking in German to her companion.

"I didn't notice what she was wearing," the Secret Service man said. "At that moment, it wasn't her I was looking at."

"Are you coming or not?" Booth yelled, honking the horn from inside the car.

"Just a minute," Soames called back. "Can we drive you to the *Sentinel*, Miss Weeks?"

"I don't work there anymore. I lost my job." Kitty hoped Soames hadn't noticed her blush.

"Any particular reason?" They made their way out onto the street.

"I was busy. I couldn't stay late like they wanted."

He turned to face her. "Did that have anything to do with us?"

"Your partner is waiting, Mr Soames."

"If there's anything you need" – Soames climbed into the driver's seat of the agents' parked vehicle – "please don't hesitate to telephone me at the Customs House."

Kitty watched the car drive away and walked home. As hellish as the worst moments of her encounter with the agents had been, life would seem empty now that they were gone.

–

Julian Weeks opened the front door. "All done?"

"All done," Kitty replied.

He enveloped her in a hug. "Thank you. I'm so proud."

She enjoyed his closeness, the familiar scent of his birch hair tonic, and then pulled away, smiling. She hadn't realized that something between them had broken when she went away to school, and now, a decade later, they were moving forward again, not just in tandem this time but in trust.

"So what's next?" he said. "Now that you don't have the *Sentinel* to go to, should I expect to have a daughter who spends every morning at Altman's?"

"I doubt it." Kitty laughed.

"Take the day off at any rate. Do something nice for yourself."

"I think I will."

Kitty decided to go riding at Durland's to work off some steam. At this time of the day, the trails would be quiet. Afterward, she could come home and take a shower and then she would see if Amanda would join her for lunch.

Kitty telephoned the Vanderwells, but Mrs Vanderwell informed her that Amanda had left for the YWCA and wouldn't be back until three.

That was quite the reversal, Kitty thought. Amanda working while she prepared to while away time.

"Thank you for your help, Miss Weeks," the usually grudging Mrs Vanderwell went on. "I do appreciate your listening to my friend, Mrs Basshor."

"How is she faring?"

"No better and no worse, I'm afraid. Still mourning her secretary."

"Did you know him well, Mrs Vanderwell?" Kitty said.

"Not really," Mrs Vanderwell replied. "He seemed a bit outspoken and overly familiar, but I will admit I would never have pegged him for the murdering type."

Kitty changed into her riding ensemble and drove herself to the stables. A groom saddled Damsel and with a leg up, Kitty hoisted herself onto the animal's back. She cantered around the park for about half an hour but found she couldn't relax. Too many thoughts crowded her mind. At first, it was Soames, then from Soames, she drifted to the concert. Then to Martha Held, the buxom beauty with the sapphires cascading from her ears. Soames had said that Aimee Cole worked for Mrs Held, who was an associate of Dr Albert's. How did it all add up?

Kitty felt certain that Hunter Cole had met Dr Albert more than once. He had told Poppy Clements so, and Dr Albert wouldn't have recalled him or launched into the lengthy diatribe justifying his desire to keep their meeting quiet if Mr Cole had only been a casual acquaintance. The murdered man had kept a syringe and vials, filled with some substance, in his toiletries case. He had been shot in a stable where, less than a week later, one of Mrs Basshor's ponies had to be put down. Kitty recalled the singing stable hand, Turnip, and his indignation at the thought that Breedlove could have stepped on a rusty nail. *Sister Susie's sewing shirts for soldiers* – she heard the song as though he were humming it right beside her.

She screwed up her face in concentration: *syringes – vials – a sick horse – Hunter Cole – stables – Dr Albert*. Could they all be connected?

She came to the end of her ride and waited for one of the grooms to take Damsel's reins.

"Frank," Kitty said, sliding to the ground. "Do you know of a disease that would make it necessary to put a horse down quickly, without any questions asked?"

"I don't understand, Miss Weeks."

"Is there something that could go wrong with a horse that the stable wouldn't want even the lads to know about?"

The groom stroked Damsel's sleek, dark neck. "Something that would scare the boys, you mean."

"Perhaps."

He bit his lip. "It would have to be something that they thought would make them sick too or infect the other horses fast."

"Exactly." Kitty nodded.

"Glanders," he said finally. "If one of our animals had glanders, we'd put it to sleep and wouldn't want anyone to find out."

Glanders. Kitty's pulse raced. Where had she heard about it before? Oh yes, that's what had killed Mrs Stepan's pony, Zsa-Zsa.

"It spreads like wildfire," Frank continued. "You get fever and chills, sores all over your body, and then, in a few days" – he snapped his fingers – "you're gone. If the boys thought we had glanders at this place? Forget it, they'd disappear in a minute." He looked at Kitty. "But not to worry, miss. There's nothing like that here."

"I know," Kitty said. "I was just curious."

She stopped off at the library on her way back home to look it up. "Glanders," she read to herself, "one of the most loathsome diseases known to mankind... Almost always fatal to humans. Death may come rapidly or gradually. Victims undergo terrible sufferings... Disease common to horses... Transmitted through cuts in skin. Not harmful if swallowed with food or water." Kitty thought of the pharmacist, Mr Murray, and felt thankful.

"Germ known for twenty-five years but still no cure has been found."

"What kind of stories are you writing these days, Miss Weeks?" the librarian asked as Kitty returned her book.

"I hardly know myself," Kitty replied.

It didn't make sense. Even if it were possible to bottle glanders germs in a vial, why would Hunter Cole – of all people – want to harm a horse? And if Dr Albert was behind it, why would he want to cause an outbreak at the Sleepy Hollow Country Club?

Just in case, as soon as she arrived home, she put a telephone call through to the Customs House. Soames would think she was crazy to call him just hours after they parted, but Kitty didn't care; she needed to be certain. The man on the other end of the line, one Agent Burke, told Kitty that Soames wasn't in, so she left a message for him to call her when he returned.

She rummaged through the bureau drawer in her bedroom, but she couldn't find Hunter Cole's vial. She ran into the pantry.

"Grace." The maid stopped folding linens. "Did you see a small glass tube that I kept in my bureau drawer? I had it beside my camisoles."

"Oh yes, Miss Kitty. The one with the cork stopper? I thought it might leak and soil your delicates—"

"What did you do with it?" Kitty said, panicked.

"It's right here." Grace opened the cabinet below the kitchen sink. She had wedged the vial upright between bars of soap and a lamb's-wool duster. "It looks like one of those chemical tubes they show in the movies, doesn't it?" She handed the vial over. "I even thought it might be dangerous." The maid laughed.

Sunlight streaming through the kitchen window hit the tube at just the right angle. The liquid inside seemed as clear and unclouded as before.

"Do you have a handkerchief, Grace?" Kitty said.

Grace handed her one from the linen pile and Kitty wrapped the glass vial before sliding it into her pocket.

"Tell Mrs Codd I may be late for lunch." Still in her riding gear, she ran downstairs and hopped back into the Bearcat.

Chapter Thirty Two

"Can I help you?" Aimee Cole's dwarfish maid peered out from behind the door.

"Is Mrs Cole in?"

"She's gone for the day."

"When will she be back?" Kitty peered past the woman and noticed sheets draped over the living room furniture.

"Later this evening. I'm not sure." The maid didn't budge an inch.

"Is she traveling somewhere?"

The servant shrugged and started to close the door.

Kitty put her foot in the way. "May I come in for a moment?" She smiled apologetically. "I'm a bit far from home and I need to... well, I need to powder my nose."

The maid stepped aside.

Kitty entered and was struck at once by the state of the apartment: sheets had been draped over every surface, even the lamps had been wrapped, and two large trunks stood in one corner.

This wasn't some temporary move; Aimee Cole would be gone for a long time.

"So, Mrs Cole plans to move back to Brooklyn?" Kitty asked.

"This way please." Without answering the question, the servant escorted Kitty directly to the bathroom and closed the door with a click.

"I'll just be a minute," Kitty called. She opened the medicine cabinet. Half of it was empty, but Hunter Cole's toiletries case remained, and Kitty pulled it down.

She undid the clasp and peered inside. Almost everything in the case was as it had been previously – but the vials were gone. Kitty replaced the case, pulled the chain to the toilet, and washed her hands.

She opened the door to the bathroom to find the maid waiting outside.

Passing through the dining room, she caught sight of a large envelope propped on the mantelpiece. She recognized the name of the rail company.

"Travel tickets?"

"Mrs Cole is going to be Pequeñita Mary."

"I beg your pardon?"

"She will be Mexico's Mary Pickford. She's leaving tomorrow."

"You're going with her?"

"No." The maid looked sullen.

"Well, please congratulate her on my behalf. I'd love to say goodbye before she leaves town."

"You won't find her here. She wouldn't want me to tell you, but I suppose it doesn't matter anymore." A look of disgust spread across the maid's face. "She's gone off to spend the day in Van Cortlandt Park with some foreigner."

"A man?"

She nodded.

"Could you describe him to me?"

"I only saw him for a minute. He was a small, dark fellow. Not a gentleman."

That didn't sound like Dr Albert.

"It's shameful." The maid pursed her lips. "And it's been barely a week since Mr Cole passed."

-

Kitty called the Customs House again, this time from a telephone at a candy store around the corner.

"May I speak to Agent Soames?" she whispered into the instrument, trying not to be overheard by the shopkeeper. "This is Capability Weeks."

"Ah, it's you again. Well, you're in luck, Miss Weeks. Soames just walked in. I'll put him on."

Kitty flashed a smile at the shopkeeper while she waited. She'd already purchased a full bag of peppermints and paid him an extra quarter to use his line.

"Is something the matter, Miss Weeks?" Kitty could hear the worry in Soames's voice.

"I'm fine, but I'd like your help."

"Can we speak later today? I'm a bit rushed at the moment."

"I'm afraid it can't wait. I'm sorry, but it's difficult to explain on the telephone. I can come meet you – I won't take much of your time, I promise."

There was a pause. "I'll take a break for lunch." He gave Kitty directions to an eatery downtown.

She hung up the telephone, thanked the shopkeeper and ran outside to her car.

Soames would help her. Soames would be able to make sense of all this. And then, if she needed to, Kitty could speak to Aimee Cole before she left town.

Kitty wove her way through the traffic, one hand on the horn like a taxi driver.

Who was Aimee with, and why, the day before her departure, would she be going to a park all the way up in the Bronx?

Some fool with a golfing cap on his head and a cigarette clamped between his teeth thought it amusing that Kitty was in a hurry and drove alongside in his roadster, winking and trying to get her attention.

When she didn't respond, he retaliated by attempting to cut her off at an intersection, but she stepped on the gas, and the Bearcat leaped forward.

Take that. Kitty arrived at her destination faster than she thought.

She hopped out of the car, passed a tobacconist's scowling wooden Indian and pushed open the door to the luncheonette.

Soames waited for her at a table right in front. Kitty took the seat beside him and pulled out the vial from her pocket.

"What this?" he asked.

"Don't laugh, but I think it might contain the germ that causes glanders and I found it in Hunter Cole's medicine cabinet."

Soames folded his arms across his chest. "This is all very far-fetched."

"I know, I know," Kitty said. "But Mrs Cole leaves tomorrow, and this may be my last chance to find out whether I'm correct. And if I am, don't you want to know where those other vials are?"

"It could be something else that affects horses."

"It could be nothing," Kitty said. "Just water. Whatever it is, I want to know for sure."

"We'd need to bring it to a lab for analysis. But that would take days, not hours."

"Can we do it though?" Kitty persisted. "If you give me an address, I'll take it across myself. You have work, but I have time."

A newsboy came through the restaurant, waving a copy of the afternoon paper and calling in a singsong voice, "'Ambassador von Bernstorff to Explain German Note Today! May Offer *Lusitania* Disavowal.'"

"They won't open the door to you."

"Come with me then."

He checked his watch and placed a couple of coins on the table. "Let's make it fast."

"Do you always drive like this?" Soames held on to his hat with one hand while the Bearcat careened along. He glanced at the road flying beneath their wheels. "There's nothing to hold you in place. You could fall right out of this thing."

"That's what I like about it," Kitty said, enjoying his look of alarm.

He motioned her to stop in front of a row of ramshackle garages on Eleventh Avenue, jumped out of the Bearcat, and rapped on one of the metal shutters that stretched from the roof to the ground. "It's Soames," he called.

Moments later, the shutter slid up a couple of feet, and a freckled fellow with curly hair ducked out. He let out a long, low whistle. "Nice wheels, Soamsie. And who might this be… a girlfriend?"

"Miss Weeks is a reporter," Soames replied dryly and introduced Kitty to Evan Monroe. "We'd both be most obliged if you could look into something that she's brought along."

"Any friend of yours, Soames, is a friend of mine." Monroe lifted the shutter all the way and led Kitty inside with exaggerated gallantry. "This way please, miss."

The garage was outfitted with rows of burners on stone counters, mazes of interlocking glass tubes, and a profusion of tongs and flasks and water baths. A fan at the rear rattled feebly as it blew away some of the noxious odors.

Soames turned to Kitty. "Would you like to explain?"

Kitty showed Monroe the vial. "I think," she said, "but I'm not sure, that this might contain some sort of virus or bacteria – the one that causes glanders, perhaps?" She suddenly felt foolish speculating in the presence of a professional. "Is it even possible to bottle a disease?"

"Glanders." Monroe tilted his head. "I'm afraid I can't help you. I'm a chemist and what you need is a pathology lab."

"Oh dear." Kitty tried to control her disappointment.

Monroe returned the tube. "But I can tell you that the vial is top quality. I'll bet you five dollars that it's made by the Krauts."

"How can you tell?" Soames asked.

"They have the best scientists, the best equipment and the best labs. If you speak to any chemist worth his salt, you'll find that he studied in Deutschland or trained under someone who has."

"Do you know any pathologists, Mr Monroe?" Kitty looked around at all the scientific paraphernalia. Surely all he needed to do was examine the liquid under a microscope or something like that.

The shutter opened with a rumble.

"Bloody furnace out there." One of Monroe's associates entered, wiping his forehead with a rag. "Beg your pardon, ma'am. I didn't know we had ladies about."

"That's all right, Tuttle," Monroe told him. "I'm sure Miss Weeks has heard worse – she's a reporter."

"Doing a chemistry story? I could tell you about the time that Mr Monroe spilled sulfuric acid on me and nearly melted my shoes off – say, what's this?" He picked up the vial from the stone-slab counter and turned to his boss. "Have the post office inspectors been back?"

"Post office inspectors?" Soames perked up.

"They brought in two tubes exactly like this a month ago."

Soames turned to Monroe. "And you didn't think to tell us?"

"I didn't know myself, Soamsie."

Soames seemed rattled. "How are we supposed to get anything done if one hand doesn't talk to the other? You know you're supposed to keep me informed about any inquiries that come your way – I don't care whether they're from the post office, the Bureau, or even Naval Intelligence. Whatever it is, we need to know *immediately*. Those are Treasury Secretary McAdoo's orders."

"It won't happen again." Monroe shot his employee a baleful glance.

"Damned right it won't, or you won't see any more of our business."

"Pardon me," Kitty interrupted, turning to Tuttle. "Did you happen to find out what was in the post office inspector's vials?"

Tuttle beamed with pride. "It took a few days, but I did, at last."

"And you didn't say anything?" His boss looked furious. "Did you even write it in the ledger?"

"I may have forgotten," he admitted. "We were busy and I didn't think we were interested in bacteria."

Chapter Thirty Three

"Are you sure you will be able to recognize Mrs Cole?" Soames asked as the Bearcat sped toward the Bronx.

Kitty kept her hands firmly on the wheel. "And here I was thinking you wanted me along for my excellent investigative abilities, or even my chauffeuring skills."

"This is no time for humor, Miss Weeks."

Kitty looked over at him. "I can see that."

The Secret Service man had telephoned his headquarters and spoken to Booth. They had left Kitty's sample for Tuttle to examine and gone to look for Mrs Cole, who, they hoped, would know about the missing vials.

"Van Cortlandt Park is huge, you know," Kitty said to Soames. "Maybe it would be better to wait until she comes home."

"By then it might be too late."

"Too late for what?"

Soames stared at the road ahead. "I'd just rather not take any chances."

"And one question still troubles me," Kitty went on. "If it is glanders, why would Mr Cole or Dr Albert want to spread the disease at a country club?"

"There's a time for questions and a time for answers," Soames replied. "But this isn't the time for either one."

"I should drop you off on the street," Kitty said. She was tired and hungry and hadn't even eaten lunch. "You go find Mrs Cole and tell me all about it."

"I'm sorry." He cracked his knuckles. "I really can't talk."

They drove along in silence.

Kitty crossed Mosholu Parkway. Van Cortlandt Park stretched out into the distance, acres of green against a cloudless blue sky. She brought the car to a halt and brushed off her sense of foreboding. "Where do we begin?"

"Let's walk and see." Soames stepped out of the car and offered his arm, but Kitty felt too shy to accept and pretended she hadn't noticed.

On one side of the path, boys played football; on the other, families picnicked on the grass. A couple of children ran along, their kites soaring in the air.

"Are you watching for Mrs Cole?" Soames said.

"I'm doing my best." Kitty thought she saw Aimee everywhere: in the woman strolling arm in arm with her companion, walking her dog, riding her bicycle, or pushing her baby along in a baby carriage.

"She's here with a friend," Soames reminded Kitty.

"As if I could forget," she replied with a touch of annoyance. Some of the ladies had their parasols open to shield their faces from the sun, while others took refuge under broad-brimmed hats. What if Aimee Cole was wearing one of her many wigs – how would Kitty recognize her then?

"You should be looking too," Kitty told Soames and tried to describe the widow. "She's about my height. Not too fat, not too thin. Medium-brown hair and medium-brown eyes."

"Middle of the road?" he said.

"Exactly. Then again, there's something about her." Kitty pictured Aimee in the brilliant red wig. "She can change. When she wants, she looks terribly attractive. I suppose that's what one should expect from an actress."

The sun beat down on them, and Soames bought Kitty a bottle of Coca-Cola to cool her off. She drank it quickly and returned the empty bottle to the vendor.

"We're never going to find her," she said.

"Never is a strong word."

"How can you be so confident?" Kitty heard the tinny sound of fairground music in the distance. The music grew louder as they walked on. Children bobbed up and down, spinning around and around, faster and faster on a carousel of gaily painted horses.

A couple trotted by on horseback. Kitty sidestepped a pile of manure. The children shrieked with joy as they clung to their wooden mounts.

Horses. It always came back to horses.

She stopped in her tracks. Why was Mrs Cole here? Why had she come to a park in the Bronx, of all places, on her last day in New York?

What was here? A golf course, a parade ground, the former Van Cortlandt residence.

She stopped a passing stranger. "Excuse me, sir. Would you know whether there are stables or riding facilities nearby?"

"I don't know about stables, miss. Are you looking for a ride?"

"I'm looking for horses," Kitty said. "Any place here that might have horses."

"Ah." He threw Soames a sympathetic glance, as if to say one never could tell with the ladies, and pointed to a corner of the park. "There's a herd corralled in the meadows back there. If it's horses that you want, there must be at least two hundred."

Kitty quickened her pace. Soames followed. She picked up her skirts and broke into a run. The horses wouldn't disappear, but if Mrs Cole wasn't with the animals, then Kitty would tell Soames that she had no idea where to find her, that they may as well sit in one spot and hope Aimee strolled by or wait until this evening and try to catch her at her apartment.

A good two hundred animals milled behind the pen. "Excuse me." Kitty approached a wiry lad hefting two buckets of water. "Why are all these horses here?"

"They're resting for a couple of days before they're shipped off," he replied.

Soames and Kitty exchanged a glance.

"Don't you know?" He put down his pails. "Our breeders send horses by the dozen to Europe. They come by rail from out west, then we put them on boats for the long journey. These beauties will be charging into battle next month."

"On whose side?" Kitty said.

"Oh." He grinned. "They're going to fight the Huns."

—

"It's absurd," Mr Weeks responded when Kitty returned home and told him what she had discovered. "Desperate though they may be, I cannot believe that the German government has a *plan* to inject glanders into horses bound for France."

"Don't you see?" Kitty said. "It follows the same principle as what they're doing with the phenol. They can't get it for themselves, so they want to make sure that the enemy can't have it."

"But spreading disease among horses?" His face screwed up with distaste. "That's fiendish."

"It's brilliant," Kitty said. "It kills the animals and spreads the sickness to the troops at the same time."

"I won't hear any more of this." Julian Weeks stood behind his desk. "And I will not allow you to spend the night with two men in Van Cortlandt Park."

"They're Secret Service agents," Kitty said. "And I won't be sleeping there."

"Oh yes." His tone was acerbic. "You will be hiding, waiting for this Aimee Cole woman. And what will you do when she arrives?"

"I won't do anything, Papa. The agents will handle it. I'll just be watching."

"And these are the same agents who, until this morning, were investigating my business affairs?" He came out from behind his desk and sat in his armchair. "You know, I think I've given you too much freedom."

Kitty couldn't take it. She had thought asking his permission would be a formality. "So it's fine for me to go out on my own for your sake but not for mine?"

"Have you lost your marbles, Capability?" her father said. "When you met them today, it was daytime, and you were gone for twenty minutes a block away from our home."

"And now I'm meeting them farther away and for longer."

"That's exactly what bothers me. I may be lax, Capability, but I'm not stupid. I know how to take care of my own child."

Kitty put her hands to her head. "This is my life. The agents wouldn't have known about Mrs Cole or the vials if I hadn't alerted them."

Mr Weeks went to pour himself a drink but remained standing, his empty glass in his hands. "It could be dangerous."

"Agent Booth and Agent Soames both agree, which is why they didn't want me to stay on in the first place, but I insisted." Booth had arrived at the park shortly before Kitty had left for home. "They've selected a spot where I am to wait. I won't move until they tell me that it's all right."

He twirled the glass between his fingers. "You remind me of myself when I was a young man."

"So you'll let me go?" Kitty brightened.

"Against my better judgment."

She stood and kissed him on the cheek. "Don't worry about me. I'll be back."

—

Kitty changed into her darkest riding skirt and a dark shirt. She put on a pair of sturdy walking boots and asked Mrs Codd to pack three sandwiches.

"You're certain you want to do this?" Mr Weeks asked when Kitty looked in to say goodbye. "Let Rao drive you."

"What, and arrive at the scene of the potential crime in my Packard with my chauffeur?"

He gripped her hand tightly. "Then tell one of those men to come back with you. I don't want you in the car on your own at night."

Much as she wanted to do this alone, Kitty didn't look forward to driving back from the Bronx unaccompanied. "That's a good idea." And before he could give her any further instructions or change his mind, she hurried out.

–

Once at the park, Kitty handed Soames and Booth each a sandwich. She'd been worried that Aimee Cole might arrive while she was away, but fortunately that hadn't happened.

"This is excellent." Booth wiped his mouth with the back of his hand.

"Do you think Mrs Cole will come?" Kitty said.

"Did you telephone her apartment from home, like I asked?" he replied.

"I did and she wasn't there."

Soames had been leaning against a tree, eating his sandwich. Now he finished it and tossed away the newspaper wrapper. He stood up straight, brushing the crumbs from his jacket. "We don't know anything about this Mrs Cole or what she might do. I know I had said it was all right, but I'd really prefer it if you went home, Miss Weeks."

A chill stole over Kitty. She wouldn't have expected Soames, of all people, to forsake her.

"Let her be, Soames." To Kitty's surprise, it was Booth who came to her defense. "It's her doing that has brought us this far, and she understands that she can't write about or even talk about anything that happens tonight. Don't you, Miss Weeks?"

Kitty nodded.

"So far, all we've got to go on is guesswork," the big man went on. "A warning to you, Miss Weeks, before you go off and hide. You're on your own until we call for you."

"Yes."

"I have a family at home." His thuggish features softened for a moment. "I should be spending this evening with them, but instead, I'm here. And while Soames may be gallant, I don't throw myself in front of a bus for anyone."

"I understand."

The sun would set after eight. The park began to clear. Picnickers folded their blankets, sportsmen gathered their equipment, and children cried tears of exhaustion as their parents pulled them away from their games. The lads looking after the horses left shortly before closing time.

Kitty took up her position in a copse of trees and watched as the sky went dark. This wasn't Manhattan, with its blur of electric lights creating an eternal day. Here in the Bronx, in the midst of the park, she could see the stars clearly. She had forgotten how much she missed them since coming to the city, but even the glories of the night sky couldn't distract her for long.

Kitty's legs ached from crouching, and she was being bitten by mosquitoes. There was nothing remotely exciting or romantic about waiting for something to happen. She must remember that for the future. Kitty stood up slowly to stretch her legs.

It must be past ten by now. It looked like Pequeñita Mary wouldn't be arriving with a syringe loaded with glanders to finish the work that her husband had started. Mrs Cole wanted to be an actress. Perhaps there was a mundane explanation for all of this – that, like many actresses, she was having an affair and had come to the park, a remote place where no one would recognize her, to spend one last day and night with her paramour.

Kitty wished Aimee luck. She felt guilty about suspecting her and speculating on her private life. Whatever Hunter Cole's involvement with Dr Albert had been would remain a secret. The dead man couldn't tell Kitty, the diplomat wouldn't tell her, and the widow would be on her way to Mexico tomorrow.

Kitty caught a glimpse of light from the direction of the carousel. She blinked and it disappeared. A few moments later, she saw it again: a yellow halo bobbing around at the far end of the meadow.

Slowly, it made its way toward the pen. At first, it was so far off that Kitty couldn't be sure of the direction. But it soon grew brighter, and the person carrying it became clearer until she could make out a hooded figure approaching the enclosure.

The lantern lowered, and the figure extracted something from a satchel and whistled softly. One of the horses ambled over to the fence.

Kitty's hand flew to her mouth as Booth and Soames rushed from their hiding places. "Don't move. Arms up," Booth bellowed.

The figure swung around, and the hood fell back. Soames raised the lantern. Even from a distance, Kitty could tell that whomever they had caught wasn't a woman, and it certainly wasn't Mrs Hunter Cole. It was the small, slight stable hand she had met at the Tombs – Marcus Lupone.

Booth slapped a pair of handcuffs on the Sicilian's wrists. Soames grabbed the satchel from his shoulders and bent to reach for something that had fallen from his hands.

Kitty remained glued in place. A featherweight mosquito landed on the side of her neck, and she brought up her hand to swat it away – but instead of delicate flesh crumpling beneath her fingers, she felt a steel needle's cold, hard resistance.

"Don't move," a girlish voice whispered in her ear.

"Aimee," Kitty breathed.

"Did you think I wouldn't notice that nice yellow car?" She tugged at Kitty's arms. "On your feet." She slid one arm behind Kitty's elbows, pinning them behind her back. "Come along." She pushed her captive forward.

"Don't do this, Aimee," Kitty whispered.

"Don't do what?" The needle hovered inches away from Kitty's throat. "Take you away from your friends? Infect you with a deadly disease? I'll try my best not to. But you will have to cooperate. So tell me, who are those men you've brought along?"

"They're Secret Service." Kitty swallowed. She could feel Aimee's warm breath in her ear.

"My, my. To think that when I first met you, you were a scared little apprentice," Aimee whispered. "And now here you are, consorting with government agents. You *were* scared, weren't you? Or was that just an act? If so, you should try your hand at the movies. Who knows? You might be better than the rest of us."

"Where are we going?" Kitty asked.

"To your car."

"And then?"

"You're going to drive me to freedom."

Kitty couldn't see more than a few feet ahead of her. She stumbled on the uneven ground and righted herself just in time. "They'll notice I'm missing," she whispered. "They'll come looking for me."

"And what will they do when they find us? Risk that I might hurt you? I doubt that. No, Miss Weeks, you are my ticket to safety, my life insurance."

"You haven't done anything wrong yet, Aimee," Kitty said, feeling the ground with her feet to make sure she didn't trip in the darkness. "Don't make this worse by bringing me into it." They were moving farther away from the enclosure, farther from any chance of assistance. "Talk to the agents. Tell them who put you up to it. Tell them that you had to finish what Mr Cole started—"

"What Mr Cole started?" Aimee scoffed. "That's a joke."

"Then why did he go to the stables at the club?" Kitty slowed down.

"Hunter thought it would be amusing to test the serum on one of Mrs Basshor's ponies, and at a July Fourth party, no less," Aimee said.

"And he was working for Dr Albert?"

Aimee was silent for a moment. "Well, aren't you clever."

"And then what happened? Did someone catch him in the act?"

Aimee didn't reply at once.

"I'm pretty sure that Mr Hotchkiss didn't shoot your husband, because Mrs Basshor told me that she was aware of his stealing. So that can't have been a factor. Who did it then?" Kitty asked.

Aimee's giggle made her shiver.

"What my husband knew about the secretary wasn't the same as what the secretary thought Hunter had discovered."

"I don't understand," Kitty said.

"The secretary had, let's say, a *fondness* for men. Hunter told him that he had found out his little secret. Of course, Hunter meant that he had overheard Hotchkiss talking to the fireworks fellows and that he had put two and two together once Mrs Basshor told us what she was paying for the entertainments. But the secretary panicked. He assumed 'little secret' meant that Hunter had found out about his secret activities—"

"What kind of activities?" Kitty said.

"You don't know anything, do you?" Aimee snapped. "The secretary was a faggot. You don't mess around with that type, but Hunter had no idea, and he never could resist the chance to make an extra buck."

"So Hotchkiss shot him?" Kitty had never heard anyone use the word "faggot" in conversation but had a vague idea of what it meant.

"That's right. Men of his kind live in terror of being discovered. I only realized the truth later and confronted him at the funeral. He folded at once. The shame of it must have been too much for him to bear, which is why he killed himself."

Poor Hotchkiss. That would explain his frantic call the day before he died.

A twig cracked beneath Kitty's foot. Aimee stopped. For a few moments, all Kitty heard was the sound of the other woman's breath. Then Aimee pushed her ahead. "You have to be more careful."

"Why didn't you tell anyone about Mr Hotchkiss, Aimee?"

"I was going to. But then he went and slit his wrists before I had a chance to speak to the police. And after that – well, they pinned the murder on him in any case, didn't they? So what would be the point?"

Kitty saw the Bearcat parked on the street. And finally, she heard Soames calling her name.

"Hurry," Aimee said.

"Miss Weeks." Soames was about twenty feet away.

Kitty's moment of relief was short-lived. Aimee Cole brusquely swung her around, and she became a shield between the widow and the agent. The needle at her neck kept her in check. She couldn't move or Aimee would puncture her skin.

"Are you all right, Miss Weeks?" Soames came closer.

"Stop right there," Aimee shouted. "I have a syringe and I'm not afraid to use it."

"I'm putting down the lantern." He bent his knees and placed the light on the ground. He stood, slowly. "Let's not panic. We can sort this out." He introduced himself. "Why don't you release Miss Weeks and we can discuss this in private, Mrs Cole? You are Mrs Cole, aren't you?"

"Who else could I be?" Aimee spat.

Soames sounded calm and steady. Reasonable. If she were in Aimee's shoes, she would trust him, Kitty thought.

"I won't hurt you, Mrs Cole," the Secret Service man continued. "Once we're done talking, I can help you. Miss Weeks tells me you're planning to go to Mexico to become an actress. I can make sure you get there safely."

"Likely story," Aimee scoffed. "Once you get what you want, you'll leave me in the lurch. I know men."

"What in God's name is going on?" Booth arrived, dragging a scowling, handcuffed Lupone beside him.

"What is happening is that I'm going to take Miss Weeks to her car, and she will drive me away," Aimee replied.

"Over my dead body." Booth raised his arm. There was a pistol at the end of it. He cocked the hammer.

Kitty gasped and closed her eyes. She would never get out of this.

"Calm down, Booth." Soames stepped into the line of fire. "Let's think things through."

"I'm done thinking," Booth said.

Kitty opened her eyes again. Were the two men playing some kind of charade to bluff Aimee into believing that Booth would shoot if she didn't do as Soames asked?

"Get out of my way, Soames. Now," Booth thundered. "Unless you want me to report you when we get back."

Soames stepped aside.

There was no one between the barrel and Kitty. If Booth fired, she would be hit. Kitty stared at his outstretched arm, mesmerized.

"My colleague has more patience than I do," Booth told Aimee. "I suggest you don't push your luck any further. Put down that syringe, and tell us who put you up to this filthy business and why."

"Never!" Aimee inched backward, pulling Kitty along with her.

Booth took aim and fired, the shot deafening.

Kitty's heart stopped. The bullet had whistled right past her.

"Bullying won't work with me," Aimee yelled. "You could ask my husband, only he's dead."

Kitty felt completely out of her depth. She saw no way out unless Aimee spoke to the men.

"Let me handle this," Soames said to Booth.

"What? And stand here all night? I'm tired and ready to go home, and I won't have my hand forced by some hysterical cow. If she wants to act like a child, I'll treat her like one. I'm going to count down from five," he said loudly, "and if she doesn't start talking, I'll shoot again. And this time, I won't miss."

He looked fierce in the light of the lantern. "FIVE," he yelled.

"Say something please, Aimee," Kitty begged. Booth didn't seem to be bluffing.

"Put the gun down," Aimee called.

The pistol didn't waver.

"FOUR," Booth shouted.

"This is getting out of hand, Booth," Soames said.

Kitty smelled Aimee's fear.

"We're running out of time," Booth boomed. "I'm at THREE."

"Please reconsider, Mrs Cole," Soames urged. "We can help you."

"Please, Aimee." A tear trickled down Kitty's cheek. "Just explain to them. Tell them you didn't understand what your husband was doing."

"I didn't understand? It's he who didn't understand, and he didn't do anything," Aimee whispered through gritted teeth. "He talked big, but he was a coward. He couldn't bring himself to hurt a horse. Not for all the money in the world, so I had to go down to the stables and do it for him."

"You injected Breedlove?" Of course, that made sense.

"It's why I left the children's tables for a few minutes. I found Hunter near the stalls with his pistol and the syringe. He was sniveling like a baby."

"And then you killed him?"

"Stop your chattering," Booth shouted.

"No one noticed." Aimee's voice was low. "Everyone looked right past me. No one – not even you – guessed that I had done it."

"TWO." The black barrel bore down on the women.

Kitty screwed her eyes shut. She was going to die.

"This is your last chance," Booth called.

Lupone slammed his head into his captor and a shot sounded as Booth's arm jerked, Soames dove forward and then the world went quiet.

Kitty yanked herself free from Aimee's grip. The widow stood still for a moment, her eyes bright, then she sighed, and her body tumbled backward. She fell so slowly, her feet coming off the ground for an instant, that Kitty felt as though she were watching a picture run by an overzealous projectionist who sped up the action once more when Soames rushed over to check Aimee's pulse.

"She's breathing." He turned to his partner. "You idiot."

"It's his fault." Still handcuffed together, Booth smacked Lupone on the head. "And besides, we needed an answer."

"*You* needed an answer." Soames applied pressure to the wound on the widow's shoulder. "You're not hurt?" he asked Kitty.

Kitty touched her neck. "I think I'm all right."

With shaking fingers, she picked up the syringe that Aimee had dropped, wrapped it in a handkerchief, and placed it on the ground beside the younger agent.

Soames took off his jacket and tied it tightly around Mrs Cole's shoulder. A hint of color returned to the widow's cheeks. "We're going to take you to a hospital."

He picked her up and carried her in his arms to the agents' car. He told Kitty to follow them. They drove to the nearest police station, where she waited in the Bearcat while Booth, Soames, and Lupone went inside, leaving Mrs Cole behind.

There were so many different Aimees, Kitty thought with a shiver. Wife Aimee, daughter Aimee, showgirl Aimee, captor Aimee. Even aspiring actress Aimee, and friendless Aimee. The only image that she had difficulty conjuring was Aimee as murderess shooting her husband through the skull. But that's exactly what Mrs Cole had done.

A police matron and two policemen arrived and Kitty watched them lift the widow onto a stretcher.

"What happens now?" she asked Soames, who came out to join her.

"Lupone goes back to prison, Mrs Cole goes to the hospital and you go home and forget everything that's happened."

"What about you and Agent Booth?"

"This won't look good on either of our records."

"You prevented a crime!"

"We injured someone and involved a civilian."

Kitty realized he was talking about her. "I won't tell."

"I know you won't, but Mrs Cole or Lupone will."
They stood alone under the stars for a few moments.

"What did she tell you before Booth fired?"

"She admitted that she had murdered her husband and that the vials came from Dr Albert."

"Oh." Soames exhaled loudly.

"I think she must have hated Mr Cole. Or hated him in that moment. It's hard to tell. She's a good actress."

The agent reached out and held Kitty's hand in his. "Well, Miss Weeks, I wish we had met under different circumstances."

"So do I." Kitty pulled away. "Goodbye, Mr Soames."

"Would you like me to follow you home?"

"I'll be fine." She climbed into the Bearcat, turned on the engine and headlamps, and drove back to the New Century Apartments.

Chapter Thirty Four

Kitty's interview appeared on the Ladies' Page the next day, just as Miss Busby had envisioned it:

> FOR AMERICAN GIRLS, BY AN
> AMERICAN GIRL: AN INTERVIEW
> WITH PHILANTHROPIST AND
> AUTHOR, MISS ANNE TRACY
> MORGAN

Kitty scanned the text, which had remained more or less faithful to her account. "Duties rather than the rights of women…with greater freedom comes greater responsibility…the girl must look into the mirror to discover who she is and what she might become." While Miss Morgan emerged from the piece a living, breathing woman with a will of her own, Kitty felt that the interviewer, referred to only as "the American girl," remained faceless and receded into the background.

"How are you this morning?" Mr Weeks walked into the dining room. He had waited for her to come home the previous night and, after she told him everything, meticulously checked her neck under the glare of his desk lamp. "You feel all right? No headaches or fever?"

"Every time I sneeze now, you're going to think I might die."

"Do you blame me?" He tucked his napkin in his collar. "I want you to stay home this weekend."

"You won't get any argument from me." Kitty finished her breakfast and returned to bed. She slept through the morning, woke up for lunch, and – since she was exhausted and nothing to do with horses would ever be the same for her – declined Amanda's offer to go out for a ride.

–

The Weekses boarded a train at Pennsylvania Station and set off for the Panama-Pacific International Exposition in California five days later. Julian Weeks had spent Monday and Tuesday at meetings, and then came home and announced that he needed a change and that they ought to leave town for a while.

Kitty hadn't heard from Soames or read anything about the incident in the park in the newspapers. Without her job to give her days a rhythm, she found herself drifting around the apartment, and new scenery sounded appealing. She had packed her bags without any argument and read old *Photoplay* magazines while the train rumbled through a tunnel beneath the Hudson.

They emerged on the other side into the warm, bright sunshine of the mainland. Clapboard houses replaced brick buildings. Lines of cable wire bordered farmland and woods, and here and there, a child on a bicycle waved to the train as it passed.

Kitty left the first-class compartment and took tea in the dining car with a group of young ladies. Later that evening, she chatted with their brothers and parents. She tried not to think about what had happened to Aimee or whether she would see Soames again. She hoped he wouldn't be punished for Booth's actions.

A few days into their trip, Mr Weeks patted the seat beside him and gestured for Kitty. "The president has sent off his third note to Germany. Listen to what he says regarding submarine warfare: 'Illegal and inhuman acts, however justifiable they may be…are manifestly indefensible when they deprive neutrals of their acknowledged rights, particularly when they violate the right to life itself. If a belligerent cannot retaliate against an enemy without injuring the lives of neutrals…a due regard for the dignity of neutral powers should dictate that the practice be discontinued.'

"And then the president goes on to say that 'the Government of the United States is not unmindful of the extraordinary conditions created by this war…nor of the method of attack produced by the use of instrumentalities of naval warfare which the nations of the world cannot have had in view when the existing rules of international law were formulated, but'" – Julian Weeks emphasized each word as he read – "'*it cannot consent to abate any essential or fundamental right of its people because of a mere alteration in circumstance.*'

"Mere?" He turned to his daughter, shaking his head. "As you and I both know, there's nothing 'mere' about the changes that this war has brought about."

The train hurtled through the heartland, and the Weekses switched to the new Scenic Limited in Missouri. It was a fast all-steel train with a glass-walled observation car, and it took its passengers on a breathtaking journey along the Meramec and Missouri Rivers, the Royal Gorge, and the Feather River Canyon.

Kitty had never seen such vistas, natural beauty on such a grand scale. She felt as though she had tumbled out of the hurly-burly of Manhattan and into a universe where diplomats and Secret Service men had no place.

She and her father disembarked in San Francisco. They set off the next morning for the Exposition, which commemorated the opening of the Panama Canal, "a historic undertaking that connects two continents and the Atlantic and Pacific Oceans," as the pamphlets said. In size and scope, the fair was the third of its class in the United States and the twelfth of its kind held anywhere on the planet.

Kitty visited the Palace of Horticulture and was entranced by the Gettysburg display. She watched the dance performances at the replica Samoan and Chinese villages, while Mr Weeks spent most of his time at the Palaces of Manufactures and Varied Industries, Machinery, and Mines and Metallurgy. Together, they attended concerts at the Festival Hall and marveled at the display of colored lights that gave the place an *Arabian Nights* air.

They posed for a photograph in front of the Liberty Bell (on loan from Philadelphia). They kept their hats on this time and appeared as they wished to be perceived: a prosperous father with his daughter on vacation. They watched craftsmen from all over the world ply their trades at souvenir stalls.

"Here you may observe up close the handicrafts of alien races," a tour guide informed them.

Julian and Kitty Weeks took a detour to Yellowstone on their journey back home. And when Old Faithful erupted, Kitty found that all the pent-up tension that she had accumulated over the past month shot into the air along with the cloud of vapor and gasses that hurtled to a height of over one hundred feet and rained back down on her like the tissue-paper nothings that fell from the skies during that fateful daylight fireworks display.

She realized that what Aimee Cole wanted more than anything was to make something of herself, and Hunter Cole had denied her that opportunity. He hadn't given her the place in the world that she craved and wouldn't allow her to try to achieve it on her own.

Thwarted women did strange things. They imploded, like Miss Busby, or exploded, like Aimee. Others were forced to channel their energies into acceptable pursuits, like Anne Morgan, and a lucky few – Pearl and Mary Pickford, for instance – found fame and fortune in the movies. But who knew what sacrifices each had to make and what injustices and indignities they put up with on the way?

She and Aimee were similar in many respects, Kitty thought. Both outsiders, both wanting to prove themselves. But what, Kitty wondered, would she do if she felt trapped? Would she be able to look another person in the face and pull the trigger?

Julian Weeks felt her shudder. "What's the matter, Capability?"

"It's nothing." Kitty took his arm, and they walked through the park in companionable silence.

–

Every day since she left New York, Kitty had scanned the papers, hoping for some tidbit of information on either Soames, Aimee, Lupone, or Dr Albert – anything, however trivial, that might give her some clue to the aftermath of what happened in the park. She found nothing and came to believe that the affair would remain buried, but on August 15, when she was just hours away from the city, the *New York World* broke a major story, exposing Germany's "secret undertakings" in the United States.

Kitty's arms felt weak as she held the paper and learned that "no less a personage than Herr von Bethmann-Hollweg, chancellor of the German Empire," had participated in the intrigues from Berlin and that "his emissaries in America included the German ambassador to the United States; his military attaché in Washington; and his chief financial agent, Dr Heinrich Friedrich Albert."

Her eyes traveled across the page.

"The *World* today begins the publication of a series of articles raising for the first time the curtain that has hitherto concealed the activities and purposes of the official German propaganda in the United States," the story began.

She glanced through the litany of charges: Dr Albert had secretly purchased a sham munitions plant in Connecticut, which took orders from the British and French governments that it never intended to fulfill. He participated in plans to foment strikes in other munitions plants across the country and plotted to buy the Press Association and so control the dissemination of war news in America.

She kept reading: there was no mention of glanders, no mention of the Coles nor of Kitty and her father, but one Mr Hugo Schweitzer was named as a participant in the nefarious proceedings. Kitty didn't find any mention of the Secret Service agents either.

Her father put down his copy of the paper. "I got out just in time."

"What do you mean?"

"Before we left town, I canceled the deal with Maitland and terminated my arrangement with Schweitzer."

"Mr Maitland can't be pleased."

"No, he wasn't, but he'll survive."

The train chugged back to New York. Kitty marveled at a facsimile reproduction of a letter between Dr Albert and one George Viereck, editor of a magazine called *The Fatherland*. "In thinking the matter over," the letter said, "I do not think that Mrs R. would be the proper intermediary, inasmuch as she doesn't attend to her financial matters herself. If it must be a woman, Mrs G., the mother of our friend, Mrs L., would be far better…" and so on and so forth.

The commercial attaché had been busy. To Kitty, the letter begged the question of how the *World* had acquired this correspondence. Had someone given it to them? Had one of their reporters stolen it? She couldn't imagine just anyone walking into the Hamburg-American building and taking private papers from Dr Albert's office.

Rao picked up Kitty and her father from the station. The traffic was terrible.

"This is nothing, sir," the chauffeur said. "Last week, twenty trucks from American Express blocked the avenue for hours. We were told that they were filled with gold all the way from England on its way to the Morgan bank."

The news at home wasn't as dramatic. Grace and Mrs Codd had managed without arguing during their absence. Grace hadn't stepped out with any young men, but Mrs

Codd had taken Sundays off to visit her daughter on Staten Island.

Grace unpacked the trunks while Kitty sorted through her letters. She had received one postmarked from Washington, along with others from her boarding-school friends.

She opened the Washington letter once the maid left the room. Soames had written to say that he had been transferred away from New York and that Booth had been placed on indefinite suspension.

"You may want to know about Mrs C," he added. "She recovered and told us what we needed. Although I think she should be in prison, she is on her way to Mexico.

"The strangest thing," he continued, "has to do with Dr A. He fell asleep on the subway, woke up with a start at his station, and rushed off, leaving behind his briefcase. When he realized what had happened, he ran back to the train, but the briefcase was gone."

Kitty began to laugh. The Secret Service had "happened upon" Dr Albert's briefcase — and they, for some reason, made the findings public?

"Capability." Mr Weeks knocked at the door, an envelope in his hands. He sounded uncharacteristically pleased as he held up a single sheet of stamped paper. "Our passport has arrived."

Miss Busby rang bright and early the next morning. "Your maid told me you'd be back."

Kitty never expected to be so happy to hear that familiar squawking voice.

"I hope you're well rested, because we have heaps of work ahead of us."

"Are *you* well, Miss Busby?" Kitty said. It was as though Kitty was back in the alcove with her editor firing off orders.

"Fine. Fit as a fiddle. Never felt better, in fact."

"You do know that Mr Hewitt let me go, Miss Busby?"

"Bah. Mr Hewitt has no say in who goes or stays at the Ladies' Page. I will tell you one thing though. I plan to keep Miss Williams. She's wonderful, that girl. A real worker. And I've realized my limits, so she will take care of the day-to-day tasks while you handle special assignments.

"That interview with Miss Morgan struck a deep chord with our readers. They loved you as a questioner. The Page was flooded with letters praising your innocence and naïveté, and it got me thinking: Why not conduct a series of interviews with other prominent women? We'll start with Dr Davis, the commissioner of corrections, and move on to Mrs Isabella Goodwin, the only top-grade female policewoman in the city's detective bureau. And I'd like to throw in a few artists and writers."

"May I have a few days to think about it?" Kitty asked, overwhelmed by the barrage of information. "I'll need to discuss the offer with my father."

"Well, take all the time you need, but make it fast. Of course, it goes without saying that I will expect you not to engage in any more of your shenanigans."

"Of course, Miss Busby. And thank you. I'm flattered." Kitty hung up the receiver.

"What a voice. I'll bet the entire avenue heard that conversation," Mr Weeks remarked. "So what will you do? Do you think you will go back?"

"Do you have a preference?"

"It's not my decision to make. However, I will say that I don't envision you spending the rest of your days planning dinner for me and bossing about Grace and Mrs Codd."

"I had considered working somewhere else."

"Where? A different Ladies' Page?"

"When you put it that way, it doesn't seem right." Kitty smiled.

Grace looked in on them and Kitty gave her the lunch order. She began to think: Dr Davis and Mrs Goodwin, then artists and writers. Maybe she could add Miss Tarbell, the journalist; Dean Gildersleeve of Barnard; Alva Belmont, the socialite and suffragist; and perhaps even an actress like Mary Pickford or Pearl White.

"What's on your mind, Capability?" Mr Weeks said.

Kitty pictured him busy in his study, Amanda headed to Europe to become a nurse, Soames posted in Washington. She saw her future unfold with Miss Busby at the helm, Mr Musser in his underground lair and Jeannie Williams scribbling away alongside her. "I think I will return to the *Sentinel*. Who knows? There might even be a story in it for me this time."

Author's Note

Much of what seems most unlikely in this novel actually happened. For instance, Dr Heinrich Friedrich Albert did fall asleep on a New York City subway in the summer of 1915 and left his briefcase behind when he woke up at his stop. Agent Burke of the Secret Service, who was tailing him, picked up the case and turned it over to his superiors. Decisions were made at the highest levels of government to leak the contents to the *New York World*.

Further Reading

During the course of the novel, Kitty reads or refers to Anne Morgan's *The American Girl: Her Education, Her Responsibility, Her Recreation, Her Future*, 1915; Arnold Bennett's *Journalism for Women*, 1898; and *Practical Journalism: A Complete Manual of the Best Newspaper Methods* by Edwin Shuman, 1905. All are available online.

Kitty also has the following guidebooks on her bookshelf: *Peeps at Great Cities: New York* by Hildegarde Hawthorne, 1911; *Vocations for Girls* by E. W. Weaver, 1913; and *The Etiquette of Today* by Edith B. Ordway, 1913.

When Kitty visits Prentiss's photography studio, she sees a clipping taken from "Bryan Admits Spies Get Our Passports," from the November 14, 1914, edition of the *New York Times*.

The news about the Morgan shooting is captured in breathless detail in "J.P. Morgan Shot by Man Who Set the Capitol Bomb; Hit by Two Bullets Before Wife Disarms Assailant" from the July 4, 1915, edition of the *New York Times*.

Highlights of the tense back-and-forth between the German and American governments include "Germany Delivers Note Tomorrow, Shuns Liability for *Lusitania*,

Proposals for Safety of Americans" (*New York Times*, July 9, 1915); "Wilson Says He Will Act Promptly After Deciding Reply to Germany; American Comment Disturbs Berlin" (*New York Times*, July 14, 1915); and "Bernstorff to Explain Note Today; May Offer *Lusitania* Disavowal" (*New York Times*, July 16, 1915).

Austria's protests are recorded in "Austria-Hungary Protests Our Export of Arms; Says We Have Means of Exporting to All Alike" (*New York Times*, July 15, 1915).

Dr Albert's activities (not all, however) were exposed in "How Germany Has Worked in U.S. to Shape Opinion, Block the Allies and Get Munitions for Herself, Told in Secret Agents' Letters" (*New York World*, August 15, 1915).

You can find full-text versions of President Wilson's speeches and responses to Germany online.

For an account of the challenges women journalists faced during the 1910s, as well as more about the Sob Sisters and the Thaw trial, see *Front-Page Girls: Women Journalists in American Culture and Fiction, 1880–1930* by Jean Marie Lutes and *Out on Assignment: Newspaper Women and the Making of Modern Public Space* by Alice Fahs.

Gail Collins offers an entertaining and informative overview of American women's history in *America's Women: 400 Years of Dolls, Drudges, Helpmates, and Heroines.*

Ron Chernow's The House of Morgan: An American Banking Dynasty and the Rise of Modern Finance *explores the legacy of the Morgan family in detail.*

Sabotage at Black Tom: Imperial Germany's Secret War in America, 1914–1917 by Jules Witcover contains fascinating accounts of some of the events narrated here and features Dr Albert, German Ambassador Bernstorff, and other historical figures of the period.

The United States Passport: Past, Present, Future by the Department of State's Passport Office provides an overview of the development and use of the U.S. passport.

There is no shortage of good books on New York City's architecture. *New York 1900: Metropolitan Architecture and Urbanism 1890–1915* by Stern, Gilmartin, and Massengale combines beautiful photographs with detailed descriptions of the development of notable buildings, streets, and neighborhoods in the city.

Photographs of New York Interiors at the Turn of the Century *and* Fifth Avenue, 1911, from Start to Finish in Historic Block-by-Block Photographs *offer a glimpse of everyday life in the city.*

Philipp Blom's *The Vertigo Years: Europe, 1900–1914* spotlights social events that illustrate the hopes, fears, and contradictions of pre-war Europe.

And finally, something to watch – *37 Days: The Countdown to World War I*, a gripping BBC miniseries set in the foreign offices of England, Germany, and Austria, chronicles the political maneuvering that led to the declaration of war in August 1914.

Harder to find but comprehensive in scope, the many "bonus material" documentaries that accompany Lucasfilm's "Young Indiana Jones" series shouldn't be missed.

For more on *A Front Page Affair* and the Kitty Weeks mystery series, visit http://www.radhavatsal.com

Reading Group Guide

1. Do you think Kitty is the kind of person who fits in wherever she is? Why or why not? What is it about her that allows her to fit in (or not)?

2. In what ways does Kitty's financial status enable her to move about society?

3. How does Kitty's father's background influence his behavior and affect his and Kitty's relationship? How does their relationship influence how Kitty investigates?

4. What drives Kitty's friendship with Amanda Vanderwell? What do you think Kitty gets out of her relationship with Amanda, and vice versa?

5. What are the characteristics of some of the powerful, independent women we meet and hear about in the novel? Think of Mrs Basshor, Anne Morgan, Miss Busby, Mary Pickford, and Pearl White. How are they similar? How are they different?

6. Why do you think Miss Busby suffered a nervous breakdown? How might this be related to her hopes, expectations and possible disappointment in Kitty?

7. How does Jeannie Williams feel about Kitty?

8. Do you think Aimee Cole genuinely likes Kitty, or does she try to turn her into a sympathetic ally for her own purposes?

9. Do you find the revelation about Hotchkiss's sexuality surprising? Do you think his contemporaries would have made similar assumptions about him as modern readers might?

10. Do you see Soames as a viable romantic interest for Kitty? What about him makes him a good match for her? What aspects of his life and career might prove problematic for a future relationship between them?

11. In her films, Pearl White plays an active heroine who never gives up but often has to be rescued from perilous situations. Are you surprised that those types of heroines existed a hundred years ago? How are they different (and similar) to action heroines today?

12. Jeannie, Kitty and Amanda inhabit different but overlapping worlds. If you could live in one of their shoes for a day, which one would you chose, and why?

13. How did Dr Albert's plan to infect the horses meet or defy your expectations of German warfare, especially compared to the torpedoing of the *Lusitania*?

14. In what ways does Kitty's world seem not dissimilar to our own? In what ways does it seem old-fashioned?

A Conversation with the Author

What was your inspiration for A Front Page Affair?

There are too many to name here, but in terms of books, I'd say E. L. Doctorow's *The Waterworks* and Alexander McCall Smith's No. 1 Ladies' Detective Agency series. I wanted to write a novel that was entertaining and very readable, yet transported readers to a different time and place.

I also wanted to create a memorable heroine – one who was determined and tenacious, but also naive about the world around her – and watch her develop as her eyes are opened to complexities of the time in which she lives.

What drew you to the 1910s as the setting for the story?

I first became interested in the 1910s when I was a graduate student at Duke University researching early women filmmakers. It came as a shock to me that so many women were directing, producing, and writing films at that time. I was also amazed to learn about action-film heroines like Pearl White, who were the stars of highly popular action/adventure/mystery series. I soon discovered that this phenomenon wasn't just limited to film: women held prominent positions in many professional fields during the

1910s and then – remarkably – starting in the 1920s, their numbers began to decline and didn't go back up again until the second wave of feminism in 1970s.

But the 1910s weren't just an exciting time for women; they were an incredibly exciting time for the country. This was the period when the United States stepped out from the shadows and moved from being a regional power to taking its place on the world stage. It was a time when much that we take for granted today – things like car culture, movies, telephones, nation states (instead of kingdoms and empires) – was taking its modern form. And the transition wasn't an easy one.

I thought it would be exciting to combine the coming-of-age story for the country with the coming-of-age story for women and to tell it through the perspective of an unlikely protagonist: a young, well-off, pretty journalist who enjoys a privileged lifestyle.

How did you do your research?

I like to use primary sources, and when I started doing my research, a lot of materials hadn't been digitized, so I had to go to the New York Public Library, which fortunately has an amazing reference collection. I spent a lot of time looking at books published during the early 1910s – decorating guides and exercise manuals, for example. I also studied floor plans of different apartment buildings and the amenities they offered to pin down where Kitty would live and what type of home she has, and so on.

When historical characters speak in the novel, I like to remain as close as possible to their own words. So, I try to read books or articles written by them or about them from the 1910s. I go to secondary sources to get a general overview, but as far as specifics are concerned, I much prefer to go back to original material because that's where you find little unexpected bits of information that add something special to a character.

I also decided that each book in the series would be set at a specific moment in time. I had read about the Morgan shooting and the whole business with Dr Albert, which culminated in his losing his briefcase. I then went back to the *New York Times* and read each day's paper in the days leading up to the shooting, through the period of my story, and right up to the date when Dr Albert lost his briefcase and a bit after. Since these little-known historical events are entwined in the plot of the mystery and aren't just a backdrop to it, I wanted to give the experience of living that history.

What do you find to be most challenging about writing a historical novel?

What's most challenging about writing a historical novel is also what makes it so enjoyable: finding the right balance between fact and fiction. I enjoy keeping dates, places, and people accurate and not altering facts to suit the convenience of the story. If Kitty lives on the Upper West Side of Manhattan and she has to drive her father to a meeting downtown, it will take her a while to get there. If J. P. Morgan was shot on the third of July and the news appeared in the paper on the fourth, then that's not going to change.

The trick is to maintain a good balance and to digest all the facts and then forget about them and allow them to flow naturally through the story. I keep a 1915 calendar beside me as I write in which I track factual events and fictional events.

What is the most surprising thing you found in the course of writing and researching the book?

How far-fetched, almost implausible, many historical events seem from our present vantage point – Dr Albert forgetting his briefcase on the subway; J. P. Morgan falling on top of the man who tried to shoot him, trapping the fellow beneath him. Accidents, sometimes absurd accidents, can have serious consequences. I like to find these seemingly trivial moments and try to understand their significance.

Real-life people, such as Anne Morgan, Nellie Bly, and Pearl White, as well as locations, such as the Colony Club and the Sleepy Hollow Country Club, appear in the book. How are/were they significant to their time? How have they changed since?

Anne Morgan, Nellie Bly, and Pearl White were all very different women. One was a philanthropist; another, a journalist; the third, an actress. But all three were very well-known in their day and provided different examples of what it meant to be a successful woman.

The Colony Club and Sleepy Hollow Country Club were both exclusive clubs, and both still exist today. I like to use real locations as much as possible because I think it creates a real geography and allows readers an opportunity to feel like they live in the world of the novel, which is something I enjoy when I read. I'm a sucker for maps in books and that type of detail.

How did you come up with the name Capability Weeks?

I wanted to find a name that would evoke something about the heroine's character – or the kind of person she aspires to be – and a name that could also be shortened into a milder-sounding diminutive. Names like Hope, Virtue, Patience, etc., seemed too soft. I don't recall exactly when I first heard about Lancelot "Capability" Brown, the famous landscape designer, but I loved that name because it sounds so competent. And I love the contrast between it and "Kitty," which sounds stereotypically feminine.

Which character do you feel most closely connected to?

All of them, really. I see the world through Kitty's eyes, but I can't help but sympathize with Miss Busby's frustration with her or enjoy her father's secretiveness and his desire to needle her a bit. I like the way Amanda condescends to her and Jeannie manages to "steal" her position. The fun thing about Kitty is that she isn't perfect, nor is she always smarter than the other characters. She's just willing to go the distance.

Writing is not your first career. How did you come to it?

At the back of my mind, I always wanted to write fiction. It was a way I could explore ideas that are interesting to me and bring together different strands that otherwise might not coexist. Fiction allows me much more freedom than academic writing, but I wouldn't have the subject matter that I do without my academic training. I chose mystery as a genre because I love to read it. It has a beginning, middle, and end – and it's all about discovery That's something I really enjoy – if a book can open my eyes to something new, for me, that's a huge bonus.

How does your background, both in film and as a woman who came from India as a teenager to study in the United States, shape the book you've written?

Without studying silent cinema, I doubt I would have discovered the 1910s as this fascinating and rewarding period in which to set a mystery. I also discovered the wonderful action-heroines and the actresses who played them, who were the inspiration for a character like Kitty.

Coming from India to attend boarding school in Connecticut on a scholarship as a teenager was a pivotal moment in my life. I was old enough to be able to look critically at the world I was entering, but also young enough to assimilate very quickly. I remember a friend telling me, "I keep forgetting you're not American." I used to keep forgetting that I wasn't American too! But it's this divided identity that gives Kitty her unique viewpoint – she can be in a certain milieu and seem like she's part of it, but she also has the perspective of an outsider looking in. This doesn't exempt her from the consequences of her actions, of course, but it does make her an effective, although unlikely, detective.

Funnily enough, I think my childhood in Mumbai helps me to imagine New York in the 1910s. I grew up among a very colorful cast of characters from all walks of life. And my family was, and is, filled with strong, outspoken women. My grandmother ran a large, rambling house in the style of a bygone era. Watching her converse with the tradesmen – everyone from the upholsterer to the fruit seller to the man who fixed broken necklaces – and hearing them talk about their families and lives gave me some insight, I think, into a more personal time. A time when you knew the person who brought your milk and sewed your clothes – although, by the 1910s in New York, that was slowly changing.

She also belonged to a country club where "everybody knew everybody." I think that's the way New York was in the 1910s (and perhaps still is now). If you were a part of a certain milieu, you knew everyone you had to know or, at worst, were just a step away from knowing everyone.

Who are some of your favorite authors?

The authors I turn to time and again are Agatha Christie and Dick Francis in mystery. Authors who create immersive worlds like Frank Herbert in *Dune* or Tolkien in the Lord of the Rings trilogy. I think I must know Jane Austen by heart. I love Gabriel García Márquez, Jorge Luis Borges, Elizabeth Gaskell, and Charles Dickens. When I was in my teens, I read everything from Isaac Asimov to *Gone with the Wind*.

What advice would you give to aspiring writers?

There's no magic to it. You have to start writing and then finish. For me, finishing and letting go is the hardest part. I never feel like I'm done, but when I start spinning in circles, I realize I must be done. I wish I had the ability to look at something I've written and feel content with it, but I'm not that lucky.

Selected References and Resources

"Austria-Hungary Protests Our Export of Arms; Says We Have Means of Exporting to All Alike," *New York Times*, July 15, 1915.
http://timesmachine.nytimes.com/timesmachine/1915/07/15/issue.html.

Bennett, E. A. *Journalism for Women: A Practical Guide.* New York: John Lane, 1898.
https://archive.org/stream/journalismforwooobenngoog#page/n8/mode/2up.

"Bryan Admits Spies Get Our Passports," *New York Times*, November 14, 1914.
http://timesmachine.nytimes.com/timesmachine/1914/11/14/issue.html.

"Full Text of Germany's Reply to the United States," *New York Times*, July 10, 1915.
http://timesmachine.nytimes.com/timesmachine/1915/07/10/issue.html.

"Full Text of the President's Note to Germany," *New York Times*, July 24, 1915.
http://timesmachine.nytimes.com/timesmachine/1915/07/24/issue.html.

"How Germany Has Worked in U.S. to Shape Opinion, Block the Allies and Get Munitions for Herself, Told in Secret Agents' Letters," *New York World*, August 15, 1915. https://en.wikipedia.org/wiki/Great_Phenol_Plot.

Morgan, Anne. *The American Girl: Her Education, Her Responsibility, Her Recreation, Her Future.* New York and London: Harper & Brothers, 1915. https://archive.org/details/americangirlhereoomorg.

Shuman, Edwin L. *Practical Journalism: A Complete Manual of the Best Newspaper Methods.* New York: D. Appleton Company, 1910. http://catalog.hathitrust.org/Record/006507340.

Acknowledgements

This book wouldn't be in its present form without the efforts of my talented and clearheaded agent, Christina Hogrebe at the Jane Rotrosen Agency, who took a chance on a first-time author.

The fabulous editorial team of Shana Drehs and Anna Michels at Sourcebooks patiently answered all my questions and shaped this into the novel that I hoped it could be. I look forward to working on many more together.

Thanks also to Heather Hall and the production and design departments at Sourcebooks.

And to Christina Prestia and Eric S. Brown on the business end.

Along the way, friends and family have come to the rescue. Mariah Fredericks, Denise Fulbrook, Julie Barer, Nicki and Henry Welt, Kelly Adams, Rebecca Gopoian and David Heatley, Marcia Lovas, Erin Toomey, Maria and Mitch Hoffman, Rebecca Gowers, Kevin Baker, Melissa Rathbone, Anandi Hattiangadi, Kiran Nagarkar, and Svetlana Mintcheva provided advice and support at critical moments.

My mother, Tulsi Vatsal, has read more drafts than I can count.

My husband, Daniel Welt, and our daughters have been there through all the ups and downs of this project.

It's been a long journey, and their enthusiasm and support have made it all worthwhile.

CANELOCRIME

Do you love crime fiction and are always on the lookout for brilliant authors?

Canelo Crime is home to some of the most exciting novels around. Thousands of readers are already enjoying our compulsive stories. Are you ready to find your new favourite writer?

Find out more and sign up to our newsletter at canelocrime.com

Lost Cause
Rachel Lynch

DI Kelly Porter has solved some of the Lake District's most gruesome murders but nothing has prepared her for the monster she's about to meet. The answers may lie with a local oddball – is he a victim, or a killer?

Lies to Tell
Marion Todd

Since she joined the St Andrews force, DI Clare Mackay has uncovered many secrets lurking in the picturesque Scottish town. When there is a critical security breach inside Police Scotland, she realises she may have put her faith in the wrong person – will it be a deadly mistake?

The Body Under the Bridge
Nick Louth

DCI Craig Gillard has spent his career hunting criminals. When a missing person case reveals itself to be far more than a routine disappearance, it isn't long before the perpetrator has another target: DCI Gillard himself. Suddenly the detective isn't just running the case – he's part of it.

A Front Page Affair
Radha Vastal

Capability 'Kitty' Weeks is determined to prove her worth as a journalist. Headlines about the Great War are splashed across the front pages, but Kitty is stuck writing about society gossip – until a man is murdered on her beat and she is plunged into a story that threatens the life she has always known.

When the Past Kills
M J Lee

The Beast of Manchester was the case that defined DI Thomas Ridpath's career, but the wrong person was convicted and only later was the true culprit put away. Now, those connected to the case are being targeted. Someone is desperate for revenge, and Ridpath risks losing more than he can stand.

Small Mercies
Alex Walters

DI Annie Delamere is off duty and enjoying a walk in the Peak District when she comes across a mutilated corpse. As the body count increases, Annie is under intense pressure to solve the case. But are the crimes the work of a deranged mind – or a cover for something even more chilling?

Home Fires Burn
Lisa Hartley

DS Catherine Bishop is dealing with the aftermath of the most brutal case of her career. Her small team is overwhelmed by an arsonist, and a new murder case provides far more questions than answers. The pieces finally fall into place, but have Catherine's demons already won?

When the Dead Speak
Sheila Bugler

Eastbourne journalist Dee Doran is investigating a woman's disappearance when the body of another is found. There are startling similarities between the dead woman and one who was killed sixty years previously. Dee is determined to uncover the connection, but sometimes the only thing more dangerous than secrets is the truth…